MAD   2010   SE

THE PROMISE OF SPRING

Seasons of Change Series

Book one: Come Next Winter

Book two: The Promise of Spring

The Promise of Spring

Seasons of Change Series: Book Two

By
Linda Hanna
and Deborah Dulworth

The Promise of Spring
Published by Mountain Brook Ink
White Salmon, WA U.S.A.

The website addresses recommended throughout this book are offered as a resource. These websites are not intended in any way to be or imply an endorsement on the part of Mountain Brook Ink, nor do we vouch for their content.

This story is a work of fiction. All characters and events are the product of the author's imagination. References to real locations, places, or organizations are used in a fictional context. Any resemblance to any person, living or dead, is coincidental.

Scripture quotations are taken from the *Holy Bible, New King James Version®,* NKJV® Used by permission. All rights reserved worldwide.

ISBN 978-1-943959-35-8
© 2017 Linda Hanna and Deborah Dulworth

The Team: Miralee Ferrell, Nikki Wright, Cindy Jackson
Cover Design: Indie Cover Design, Lynnette Bonner Designer

Mountain Brook Ink is an inspirational publisher offering fiction you can believe in.

Printed in the U.S.A. 2017

CHAPTER ONE

July

"YOUR MOMMA WANTS TO MEET ME?" Millie Drake's heart rate quickened and her knees grew weak. She plopped on a park bench and covered her warm face with her hand. "What have you told her, Lou?"

"She knows I think you're pretty special and that we've been dating for six months. I told her you have a gentle smile, warm, chocolate brown eyes that entice me, and soft lips that beg to be kissed."

"Lou, you didn't!"

"Sure did. Okay, maybe not the part about your lips. She doesn't need to know everything." He cracked his knuckles, sat next to her, and draped his arm on the back of the bench. "Don't worry, she won't be here until October. I'm kind of surprised your parents haven't asked to meet me yet."

Lifting her head, Millie gazed at him while her mind waded through a quagmire of emotions. Mother would be infuriated when she learned of their well-guarded romance.

Millie had labored over forty years to stay on her mother's good side. Today she faced the difficult task of coming clean about her secret relationship with Lou Blythe.

She flipped her dark hair over her shoulder and

opened the back door. "Dad, lunch is ready."

"Millicent!" an angry voice growled behind her. "Will you close that patio door? You're letting in hot air."

"Sorry, Mother." Millie's shoulders drooped as she pulled the glass door shut and headed to the kitchen table. Their mother/daughter bond had always lacked the warmth and closeness she longed for. Even as a child, she was required to call her 'Mother.' Penelope Drake deemed any other title highly undignified.

With sweaty palms, she smoothed her raspberry-colored blouse over her slight frame. In the best of times, soul-baring conversations with Mother never ended well. She'd take your naked soul and ram it through the meat grinder. At least Dad could be trusted to stay cool, calm, and clever.

Millie scooted her chair closer to the table. The Lou bomb had to be dropped with caution during lunch because she had a date with him tonight. The Grand ol' Duchess needed to be carefully primed before anyone dared to ask for favors. She grinned. Dad's royal title for Mother was very fitting. Thanks to him, she'd learned to start the groveling process with a compliment.

"Umm. Mother, I'm glad we're having tossed salad today." That wasn't much of a rave review. Seconds passed. Finally, inspiration hit. "Have I ever told you how much I love your homemade salad dressing?"

"You sound like your father when he wants something, Millicent." An annoyed sniff followed as she scooted into her chair. "Where is that man, anyway?"

"I'm coming, Penny." Stuart Drake joined the family. He pushed his sunglasses on top of his balding cranium. "Everything smells delicious. Let's thank the Lord for our lunch."

With head bowed, Millie gripped the hands of her parents while offering a silent prayer for courage to complete her mission.

". . . and bless this food for our nourishment. In the name of Jesus we pray, amen." He looked at his wife. "Penny, you were at the flower shop this morning. Did you happen to notice anyone lurking around the desk?"

"Stuart, please." She jabbed a slice of roast beef. "Do you think I pay attention to every little thing that happens there? I'm not a store detective, you know. All I remember is your niece haggling with the mayor's wife."

He cleared his throat. "Carol wouldn't do that. She called and said several raffle tickets were missing. If they don't turn up, I'll have to pay for them."

Penny's eyes met his. "Have you checked her pockets? That woman takes things that don't belong to her. Do the words 'Pastor Frank' ring any bells?"

Millie shook her head. "Let it go, Mother. Carol didn't take Pastor Frank from me. He was never mine in the first place." She bit into a carrot. "By the way, Dad, what's the raffle for?"

"The Chamber of Commerce is trying something new this year to raise money for the hospital. KAPP-TV news team has agreed to be auctioned off as dates."

"Just think, Millicent, some lucky girl will win a date with that hunky head anchorman, Kent Sheridan." Her chin lifted. "We'll make sure to get several tickets for you."

Stuart's eyes narrowed over his drinking glass. "Penny, did you—"

"This topic is boring me." She waved her hand dismissively. "Let's talk about something else." After pouring blue cheese dressing on her salad, she covered the delicate container.

Great. Millie closed her eyes and took a deep breath while doom circled overhead like a vulture. All signs pointed to Mother manipulating the raffle to win the newsman for her. But, how could she ever think of dating someone other than Lou? She swallowed. The time had come to drop the bomb and show Mother that her daughter could get a man on her own.

Hands shaking, she clenched the napkin on her lap. "I turn forty-three next Saturday, and I only have one birthday wish." Her gaze nervously zeroed in on her mother, sitting across the table in a flamboyant purple lounging robe.

"What is it, Millicent?" Her mother's brow puckered above her red-rimmed glasses. "Did your book club subscription to Bleeding Hearts in Duluth expire?"

"I've been too busy to read lately." Millie stared at the fluted meat platter and nibbled her bottom lip. Could she pull this off? "Since we usually have a cookout for my birthday, I'd like to invite a guest this time. Dad, you make the best grilled steaks in the world, and Mother, everyone knows there isn't a better cook than you." Did that sound more sincere than her last compliment?

"Why, thank you, dear." She smiled, took a sip of lemonade, and set the glass down. "It's not your cousin, is it?"

Millie swallowed a bite of roast beef. "Don't worry, it isn't Carol."

"Well, that's a relief. What's your friend's name? Do I know her?" A string of creamed spinach dangled from her fork.

"You know of *him*. He goes to our church." She squirmed in the chair, adjusted her blouse, and gauged her mother's reaction. "As a matter of fact, Carol and I sit with him during morning worship when he's in town."

"You mean that odd man in the church balcony? Oh, Millicent, that heavy brow makes him look like the missing link."

Her caustic reply hit Millie like a sack of fresh fertilizer on a sweltering day.

Stuart frowned. "That remark was totally uncalled for,

Penny."

Peace-loving Dad rarely called her out. Millie winced and waited for creamed spinach to hit the fan.

Her mother's fork clattered to the plate. With a lowered voice, she pecked her finger on the table. "Your daughter and niece made spectacles of themselves when they sat with him in the church balcony last winter. They giggled, dropped things over the ledge, and shamed our family. Do we want Millicent involved with such a bad influence? Of course we don't."

"His name is Lou Blythe, Mother. He's wonderful, handsome, and loving, exactly like Stoney Rhodes on Crest of Love."

"Oh, puke. You should write for Hallmark, Millicent."

Stuart shot his wife a dark, angry frown, which she quickly dismissed with a snort.

"It would be nice for the two of you to meet him." She smiled at her dad. "We're going to celebrate six months of dating this evening, and I'd like to invite him to the cookout."

An exaggerated huff came from Millie's left. "I'm your mother, Millicent Marie. You've hidden this from me for half a year?" Her eyes narrowed. "Didn't I warn you that as long as you live under my roof, you were never to hide anything from me?"

"When will I gain the right to my own life?" Millie gulped when she realized she'd actually exposed her thoughts. She'd never stood up to Mother before. Her eyes searched the ceiling for lightning bolts.

"Maybe when you start making intelligent choices." Her mother sneered. "Lou Blythe is not one of them. He's a plain, ordinary repairman who looks like a mangy orangutan on National Geographic." She pressed on her abdomen and pushed her still-filled plate away. "I don't want to discuss it anymore. The thought of him with you makes my stomach wrench."

Her dad cleared his throat. "We're getting off topic, ladies. The question was if she could invite Lou to the cookout. I vote yes."

Millie crossed her arms and focused on her mother. "He not only has a good business repairing office equipment, he's a computer tech, and sings bass in a gospel quartet." She grinned. "Carol said his voice is so deep, it'll melt the polish off your toenails."

"Millicent Marie! Watch your mouth in front of your father."

"You know, she's right." He chuckled. "I heard his group sing at one of our men's breakfasts. I guarantee there wasn't a speck of polish left on my toenails." He paused before continuing. "Lou's a nice guy but kind of backward."

"Don't encourage her, Stuart." Penny slammed her fist down with enough force to rattle the ice in their glasses.

Millie sent her kind-hearted dad an appreciative smile. "Lou is shy, but once you get to know him, I'm sure you'll love him."

"Ha! I certainly wouldn't count on that happening any time this century."

Ignoring her mother's rudeness, Millie continued. "His mom's coming for a visit soon, and he wants us to meet her."

"Meet his mother? Stuart, do something. This relationship is moving too fast." She glared at Millie. "Did that knuckle dragger even notice you before you started wearing Carol's war paint? Of course he didn't. He's used to all those worldly hussies in the music industry, and you're fitting right into their mold."

"Mother, please. It's gospel music." She frowned and chomped the last bit of her salad to keep from lashing back at the offensive remark.

A teasing smile tugged at the corners of her dad's mouth. "I'd hardly call that a hussy haven, Penny."

"Be that as it may, he'll have his way with our daughter and then bolt like a bat out of you-know-where." Her gape locked with his and her voice raised an octave. "And then no other man will want her because she's been soiled like Fanny Woolsey on Frontier Passion."

"Penelope, drop it." The veins in his neck bulged. "Our Millie has a nice young man who loves God and is interested in her. What more could we ask?"

She pinned him down with eye daggers. "Hush, Stuart. Next thing you know, Fred Flintstone will take her to some liberal church that prays to goddesses with rainbows and unicorns circling their heads. They'll have those cheesy fish crackers and wine coolers for communion. I demand you put your foot down."

Millie fork-jabbed her baked potato right between its eyes. Her dad's good-natured belly laugh was the only thing that protected Mother from a similar fate. Would she ever be out from under that woman's oppressive thumb?

"The boy has my complete blessing, dear." He patted Millie's shoulder. "Lou's in love with our girl, so are you going to deal with it, Penelope?" He raised his voice and frowned. "Of course you are."

She pushed back from the table and rose with her hand pressed to her stomach. "Stuart Thomas Drake! Are you using a *tone* with me?"

CHAPTER TWO

LATER THAT NIGHT, APPETIZING AROMAS MADE Millie's mouth water as she and Lou followed the maître d' into the dining area of the Grand Oasis Inn. The setting sun cast its rays on the crystal chandelier sending red, green, and violet sparkles throughout the room. Waiters in white shirts, black dress pants, and suspenders scurried from table to table. This swanky restaurant offered the perfect ambiance to commemorate six months of dating. He was only a copier and computer tech. How could he afford this place on his salary?

Soft background music helped to ease her nerves as they followed the man to a secluded table for two. The white linen tablecloth and crisp matching napkins indicated the elegance of the establishment. Millie straightened her light green dress and settled into the curved back seat. Lou slid her chair in and took his place across the table.

"Mother hasn't been feeling well lately." She placed her cell phone beside her napkin. "Dad asked me to keep this handy."

A thin young man sporting a wannabe mustache, came to their table with a water pitcher. "Hello, my name is John. I'll be your server this evening. May I get you something to drink?" Ice clinked as he filled their goblets with water. After Millie and Lou gave their beverage orders, the waiter nodded briefly and hurried off.

Millie opened the black and gold menu and stared at the list. "Everything sounds so good. You've been here before, Lou. Do you have any suggestions?"

Lou pointed at the menu's dinner entrée list. "You might enjoy the grilled chicken plate or the pork chop with roasted vegetables."

A few minutes went by before the smiling waiter reappeared and placed their drinks on the table. "Are we ready to order?"

She handed him the menu. "I'd like the grilled chicken plate with the house salad, please."

He turned to Lou. "And you, sir?"

"Your Porterhouse steak is the best. I'll have that, a loaded baked potato, and green beans. Thank you."

Millie took a sip of water after the server disappeared. With her fingers still wrapped around the glass, her eyes locked with Lou's. A sense of intimacy grew between them. "What an enchanting restaurant."

"It's the perfect place to celebrate us." He winked. "I never dreamed I'd have a chance with a beautiful lady like you."

Lou Blythe was such a romantic. He reminded her of Stoney Rhodes, Tawny Lamour's heartthrob on Crest of Love. Her heart fluttered as she peeked over the crimson candle flickering on the table. He never looked more handsome than he did this evening in the charcoal suit and lavender shirt.

As he offered his outstretched hand across the table, the faint ringing of a phone broke the spell. He shook his head, pulled the cell from his pocket, and read the caller ID. "It's Dooley Overton from the quartet. Sorry, I have to take this. I'll try to make it quick." He excused himself from the table.

Millie accepted the explanation with a nod. She watched him head for the foyer where the brass chandelier highlighted his dark hair and broad shoulders. With the phone to his ear, he threw his head back and a deep, bass laugh came from his chest. She grinned. That was her man.

How dare Mother consider Lou an unworthy suitor when she hadn't even met him? No matter the cost, Millie was determined to protect their love life. A wave of heat warmed her neck as she stiffened at the challenge. What kind of plan would she need?

Tawny Lamour faced similar problems on *Crest of Love*. Millie gulped. A lot of innocent people were hurt by Tawny's selfishness. She didn't want to destroy anyone, but simply safeguard their love. After all it was true love. Or was she going out with Lou for the thrill of defying her mother? Her conscience twitched. It was true love for sure. Defying Mother was only a gratifying bonus.

She'd spent too much time devouring the passionate love in her mother's romance novels and soap operas. Life wasn't a soap opera, but it was all she knew. No, that wasn't right. The relationship Aunt Sylvia and Uncle Max shared for so many years had been a great example of lasting devotion. Obviously, Pastor Frank and Carol enjoyed the same genuine love.

What kind of bond did she and Lou have? Sure, he called her Sweet Cheeks and his smile made her heart dance. She felt safe and comfortable with him. They definitely had a connection, but was it worth fighting for?

Millie chewed her lower lip and observed the couple at the next table. They were in their own little world as they held hands and looked deep into each other's eyes. Would Lou ever be that entranced with her?

"Excuse me, ma'am." The waiter's voice broke in on her thoughts. "Your chicken plate and salad." He placed the dinner in front of her.

"Thank you. It looks delicious."

The waiter set the other plate on the table. "And one Porterhouse steak, potato and vegetable. May I get anything else for you?"

"We're fine, thank you." She struggled to keep from looking at the time but eventually gave in and glanced at her watch. Twelve minutes had crept by. No wonder her patience was wearing thin. She realigned the silverware on her napkin one more time. Lou would have to unlearn his bachelor mentality.

She breathed a sigh of relief and cleared the edgy thoughts as Lou approached. He pulled out his chair to join her.

"Dooley shared the best news! I'll fill you in after we say grace." He bowed his head, took her hand, and offered thanks. Once his prayer was finished, he gave her hand a quick squeeze before releasing it.

Millie picked up her napkin and swallowed hard, hoping their group wasn't going on the road any time soon. She missed him when he was away. "So, don't keep me in suspense. What's your big announcement?"

"The Warble-Heirs have a great opportunity for the rest of the summer." Lou's eyes sparkled as he adjusted his purple and gray tie. "This is the first time our gospel quartet has been invited to perform on a luxury cruise liner. There was a last minute cancellation, and we've been booked on three back-to-back tours on the Caribbean Breeze." His smile deepened. "We'll be gone through Labor Day weekend. That's six weeks."

Millie's chicken-laden fork stopped halfway to her mouth. Romantic cruises for six whole weeks? Her shoulders slumped as she struggled to breathe. She pictured Lou drowning in a sea of voluptuous babes lurking in skimpy bikinis on the Lido Deck. Champagne would gush from bubbling flamingo fountains with everyone having their fill.

And then there was Lou, the only single man onboard.

"Doesn't that sound exciting?" Lou said between bites.

"I can't believe it. We've never had a break like this." He grew quiet and concentrated on his meal.

Millie watched as his steak, potato, and dinner rolls ceased to exist. How could the man eat like that when they were going to be apart for so long? Oooh. Her stomach pitched as a bout of seasickness overwhelmed her, and she wasn't even on a ship. She scooted her dinner roll plate toward Lou.

Her voice finally found life again. "Are the wives going?"

"Lonnie and his wife, Dena, are retired, so she's going. She's also our manager and goes with us most of the time." He drained his water glass and reached for her untouched roll. "My dog, Farfel, always stays with Dooley's wife. She enjoys his company, and he loves her cooking."

The idea of Lou leaving for so long shook her. Millie half-heartedly poked the cherry tomato in her salad. "When do you leave?"

"Next Saturday." He popped the last bite of well-buttered dinner roll into his mouth and licked his fingers.

Next Saturday? She'd looked forward to this birthday, her first with a sweetheart, and now he wouldn't be there. Her lower lip quivered. A pout welled up as loneliness, confusion, and frustration fused together in one stinkin' flash. Should she take cues from Mother and mention the cookout to make him feel like a first-class heel, or be more like Dad and take the disappointment in stride?

"Would you like dessert before we go?" He wiped his mouth. "The Oasis is known for their lemon meringue pie."

Millie tucked a lock of hair behind her ear. "I'll just have coffee, but go ahead if you want a slice."

"Don't mind if I do." Lou motioned for the waiter, ordered the coffee and dessert, then turned his attention back to Millie. The crimson candle flickered as he scooted it aside and rested his open hand on the table.

An unwelcomed mix of emotions brought warmth to her cheeks. Here they were celebrating their sixth month anniversary and now, he wanted to leave her? She reluctantly touched his palm as an awkward silence settled between them.

"You're awfully quiet, Millie. Are you okay?" He squeezed her hand.

"I'm fine. Your news caught me off guard, that's all." She quickly lowered her head to hide the disappointment and threatening tears. "I'm happy for your opportunity, but I'll miss you, Lou."

He cut her a glance and rubbed his forehead. "I get it. We're going to be separated for six weeks."

"Exactly." Pain stung her heart.

"I'm so sorry, honey. I was only thinking of this once-in-a-lifetime adventure." His head popped up, and he offered a remorseful smile. "I've been a lonely bachelor for so long, having a girl in my life is still new to me."

His sad-eyed expression sent her emotions into a tailspin. "I understand. I'd be excited too." Millie gave a crooked smile. While she admired Lou Blythe and his unselfish goal to serve the Lord, the fact remained he'd forgotten about her.

The waiter brought Lou's lemon pie and two cups of coffee. "Anything else I can get you?"

Lou sent a questioning glance her way.

She feigned a cheery smile and shook her head. "I don't think so, but thanks anyway. This is fine."

While Lou licked his lips and dug into the lemon meringue, a burst of thoughts assailed her mind like bullets from Al Capone's Tommy gun. If they got married would he always leave her behind when he went on tour? Even special things like this cruise? Surely, he'd invite her along.

Staring into the candle flame, Millie envisioned Cap'n

Lou Sparrow's arm around her cinched waist as they leisurely strolled around the mizzenmast on the moonlit deck. The bearded buccaneer stopped and pulled her near. Her eyes closed as she leaned in for the kiss that was sure to shiver-her-timbers.

Popping noises grew louder, ripping her from the swashbuckling romance. She blinked herself back to reality, looked around, and offered a sheepish smile.

Lou cracked his knuckles. "You're so beautiful tonight." He reached for her hand. "I wish you were going to the Caribbean with me."

An ache filled Millie's throat. He was going to miss her after all. Her heart did an Olympic-worthy somersault as she smiled and brushed pie crumbs from his smooth chin. She liked him better without the braided pirate beard.

"Someday we'll do everything together." He offered her a bite of pie.

She placed her hand on his and helped guide the lemon cream into her mouth. In spite of the initial disappointment of the cruise, the evening had finally turned romantic. The surroundings blurred as the sense of seclusion and intimacy intensified between them.

The waiter discreetly placed the bill on the table.

Lou inserted cash into the black and gold folder and pocketed his billfold. "Don't forget your cell." He picked up her phone and handed it to her.

She smiled and put it in her purse. "I'm always forgetting this thing."

His arm held her tightly as they left the restaurant and walked into the waning heat. He opened the van door and with a peck on the cheek, helped her inside.

Silvery moonlight peeked from behind the clouds creating a purple and mauve hodgepodge in the desert sky.

Millie was thankful he liked her suggestion to take the

long way home. The evening was nearly over, and she still hadn't decided whether to mention her birthday cookout.

Headlights from an oncoming semi brightened Lou's profile. The passionate rhythm of her pulse escalated as she relived her man's promising affection. Tonight he had strummed the romantic strings of her heart, which rendered her rather frisky. No, no. Make that *significantly* frisky. She squirmed in her seat. *Slow down, Millie. You're not some starry-eyed serving wench like Portia Claremont in Pillagers of Desire.*

By the time they turned into her cul-de-sac, Millie decided to forget about bringing up her birthday. No need to put him on a guilt trip and ruin his cruise. However, she fully intended to lavish him with kisses, enough for him to relive during the six weeks without her. She rolled up her sleeve, administered a quick swipe of Lippity-Dew, and mentally set her smooch-gauge to zealous.

"I don't want Mother to see your van, so let's pull over in front of the bushes."

The van sputtered to a stop by the Arizona Rosewood near the Drake home. Thank goodness, the porch light wasn't on to distract from the soft veil of moonlight. The kissing ambiance was perfect. A healthy dose of hope mounted in her chest as he leaned over, filling the space between their seats.

"Thank you for the romantic evening, Lou." She scooted in his direction and closed her eyes, anticipating the perfect kiss. One like Sir Lance Lambert planted on Lady Viola in her last romance novel. Tonight, she'd immortalize every amorous moment in her diary.

Lou cleared his throat but said nothing as he took her hand.

In the darkness of the van, she waited, lips scrunched, for that monumental kiss. Seconds passed before something soft brushed her forehead. Her fervent pucker fizzled, and her left eye popped open.

With a deep sigh, Lou moved away and settled back into his seat. The silence lengthened between them, making her uncomfortable.

Was this the same Romeo she just had supper with? What caused the sudden arctic clipper? His familiar knuckle cracking broke the stillness, and Millie put her hand on his to muffle the percussion solo. "What's wrong, Lou?"

"I'm not sure."

Her heart dropped as insecurity set in. Had she prematurely puckered and turned him off, or was this his way of dropping her as Mother predicted? Couldn't be, he hadn't even tried to have his way with her yet.

"Did I do something wrong?" *Please say no.* "I'll try to do better."

"It's not that, Millie. I love your kisses." He massaged her hand. "I've never asked this, but is there a reason you've never introduced me to your parents?" He faced the windshield. "Do I embarrass you?"

She gasped. "No. Don't even think that."

"Then why didn't you want your mother to see my van?"

"Uh—" Did she have the pluck to say she wanted him to kiss her good and proper . . . or improper for that matter? "I hoped a little privacy was in order." She looked out her window then turned to face him. "I was also waiting for the right moment to invite you to my birthday cookout next Saturday to meet Mother and Dad. But now you're leaving on that cruise and won't be able to come." She sniffed. "I didn't want you to feel bad."

"I'm sorry. I shouldn't have jumped to conclusions. Listen, my flight is late in the day." His voice reflected hope as he pulled her close. "So if your cookout is early enough, Sweet Cheeks, I can make it."

"You can? Really?" Millie wanted to rejoice, but the thought of him meeting her belligerent mother was nerve-racking. It was like dipping him in bacon grease and tossing him into a lion's den. If their promising relationship was going to move forward, Lou deserved an explanation. "The fact is I put off having you over because of Mother. She's not the easiest person to please." Her hand went to his shoulder. "I wanted to protect you from her harsh and unreasonable attitude. I was afraid of losing you."

Lou shrugged. "Come on, honey. I know your mother has a strong will, but she can't be as bad as you're insinuating."

And that quick, Lou Blythe crossed the line. The atmospheric pressure in the van changed. Millie trained her eyes on him like twin barrels of a shotgun.

Her cheeks flamed as she choked back the angry knots threatening to strangle her carotid arteries. "Y-You haven't witnessed the destruction Mother's capable of."

Uh-oh. Forty-three years of fiery magma had finally reached the boiling point, and Mount Millicent was about to erupt.

"I've suffered under Mother's controlling and conniving ways my whole life." She clenched her teeth. "It doesn't matter how much I try to appease her. She manipulates people and situations to get her own way and doesn't care who gets hurt. Ask anyone."

Millie stiffened. At what point had she grabbed his necktie? She released her hold and frantically tried to smooth the wrinkles. A prickly silence descended on the van. Had she hammered the final nail into her romantic coffin?

She turned from Lou wanting to disappear. Instead, she'd have to settle for ejecting herself from the van. "I need air."

Squaring her shoulders and clinging to what little dignity she had left, Millie gave the door handle a good yank. It held firm. She bit her lip to fight back a sob and feverishly shoved a shoulder against the rigid and unyielding metal.

Tap-tap-tap.

She looked to the window where Lou's solemn face stared back at her.

"Millie." He pointed to the door. "It's jammed. Let me help." The metal hinges moaned as he jerked it open. In one forward motion, he pulled her into an embrace. "I didn't realize how much your mother upsets you. I'm sorry. Do you still want me to come to your cookout?"

She turned into a gooey mass of remorse, still unable to return his gaze. "Oh, yes. I really want you there." She chewed on her lower lip and cleared her squeaky voice. "I'm the one who's sorry. Forgive me for being so childish."

"I can't imagine anyone coming between us." Lou worked the knot in his tie loose. "Especially your mother." His hand went beneath her chin and gently raised her face so she had to look at him.

Eyes blurring, Millie melted into his arms. She became lightheaded as soon as their lips touched. *Don't swoon.* She returned his kiss, savoring every second.

Lou whispered her name again and looked longingly into her eyes. "I-I-I love you."

CHAPTER THREE

DEAR DIARY,

TODAY IS MY 43RD birthday. Each birthday is a blatant reminder of being another year older and still unmarried, and Mother never lets me forget it.

This is the last time I'll see Lou until after Labor Day. I'm going to miss him dreadfully. I'm not looking forward to my birthday cookout, but meeting my parents was his idea. More than anything, I want this initial meeting with Mother and Dad to be a positive experience for him. However, Mother's narcissism is a one-note chord, a constant bellyaching that smothers any intimate or casual conversation. Is it possible for anything to end on a high note when Mother's involved?

I have always envied the bond Carol has with her mother. She and Aunt Sylvia have a closeness that fosters love, acceptance, and understanding. But my fumbling, well-intended efforts to imitate that bond with my own mother always seems to miss the mark. She always expects me to jump to attention whenever she calls. No questions asked. It's getting old and I don't know how much more of it I can take.

One more of her nasty comments about Lou being a Neanderthal or caveman and I won't be responsible for the outcome.

A blistering blast of hot air beneath the late-July sun showed promise of the scorching weeks to come.

Sitting on the front steps of the house, Millie readjusted the buckle on her beige sandal while waiting for Lou to arrive. Her mind was a conglomeration of hope and fear as she thought of him not only facing Mother today, but also preparing for his extended trip.

The red van rumbled to a stop in the drive, and Lou jumped out and pulled a single rose from behind his back. "Happy birthday!"

Tears formed in her eyes and her heart melted. Her first birthday with a sweetheart, and he was trying to make it perfect. Millie flew down the driveway to his side, accepted the rose, and welcomed him with a kiss.

Their smooch came to a quick demise when heavy breathing from the van caught her attention. She frowned and peered over Lou's shoulder. Was that a drooling basset hound she saw hanging out the window? Her nerves zinged. Lou brought Farfel.

Millie opened her mouth and shut it. She couldn't scold him for bringing his beloved pet, but Mother was not going to be happy. The dog's head bobbed as she patted him. "Hi, boy. I didn't know you were coming." Chewing on her brittle smile, she was amazed her voice was sweeter and calmer than expected. "Lou, I need to remind you, Mother isn't an animal lover."

"I know." He nodded and took her hand. "Sorry, but it couldn't be helped this time. I have to take Farfel to Dooley's house. His wife is going to dog-sit. For now, he'll be on his leash."

"Okay. But please, we have to keep Farfel as far away from my mother as possible, for all our sakes."

"I promise you, I'll do my best." He leaned in for another kiss.

Millie placed her hand on his waiting lips. "One more thing." She looked deep into his blue eyes. "Remember when I said Mother can be hurtful? Be prepared because it's bound to happen at least once. Don't take it personally. Smile, look at me, and—" It was her turn to say it. She cleared her throat. "Please remember I love you."

Unbelievable. She actually managed to say the three little words, which up until now, had been reserved for select family members only.

"Really?" An easy smile played at the corners of his mouth. "I was hoping you'd say that before I left. Now, where's my kiss?"

Millie stood on tiptoe and pressed her lips to his.

He whispered in her ear. "By the way, Sweet Cheeks, you're beautiful."

The sensation of having beauty made her face warm. To think a man would pay her such a compliment.

She stepped away and drew a breath while he leashed Farfel. Thoughts of Mother's reaction to the dog brought on a sick feeling. This little snag had birthday damper written all over it.

The trio headed for the backyard where her dad stood guard over a sizzling grill. Stuart Drake smiled through a cloud of barbecue smoke, placed the long-handled tongs on the table, and wiped his hands on a towel. "Afternoon, Lou." He greeted the younger man with a handshake, and then bent down. "And who do we have here?"

"This is my buddy, Farfel. Thanks for inviting us today."

"Our pleasure." Stuart rubbed the dog's belly. "Oh,

boy. Wait until Grandma sees you."

The patio door slid open. "Millicent!"

Millie jumped at the sound of her mother's voice. She gave Lou's arm a squeeze and hurried into the house to help the family's relentless drill sergeant.

"Well, it's about time you got in here. I'm doing all the work in this hot kitchen, and it's making me lightheaded. The least you can do is tote things to the patio table. After all, he's *your* guest."

The sight of her birthday cake caught Millie's attention. "What a beautiful masterpiece. You must've worked all night to make those lilacs so perfect. I hope you've taken several pictures of it."

"I haven't had time to take any pictures." She planted her fists on her hips. "We'll do that outside in proper lighting so it picks up all the minute details of the petals and leaves. I hope you and your caveman appreciate all my hard work to make your day special."

There it was. Mother said caveman. It was becoming more and more difficult to keep quiet. Millie's blood boiled as she pressed her lips together and tried to maintain her composure. One day Mother would get what she deserved, and that was a scary thought.

Millie slid the glass door open, grabbed the tray of condiments from the counter, and stepped out to the patio. After setting the tray on the table a little harder than necessary, she drew a deep breath. The smoky aroma of sizzling steaks eased her jangled nerves. A diminutive speck of hope rose in her chest when she watched her dad give Farfel a juicy nibble. Maybe the day would turn out okay after all.

Stuart wiped at a stain on his shirt, and then handed the tongs to the younger man. "Will you watch the grill for me, Lou, while I change my clothes?"

"I'd be glad to." Lou smiled and put his arm around

Millie's shoulder. "I don't know what you were so worried about, honey. Things are going great."

"I wasn't worried about Dad." She patted his back. "You haven't met—"

An ear-hemorrhaging shriek came from the house.

"Oh, Lou, Dad left the patio door open!" An empty leash lay on the ground next to the patio table. "Where's Farfel?"

They hurried to the kitchen where her mother was still screaming. She awkwardly held the birthday cake to one side as the long-eared basset hound circled her legs.

Lou reached for Farfel's collar and missed. The dog's head came up, collided with Penny's arm, and pushed her off balance. The cake launched upward, and hovered as if in slow motion. Her fanny hit the floor first, followed by the plummeting purple confection, which knocked her flat.

Frosting lilacs plastered her face as she lay sprawled on the kitchen floor. Her arms and legs flailed between each lung-filled squawk. The sugary mess had become a tongue magnet for the tail-wagging hound. In spite of Lou pulling on Farfel's collar, the hound's short, stocky legs anchored the woman as he doggedly licked purple goo from her neck and shoulders.

Stuart burst into the room. "What's going on?" He skidded to a stop then pointed to his wife on the floor, doubled over, and howled with laughter.

"This is not funny, S-S-Stuart." She hissed his name and gasped for air. "Get rid of this hideous beast. Now!"

The drooling dog pounced to her cake-covered mouth where his lavender tongue pilfered the mess in several quick swipes. Penny released another siren-worthy screech. She spat and sputtered, as she smacked the floor with her hands.

"Get down, boy." Lou grabbed Farfel's collar as Penny

spit and gagged. He wrestled the dog away and dragged him outside, leaving purple and white skid marks in their wake.

By this time, Stuart had regained enough composure to help Penny to her feet. "Millie, take your mother upstairs and help her clean up. I'll tend to the steaks." He stifled another chuckle. "I'll help Lou hose a couple layers off the dog too."

A slap on the hand greeted Millie as she reached for her mother's arm.

"Do not touch me, Millicent." Penny headed for the stairway. "I can go by myself, thank you very much. Have your father remove that animal and his dog from the premises immediately."

This nightmare was all she needed. The Mother/Farfel apocalypse would certainly lower Lou's approval rating. Tears welled and Millie's throat tightened. "Mother, you can't blame Lou. This is life and accidents happen."

"That mangy beast licking my lips shall haunt me until the day I die, which will probably be soon because dogs have worms." She stopped on the stairs and shook her finger at Millie, standing a few steps behind her. "And if you think I want all of Apache Pointe to know I had to be de-wormed, well, girlie, you have another think coming."

Writhing with temptation to be the cheeky de-wormer, Millie clenched her fists and followed her angry parent into the bathroom. "Mother, I've had my fill of your hysterics. You're ruining my birthday."

"I'm ruining it? Everything was flawless until that beast showed up. My cake, my kitchen, my outfit." Penny stared into the mirror and screamed. "Look at my hair! I had it done this morning. Forty-nine dollars down the drain. Plus tip."

"Let me help you." Millie reached for a washcloth from

the linen closet.

Penny raised her crepey arm to stop her. "I said don't touch me." A double chin formed as she lowered her head, pulled creamy clumps of purple frosting from her maroon-colored coiffure, and threw them into the sink. "I spent hours on my beautiful lilac cake, and I didn't get one picture. Who ruined what, Millicent Marie?"

"Everything always has to be about you. Why are you so hateful?" Millie had never been so furious. She suppressed the urge to clamp her hands around her mother's neck. Fists clenched, she stomped to the top of the stairs, turned, and shrieked, "You make me sick!"

With her eyes taking on the predictable rattlesnake glower, Penny bared her fangs. She was ready to strike. "How dare you bring your Neanderthal boyfriend into my home?"

Millie's voice cracked as it elevated. "May I remind you, I love that Neanderthal?"

A hairspray can flew past Millie's head, hit the wall, and thumped down the steps. "Get out of my sight, you ungrateful brat."

A second of unprecedented headiness flared in Millie's chest before realization hit. She'd actually yelled at Mother and even considered choking her. As long as she could remember, Millie prayed to not become a Penny clone, and yet today, anger surfaced as if it were second nature.

Scurrying to put distance between them, she took the stairs at a fast clip. Visions of turning into a pillar of salt kept her from looking back.

Her breath caught when she nearly collided with Lou standing at the bottom step. Shock etched his face. He turned and marched out the door without a single word.

Icy prongs stabbed her heart and her body trembled. A firm click of the door's latch ended any promise of romance.

CHAPTER FOUR

A GUST OF WIND MESSED LOU'S hair as he plopped on the park bench, angry and defeated from the frenzied scene at Millie's cookout. His stomach clenched. How did her dad stand the chaotic tension with two women going for each other's throat? He cracked his knuckles. Stuart Drake had to be on the short list for sainthood.

Exhausted from the trials and emotional seesaw of the afternoon, Lou rested his elbows on his knees and moaned. Farfel, still sporting a dark purple tongue from the birthday cake, nuzzled between his master's arms. Lou scratched the dog's ears and picked some of the lingering frosting lilacs from the fur. "Face it, boy. You and your sweet tooth own some of the blame for this fiasco."

He had known Millie for several years and dated her for six months. She was always sweet and even-tempered. Within the last week, she'd exploded, not once, but twice. Was that the true Millie surfacing? Did he want to spend the rest of his life dodging anger and flying projectiles like Stuart Drake had for years?

"Hey, Lou!"

With a slight huff, Lou wiped his eyes with the heel of his hand and looked over his shoulder. Of all the times for Pastor Frank and Carol to come by. He didn't want to talk to anyone, but scooted over on the bench to make room for the couple anyway. "What are you and Carol doing here?"

"We're enjoying a nice afternoon together." The pastor motioned for Carol to sit beside Lou. He took a bite of ice cream and sat next to her. "What's wrong? Weren't you supposed to be with Millie today?"

"We were there all right." His face turned into a hard-lipped scowl as he patted his dog's head. "Then we left."

Frank hesitated for a moment, and then chuckled. "We? You mean you actually had the nerve to take Farfel? Didn't Millie warn you that Penny hates animals?"

"Not one of my smarter moves, was it?" Lou shook his head. "She told me. I had no choice but to take him with me."

"I see." Carol licked a drip from her Pudgy Fudgy Bar. Farfel crouched at her feet and smacked his lips while his tail thumped the ground. "And you bore the brunt of Aunt Penny's finely tuned social graces, didn't you?"

Lou raked his fingers through his hair. "I sure did. And let me tell you, that daughter of hers came in a close second in the battle of the banshees."

Frank's eyebrows shot up. "Whoa, wait a minute, Lou. That can't be right. Millie Drake has been my secretary for years and has always been soft spoken."

"That's what I thought, but I've seen another side of her. Twice." Lou cracked his knuckles. "You know the old saying about the daughter taking after the mother. Well, I believe it." He lowered his head. A mixture of anger and confusion flared in his chest. "Who wants to be tethered to someone that harsh and controlling?"

"For years Uncle Stuart's been too lenient in dealing with Aunt Penny." Carol shook her head and frowned. "She should've been reined in a long time ago, but he lets her get away with things to keep peace."

"Keep peace? I saw the results of his arbitration skills today when a hairspray can went airborne and hit the wall." Lou rubbed the back of his neck.

"Aunt Penny's self-imposed authority has ruined any decent relationship between them. Poor Millie's dealing with a lifetime of oppression. If I saw a hint of my cousin morphing into her mother, I'd warn you and the world."

"Meanwhile, we'll help you pray about it." Frank stood and handed his business card to Lou. "My cell number is on here. Carol, Andy, and I are leaving this afternoon to visit my daughters for a couple of weeks, but you can still call or text anytime."

"Thanks. I'll pray for your travels." Lou took the card, hunched over, and stared at his basset hound. "I was beginning to think Millie cared for me."

Carol looked squarely at him and placed her hand on his shoulder. "Trust me, Millie and I have talked about your romance, and it's more important to her than anything else. Her stress load is over the top, Lou. She never had the nerve to stand up to her mother before. It sounds to me like she's actually fighting for you."

"Thanks, Carol. You've given me a lot to think about for the next six weeks." He looked at his watch. "Sorry to gripe and run, but I've got to get Farfel to Dooley's house, and rush to Sky Harbor Airport."

Frank shook his hand. "That's right. You're going on that cruise. Like I said, we'll be praying that you and Millie can work things out."

As Lou and Farfel made their way across the parking lot, Millie's previous words of warning came back to taunt him. *Mother can be hurtful. Smile, look at me, and remember I love you.*

He put the dog in the van, climbed into the driver's seat, and rested his forehead on the steering wheel. "I'm such a meathead, Farfel. After all this time, Millie admitted she loves me, and what do I do? I leave her to face her mother alone."

Lou followed the other Warble-Heirs through the Jetway

to their plane. After checking his ticket to Tampa for the seat number, he headed for the already filled coach section. He stared incredulously at the miniscule spot that corresponded with his number. He crammed his long body into the aisle seat, thankful for the extra legroom.

Once settled and seatbelt on, he nodded to the old man on his right and the expectant mother seated by the window. The straggly bearded man looked like a long-lost relative from Duck Dynasty. His wiry, gray facial hair had two reddish-brown streaks coming from the corners of his mouth.

The mother-to-be wore a flowered dress and continuously rubbed her swollen stomach. She reached into her green straw bag, pulled out a pack of Black Jack chewing gum, and offered a stick to her seatmates. "Here, this might help to keep your ears open."

Lou reached across Mr. Whiskers to pull a stick of gum from the blue and black jumbo pack. He smiled and thanked her.

The old man, however, waved her off and pulled out a small bag of George's Jerky from his back pocket. He thumbed a few pieces, decided on the largest, and gave Lou a snaggletooth grin. "Might wanna play your man card and try one of these instead of that chewin' gum." He held up the bag.

"No thanks. Maybe later." Lou settled into his seat as the plane taxied down the runway. Too bad the others in the Warble-Heirs group weren't sitting closer. He scratched the back of his neck. This might be a long four hours. Who was he kidding? This was going to be a long six weeks.

Across the narrow aisle, Lou noticed a younger couple holding hands during takeoff. Their heads touched as they gazed into each other's eyes.

A short time later, the flight attendant stopped at their seat. "Congratulations on your wedding, Mr. and Mrs.

Walburn. I hope you two have a great time on your honeymoon."

His seat had to be next to newlyweds. Of all the luck. Bitter loneliness enveloped him. He was trying to keep his mind off Millie, but everything seemed to remind him of their injured relationship. Without her, his whole life was thrown out of sync.

Lou combed his fingers through his hair. No matter how hard he tried, his mind kept wandering back to Millie and her party. Would the day have ended any better if he hadn't taken Farfel to the birthday cookout? Probably, but from what Carol and Frank said about Millie's unpredictable mother, it was highly unlikely.

The main question on his mind was how he would be able to sing of God's love and grace to an audience when he still carried the guilt of abandoning Millie.

If only she'd answer the phone so he could make it right with her.

CHAPTER FIVE

AFTER A SHORT BOUT OF FEELING sorry for herself, Millie sat up on the bed and straightened the wrinkles from her blouse. A prolonged pity-party wouldn't solve anything. As she tried to compose herself, a spontaneous gulp of air caught in her throat. She scooted from the bed determined to make permanent changes in her life.

Yanking her berry-colored suitcase from the top shelf in the closet, she plopped it on the bed and began to fill it. After setting various bathroom items on the counter, she slammed the medicine cabinet door and frowned into the mirror. "Well, you really did it." She shook a finger at herself. "Forty-three years of Mother's manipulation and you wait until today, of all days, to sink to her level. Thank you very much, Millicent Marie."

She'd only gone ballistic twice in her life and both times in front of Lou.

Her jaw tightened as she hurled a can of hairspray onto the bed. She gasped. That's what Mother did in their fight that afternoon. The woman's angry, contorted face flashed before Millie's eyes. Was that vile disposition taking hold of her too?

The time had come to make a decision. Leave home or risk turning into Mother's clone permanently. She crammed the hair blower into the suitcase next to her socks, causing the lid to shut on her pinkie.

A knock on the door made her jump. She rubbed the throbbing finger. "Who is it?"

"It's Dad. Mind if we talk?"

"It depends. Are you alone?"

"Yes, Princess." He laughed. "I took your mother to the beauty shop for a major overhaul. It's a small price to pay for a little peace and quiet."

Tears welled as Millie opened the door and flew into his arms. "I'm sorry, Dad. I didn't know Lou was going to bring Farfel. He had no choice. After the cookout, he had to drop the dog off and get to the airport."

"It isn't your fault or his. You've endured years of your mother's harshness, so it was bound to come to a head one day." He gave her a tight squeeze, turned the desk chair around, and sat facing her. "I'm the one who should apologize for letting your mother's offensive behavior go on so long. It was easier to turn a deaf ear and ignore her rants. I regret not being firmer for your sake. We're both paying for my silence."

"I've never blamed you. In fact I need to thank you because your patience taught me how to cope when life gets overwhelming." Millie shook her head. "Am I turning out to be like her?"

"I don't want you to ever think that." He pointed his finger at her. "You're more like your Grandma Drake. She was known for her kindness and encouragement."

"Thank you. If only she'd lived long enough for me to know her." Millie stared at the floor. "What possible attraction did Mother have that made you want to marry her?"

"Think about it. I was a young, green soldier in South Vietnam. Lonely, scared, and homesick. Seemed like everyone else had sweethearts to brag about, but the only mail I received was from my mom and your Uncle Max. When I got that first post from Penny, I was hooked." His eyes glazed, then he grinned and shook his head. "Oh, my, can that woman write a good letter."

"Didn't you see any obvious red flags when you met

her face-to-face?"

"I was nineteen and saw some of my buddies killed right beside me. But, I finally made it home safe and my sweetheart said she loved me." He shrugged. "That's all I cared about at that time. Unfortunately the red flags didn't show up until after the knot was securely tied and the ring was in my nose."

Millie shook her head. "I'm sorry. Sounds like you left one war zone and came home to another."

"I'm okay. The Lord helps me through it." He put his hand on her shoulder. "I want to warn you about a couple of things. First, unrealistic expectations are dangerous. Real men don't wear shining armor like romance novel heroes."

She kissed his cheek. "It's going to be hard, but I'll try to remember your sage advice."

"You do that." He chuckled. "Another thing, I know Lou believes in God the same as we do, but if things don't work out with him, never settle for someone of a different faith. Make sure he has a personal relationship with the Lord and not just a Sunday pew warmer."

Millie nodded. "I understand."

He glanced at the luggage on the bed beside her. "Going somewhere?"

"Only for a couple of weeks. Pastor Frank and Carol plan to visit his daughters. She asked me to house sit her place until they get back. The solitude will help me think things through and put it into perspective." She shrugged. "After that, my arrangements are nonexistent, but I'd love to find a place of my own."

"I'm going to miss you, but I understand." He took her hand. "When the time comes, if you need help with a deposit on an apartment, let me know. Promise I can visit when needed?"

"Promise." Millie laughed through tears and then grew

serious. "What about you? Are you going to be all right here with Mother?"

"The weekly therapy sessions for her increasing anger issues haven't been working. She threatened to sue the entire staff for negligence. Her counselor said the next step might be taking her to Arizona State Hospital in Phoenix."

"I remember you mentioned that to me after her last appointment. Mother's going to flip out when you tell her."

"Looks like I'm going to have a lot of overtime in my future."

"I hate it's come to this, but we can't go on sweeping it under the rug, Dad. She needs help." She paused. "You can't live the rest of your life under her dictatorship."

"True. I've had my fill." He rubbed his chin. "Seriously, if she needs time in the hospital, I might take advantage of it and go on a short-term mission trip. I've wanted to do that for years."

"What a good idea. Why don't you talk to Ethan? He and his fiancé work summers at a reservation outside of Phoenix. Carol says they have another three weeks before returning to college."

"That's right. I'll get in touch with him, and maybe I can meet his girl too."

"There is something you can do for me. I'd appreciate your prayers for my courtship with Lou."

"Anything in particular?"

"He saw a side of me even I didn't know existed. My inner-Penny shot forth in flames. It tore me up to see the broken look on Lou's face when he walked out. That's when I realized how deep my love went." She swiped her nose. "And now I might have lost him."

"Trials help us grow stronger if we trust the Lord. He'll take care of you and Lou." He pulled her into a protective daddy hug. "I couldn't be prouder of you, Princess. Meanwhile, due to technical difficulties, neither of us had lunch. Come downstairs with me. I managed to salvage a couple of the steaks for sandwiches and the coffee is ready. I'd appreciate some pleasant company, because from here on out that might be a rare commodity."

"You're probably right. Not sure I can eat, but coffee sounds good." Following him, Millie bypassed a dented can of Teeze 'n' Freeze hairspray resting on the fourth step. She even refused to glance at the front door where Lou stormed out of her life like Marshal Buck did to Darcy May on *Frontier Passion.*

Stuart pointed to the tile floor in the kitchen. "Watch your step. I tried to clean the point of impact after taking your Mother to the hairdresser." He grabbed a potato chip bag from a cabinet and pulled sandwiches from the refrigerator.

"You did a pretty good job. When we get done eating, I'll work on the cupboards and get Farfel's nose prints off the glass door." Millie took a sip of coffee and put a sandwich on a paper plate. Her shoulders relaxed a bit. "Maybe you could finish the floor while we wait for Mother's call."

"Sounds good." Stuart glanced at the clock. "It's almost five. By my calculations, we have about an hour and a half."

"A little teamwork and we should get it all done." She spread a dab of mustard on her bread.

After a short blessing over their food, he popped a potato chip into his mouth and added a few to his plate. "Eat up. You'll feel better."

"I love you, Dad. Talking to you helps." Surprised at her recovering appetite, she took a small bite of her steak sandwich and returned it to her plate. She couldn't wait to get out of the house but felt a little guilty about leaving her father behind. "Why are you frowning?"

He took a gulp of coffee. "Have you noticed how often

your mother complains about her stomach lately?"

"Not really. She complains about everything so I rarely pay attention any more. Why?"

He licked his fingers. "Maybe it's my imagination, but she hasn't been eating much, either. She's eased up on her chocolates too."

"The only thing I've really noticed is that she gets tired easily. I've seen her fall asleep in front of her favorite shows or while reading a book. That's not like her." Millie took another bite of her sandwich.

"She's way overdue for a checkup. Guess it's time for me to poke that ol' bear again." Her dad finished his sandwich and then grabbed the mustard jar and loaf of bread. As he put them away, his attention shifted to the kitchen clock. "Look at the time. She'll be ready to come home in an hour."

A sense of urgency prompted Millie to push away from the table with half a sandwich in her hand. "Ready to work. I'll set the timer for forty-five minutes."

"Rags and cleaner are by the fridge. Let me get my workin' music on." He cranked up a Herb Alpert and the Tijuana Brass CD, then grabbed the mop and filled the bucket with hot water. "I'm goin' in."

The father-daughter team rushed through their tasks at breakneck speed. It wasn't long before the timer went off and still no phone call. Mother must've required fine-tuning.

Stuart wrung out his mop, emptied the pail, and set both outside to dry. "You missed a swath of dog slobber on the patio door. I'm going upstairs to get a clean shirt."

Millie wiped the perspiration from her forehead and groaned. Why hadn't she tackled the door first? Any trace of dog would upset Mother, so those nose prints should've been priority one. She poured vinegar into the hot water.

The initial layer of frosting on the glass melted away without much effort, but Farfel's snot proved more stubborn.

Hotter water, ammonia, Mother's plastic scrubby, and a roll of paper towels should do it. Another mad dash to the door and a five-minute scouring ensued.

The phone rang. Millie cringed and kicked her scrubbing into fourth gear.

Her dad poked his head around the corner. "Guess who. I'm going after her. Don't worry about putting stuff away. I'll get it."

"Please take your time. By the way, I think it's a nice day for an extended drive, don't you agree?"

He presented a thumbs-up and headed for the door. "Good thinkin'. You just got yourself an extra half-hour."

Millie wiped her eyes and reset the timer for fifteen minutes which offered her enough time to get away without encountering more maternal hostility. She went back to work on the slimed patio door.

Her wounded heart screamed to escape her mother's constant rants. Millie took a deep breath. Moving to her own place was the perfect solution for a chance at a normal life–whatever that was. She wanted that normal life to include Lou, but would he forgive her? Could she win his love back?

The buzzing timer warned that her folks would be home shortly. She stood back and looked at the door from different angles. Four snout spots remained. Too bad.

Millie tossed the empty ammonia bottle in the trash and managed to put the remaining cleaning supplies away. She ran upstairs, grabbed her luggage, and raced to the car before The Duchess returned to her palace.

CHAPTER SIX

Last week in July

THE SHIP'S FLAGS FLAPPED IN THE wind as Lou followed the other Warble-Heirs through the crowd and up the short walkway. Seagulls squawked and circled overhead as the tourists boarded the Caribbean Breeze.

Lou shoved the cell phone into his pocket and wiped his sweaty palms. He had let the last call to Millie ring ten times, and she still wouldn't answer.

"Come on, boy. Pick up your pace. We don't want to miss the lifeboat drill." Lonnie Chandler reached past an older lady in a hibiscus print muumuu and casually punched Lou's arm.

"Don't worry." Lou adjusted his backpack. His misunderstanding with Millie had snuffed the fun out of this adventure before it even started. "I'm right behind you."

"Hope you have your boarding pass ready, and whatever you do, smile when they take your photo ID." The older man put his arm around his wife, Dena, as they stepped onboard the ship. "We are going to have so much fun."

"Hey there, cowboy!" A firm hand came out of nowhere, grabbed Lou's arm, and squeezed. "Do you mind if I hold onto your left gun?" She tightened her grip. "Appears to me like it's fully loaded."

His back stiffened as he gaped at the presumptuous woman hanging onto his bicep. She wore a white cowgirl hat, and a bright red plaid shirt tied at the midriff.

"My new boots are killing me." She wrinkled her nose. Her grip tightened on his arm as she held up a foot. "Do you like them?"

He looked down at the fancy cowgirl boot with its sharply pointed toe. "It looks pretty painful to me."

"My name is Betsy Barnum, by the way." She lifted her sunglasses and batted her heavily lashed eyes. "Are you one of the singers for this cruise?"

"Yeah, I'm with the Warble-Heirs Quartet." He wished she'd loosen her grip before his gun went numb.

"I'll be checking your group out." Betsy flashed a grin. "Look for me in the front row, good-lookin'." She released his arm and gave it a rub before boot-scooting on her way.

He supposed her less-than-bashful charms attracted certain men, but he wasn't one of them. It didn't matter how many times the cowgirl sent him one of those come-hither looks. Millie was the one who had lassoed his heart.

Marv, with zinc oxide on his lips and nose, hurried to Lou's side. "There you are. Go get checked in. We're on the Baja Deck. I can't wait until you see how small our cabin is. Dooley's sacked out for a while. I *told* him not to eat so many burritos for breakfast." He laughed. "You probably won't want to stand next to him during the lifeboat drill."

Waves slapped the side of the Caribbean Breeze as it pulled away from the dock in Tampa, Florida. Noisy seagulls swooped as Lou leaned on the cruise ship's brass railing, trying to stay under the cowgirl's radar.

The crowd of excited vacationers loudly maneuvered to get their pier-side positions. They swarmed around Lou cheering and waving goodbye to friends and family below who were wishing them bon voyage.

The mournful blare of the horn accentuated the loneliness lodged in his chest. Being away from Millie was bad enough, but here he was, out at sea, unable to contact her. He closed his eyes, clenched his fist, and hit the railing in front of him. How could he make things right after walking out on her without a word? Taking a deep breath, he released it slowly in an attempt to calm his queasy stomach.

This six-week cruise was supposed to be the trip of a lifetime. He was singing for the Lord and hanging out with his buddies. He didn't want to ruin it for everybody.

"Lighten up, boy. Don't look so tormented." The baritone voice whispered in his ear. "At least pretend you're having fun."

Lou rubbed his forehead and glanced at the oldest Warbler standing beside him. Lonnie Chandler was a tall man with gentle blue eyes, a white goatee, and mustache. He and his wife, Dena, usually wore matching outfits. Today they wore white slacks, peach-colored shirts, and white hats.

"Sorry, Lonnie. I don't mean to bring everyone down." He rubbed the back of his neck. "Guess I'm not in a very good mood."

Lonnie angled his white Panama hat and placed a hand on Lou's shoulder. "God will see to it that things work out with Millie one way or the other. But for now try to keep your mind focused on why we're here."

"I messed up, man. What does she think of me or worse, does she even think of me at all?" The wind ruffled Lou's dark hair as he pulled his gaze from the vanishing shoreline. "Millie Drake is the only woman I've ever truly loved. We were so sure this relationship was the Lord's will for us."

Dena held onto her hat. "Go easy on yourself. All

couples have disagreements, so don't think the Lord didn't bring you together." She took her husband's arm. "Did you attempt to contact her?"

He nodded. "I called her cell and even the church several times, but didn't get an answer either place. So before getting on the ship, I called their house phone to leave a message with her mother. All I heard was a grumble and whoever answered hung up."

Lonnie buddied up shoulder-to-shoulder. "Trust me. Your girl just needs a little time." He rubbed his white goatee and lowered his voice. "Get used to it. Women are like that."

He let out a grunt as his wife elbowed his gut.

Dena turned to Lou. "You might be able to contact her when we hit St. Thomas and St. Lucia." She smiled. "In the meantime, we'll help you pray about it."

"My wife might only be five foot tall, but when she's on her knees she's taller than trees." He pointed to the door. "Let's go check on the other guys. Poor ol' Dooley went to his cabin because he couldn't get his sea legs. But Marv may want to join us for Cuban sandwiches in the Ocean View Grill. We all know he's never missed a meal."

With his stomach twisted in a tight knot, Lou shuffled behind the Chandlers as they headed to the elevator. Cuban sandwiches? He swallowed a few times. Was his lack of appetite due to the constant rocking motion of the ship or because of losing Millie? It didn't matter. At least he had the hope of calling her when they docked in St. Thomas. He might try the Cuban after that.

The idea of sharing a tiny space with Marv and Dooley Overton and their sophomoric hijinks, made Lou cringe. One week of their tour bus snoring, dirty sock bombs, and smelly T-shirts was difficult. But a month and a half of the Overton brothers would be like enduring Chinese water torture.

Memories of his three older brothers constantly teasing him came rushing back in a flurry. Having no athletic ability, loving music, and being a computer nerd made him an easy target at school and at home. Still to this day, he never learned how to get revenge. One thing for sure, he could kiss solitude goodbye for the duration of the cruise.

Lou cracked his knuckles and gave a quick knock on the cabin door before opening it. His hand came back sticky. The shenanigans had begun. He took a step inside the room. "Thanks for the warm welcome, guys." He wiped his hand on a nearby elephant origami towel. "We stopped by to see if you wanted to get a Cuban sandwich with us. Now, I'm not sure I want you to come."

A concerned look crossed Marv's face. "Want me to stay here with you, Doolely? I'd be happy to even though I'm hungry."

"No." Dooley sipped his iced drink and waved him on. "Please go, Marv. I need peace and quiet."

"Guess I'm available, Lou." Marv stepped into his shoes and followed the others. "I'm glad we're not going to eat big now, I don't have my buffet pants on yet. But, I'll be ready later tonight."

The muscle in Lonnie's jaw flexed as they walked down the hall. "With Dooley down, we're fortunate the quartet doesn't have to sing this evening."

"I feel so bad for him." Dena raised her hand to stop them. "Before we fill our own stomachs, or Dooley empties his, we need to go to the pharmacy and get the poor fellow something for his tummy."

"He's my brother. I'll get the stuff for him and you all go ahead without me. Order me one of those sandwiches you were talking about. I'll catch up."

The Sea View Grill's rustic nautical atmosphere welcomed them in. After Lonnie placed their orders at the counter, the trio scooted into a booth to wait for Marv.

A few minutes later, the waitress came to the table. She was dressed as a medieval serving wench in a red gathered skirt and white blouse with balloon sleeves. Her wood-like tray held their soft drinks in chilled steins and large pretzels sticks in a pewter bowl.

As they nibbled on the pretzels, Dena pointed to various nautical items decorating the walls. "I need to take pictures of this for Aunt Daisy." She pulled out her cell phone and walked around the room.

Marv and Dooley joined them. "That was a wasted trip. Dooley was already feeling better when I went back." The brothers slid into the booth next to Lou.

"After you guys left, I remembered I had Gas-X in my backpack." Dooley reached across the table for a large pretzel. "It worked fast for me."

Dena returned from her photography session and patted him on the back. "I'm glad you're feeling better."

The waitress returned with a filled tray. "I have hot sandwiches for all. Fries for the men, and slaw for m'lady." She looked at Dooley. "An' what might ye be havin', gov'na?"

"Normally, I'd have what they're having, but I'm still a bit woozy. Could I have water, please?"

The raven-haired woman nodded. "It don't take long fer most chaps t'feel better." She stuck a pencil behind her ear and scurried off to the kitchen.

After Lonnie said a quick prayer, they dug into their meals.

When the waitress came back, Dooley took the glass of ice water and thanked her. He placed his elbows on the table and leaned forward. His large belly kept him from moving in closer.

Marv picked up his sandwich and nudged Lou. "Have you tried to call Millie?" Without waiting for a reply, he took a generous bite and wiped the sauce from his mouth.

Lou shrugged and lowered his head. "No reception onboard ship. I have to wait until we dock in St. Thomas."

"That's a couple of days away. I'm sure she'll be excited to hear from you."

The other three grew quiet and stared at Marv. Lou looked away trying to swallow the lump of cheesy ham lodged in his throat.

Marv looked around. "What?" He leaned toward Lou. "Sorry. I must be out of the loop. Somebody wanna fill me in?"

Betsy, in her cowgirl boots, clomped into the restaurant with another woman. They stopped at the Warble-Heirs' booth. Betsy pushed the brim of her white hat above her eyebrows. "Hi, again, Lou. Why don't you introduce us to your friends?"

Relieved Betsy interrupted Marv's interrogation; Lou motioned to the older couple. "This is Lonnie and Dena Chandler." He pointed to the brothers. "Next to me is Marv and Dooley Overton."

"Hi, I'm Betsy and this is my friend, Nadine. We look forward to going to your shows." She shook their hands, cupped Lou's chin, and winked. "I'll catch you later, guns."

The two gals sat a table next to the booth. Betsy rested her chin on her left hand and wiggled her fingers at Lou.

Heat rose in Lou's neck. He never dreamed he'd have problems with women at this stage of his life. Maybe Betsy's arrival would make them forget about his breakup with Millie. He held up his Cuban sandwich. "I'm glad you suggested we try these, Lonnie. They're really good."

Marv turned to Lou. "You never did answer my question about why you haven't called Millie. What's up?"

"We'll talk about it later." Dena frowned. "Now, eat your fries before they get cold. You want ketchup?" Without waiting for an answer, she took the condiment bottle, shook it, and squirted it on his plate.

Lou fussed with a napkin and faced him. He didn't want Betsy and her friend to take the news as an invitation. He kept his voice barely audible. "Millie and I broke up. At least I think we did." His chin slackened with the confession.

"Oh, come on! You don't know if you broke up?" Dooley chuckled. "Seems like you'd remember something like that."

"Pipe down." Lou motioned to the cowgirls. "Millie and her mother were throwing things and squawking like a couple of screech owls. I couldn't stand the racket, so I walked out." He slouched and crossed his arms. "That certainly isn't the happily ever after I'm looking for."

Dena tapped a bright red fingernail against the tabletop. "All families are different, Lou. Millie and her mother apparently have a volatile connection."

"That's what I'm afraid of. Everyone says Mrs. Drake is difficult, but does Millie take after her mother when things don't go her way? She got angry once before and grabbed me by the tie."

Dena laughed. "What did you do to the poor girl?"

Lou ran his hand through his hair. "All I did was stand up for her mother."

"Yikes! You took her mother's side over hers?" Lonnie clucked his tongue. "That wasn't your brightest move, sport."

"I know. Talk about learning my lesson the hard way. I tried to call Millie to apologize before we boarded ship, but she won't answer." He spooned a chunk of ice from his drink and chomped on it, in hopes of shaking off the rising depression. "Sorry. We'd better change the subject before everyone's trip is ruined."

Marv put a hand on Lou's shoulder and looked him straight in the eye. "Tell me this, is she worth the trouble?"

"In spite of everything, I love her." Lou choked. "But she may not take me back."

Later that evening, Lou wandered back to the secluded deck railing. He found it a quiet place to be alone with God. The forceful wind and waves attested to His mighty power, wisdom, and love. Right now, Lou needed to force Millie from his mind and feel the presence of the Creator, Who had control of all things. He'd been taught that surrendering his life would lead to true peace.

In a soft whisper, he offered a prayer. "Lord, I know all my hopes, dreams, and even Millie are better off without my interference. Only You can put all the broken pieces in place. Take it all, Lord. Help me not to doubt for Your word says, hope is the anchor of our soul. In Your name, Amen."

His attention went to the vast array of stars overhead. If God could speak them into being, who was he to doubt His power to move mountains? Even Mount Penny.

"Ya have my private spot, don't ya know?"

Lou glanced back at the youthful blonde speaking behind him. "I'm sorry. I'll find another place."

Her soft, tittering laugh made him smile.

"Ya don't need to move. I was pullin' your leg. I'm Gemma Carr, the ship's cruise director. What's your name?"

"Lou Blythe. Happy to meet you." He offered his hand.

She shook his outstretched hand. "Are ya one of the gospel singers or a regular passenger?"

"I'm with the Warble-Heirs quartet." He turned to face the water.

"You're out here all by your lonesome, Lou. Anything wrong tonight? Are ya feelin' poorly?"

He shook his head. "I had a pretty rough day and need to sort things out."

"Okay then, I'll leave ya with your thoughts. I hope we run into each other another time." She paused. "A word of warning. Watch out for Betsy Barnum. She and her friend are on these cruises every year, don't ya know, and they always latch on to some unsuspecting guy. It never ends well."

"Thanks for the heads up. She is rather pushy."

"Listen, Lou, if ya ever need anything, don't hesitate to contact me. Use any of the ship's phones. Remember, my name's Gemma Carr. I'll try to save ya from Betsy's clutches the best I can."

The urge to watch the pretty cruise director walk away hit him. Twice. He forced himself to keep his eyes focused on the full moon's reflection bobbing in the ship's wake.

CHAPTER SEVEN

First week in August

RAIN PELTED THE DISPLAY WINDOW OF Floral Scent-sations flower shop. Millie closed her eyes and pictured Lou on the ship. He was probably devouring chunks of juicy passion fruit hand-fed by voluptuous mermaids wearing coconut shell bras. She sniffed and crossed her arms. They probably smelled like Chicken of the Sea. At least she hoped they did.

The image of Lou's endearing features rose in her memory. The last time she saw him, a deep frown of disgust had marred his face. He stomped from the house not caring to say good-bye before leaving on his precious, six-week Caribbean trip.

As the shop's only customer approached the counter, Millie's attention was diverted from her brooding.

The woman was a frequent patron and had become like a grandmother. She had an aging Barbra Streisand face and wore her dark hair short and curly. Setting her armload of items down with great care next to the cash register, she offered a bright, toothy grin.

Millie rang up the stained-glass sun catcher, moved it aside, and then reached for the five cinnamon-scented pillar candles. "Did you find everything you were looking for, Mrs. Eichenbaum?"

"Oh, my. I sure did and more. You have so many beautiful things here." The older woman peered through glasses secured on a chain dangling by her amply-rouged cheeks. "Word around town is you've snagged yourself a man. So, is it getting serious?"

"Lou and I have been dating for quite a while. Unfortunately, we're going through some tough times right now."

"A little glitch in your romance?" She patted Millie's face like a doting Jewish mother. "It'll pass, of this I am sure."

"I hope so. Lou and his quartet will be gone for six whole weeks." Tears rose in Millie's eyes, and she wiped them away as they rolled down her cheeks. "Oh, Mrs. Eichenbaum, I miss him like crazy."

The older woman pulled a crumpled tissue from her large embroidered purse and offered it. "No need to get verklempt over a man. If he's worthy of your devotion, he'll be back on bended knee quicker than you can say lox and bagels."

"But there are so many beautiful women aboard a luxury liner. What if he succumbs to all their flirtations?"

"Oy vey. You want I should put the word out you're in the market for a nice middle-aged kosher man? As they say a little jealousy never hurts. That's how I managed to catch my wonderful Mordechai."

"Thank you, but please don't." The last thing she needed was another older woman offering advice to the lovelorn.

Mrs. Eichenbaum pulled a credit card from her paisley billfold and presented it with a devious smile. "Who knows? Dating another man just might be the way to capture your Mr. Right."

Millie dabbed her nose with the well-scented tissue. She didn't need to search any more. Lou was Mr. Right. "Not that I don't appreciate it, but I'll have to pass on that offer." Before she could swipe the gold card, a bolt of lightning flashed followed by intense thunder that rattled the front window.

The heavyset customer held her hands over her ears.

"Looks like the first storm of monsoon season has reared its ugly head." Millie ran the credit card through the scanner and handed her the receipt to sign. "Would you like to register for the Chamber of Commerce charity raffle?"

"Oh, that's right. The charity raffle. Mordechai told me they were trying something different this year, but I was talking to my mother on the phone and didn't hear what he said. Do you know what it is?"

Millie smiled, wrapped the delicate sun catcher in pink tissue, and carefully bagged it. How could she avoid answering that question? "They're only ten dollars a ticket and it's for a good cause."

"It's only my tchotchke money." She signed the receipt and pulled a twenty-dollar bill from her wallet. Her dark red fingernails were short and stubby, but her manicure looked pricey. "Where are the proceeds going this year?"

"They're renovating the chemo bays at Apache Pointe Hospital. I've heard it's going to be state-of-the-art."

"Well, that is a good cause. Better let me have two tickets." Her brown eyes twinkled. "Now what did you say the grand prize was?"

Millie met the woman's inquiry with a forced smile. "Mother told me they're raffling off dates with the Channel 2 News team."

Mrs. Eichenbaum's charm bracelet jangled as she raised her arms over her head. "Woo-hoo! That Kent Sheridan is such a charmer. I don't mean to be a smothering yenta, dear, but you're still single. You and Kent would be a cute couple."

"I appreciate your efforts, but I'm really not into a man hunting expedition or a wild-goose chase right now."

"Maybe these tickets will bring you a lot of luck." She

winked, wrote Millie's name on them, then kissed both with her cherry red lips. "Mind you, if I was only a few years younger and not married to my man, Mordechai, I'd be writing these for myself."

Millie's face burned. She glanced to the workroom. Dad and Uncle Max had to hear this conversation, so why weren't they rushing in to rescue her? Men!

The woman's rouged cheeks dimpled as she presented a wide smile and dropped her raffle tickets into Kent Sheridan's fishbowl. She was clearly taking too much pleasure in her matchmaking skills.

"You didn't need to do that, Mrs. Eichenbaum, but thank you."

"Oh, bubbellah, I'm telling all the girls in my canasta club to come down here and fill up this container a couple of times over. We'll get you married off so quick you won't know what hit you. Mazel tov."

"Thanks again. Be careful driving home in this storm." As soon as the door closed, Millie turned, rolled her eyes, and grumbled under her breath. "She acts like I'm the charity case instead of the hospital."

A mixture of hearty laughter and snorts came from the back room, embarrassing Millie that much more.

She fisted her hands and placed them firmly on her hips. "Were you and Uncle Max listening to all of that, Dad?"

He entered the showroom with his arms lifted high overhead. His lips pulled into a lopsided grin. "Oy! You bet your sweet gefilte fish. Your Uncle Max and I had a great time listening in."

His brother joined him at the workroom door. "We heard every single word, bubbellah. We're going to pass along her inspired suggestion to our bowling league." He laughed and wriggled his eyebrows. "That should score you a few extra tickets for a rendezvous with that Kent

Sheridan fella."

"Whatever you do, don't give Mother any more ideas. She's in five book clubs, for crying out loud." Millie frisbeed a cork coaster at them to stop the tomfoolery. "You guys had better get back to work. Do you realize the charity dinner is this weekend?"

"That girl of mine is right." Stuart pointed to the workroom. "Let's get crackin', Max. We still have another half dozen table arrangements to make."

She reached for a spool of ribbon. "While you guys are doing that, I'll finish the Shingledocker anniversary corsages for this afternoon's pick-up."

Following his brother to the workroom, Stuart stopped at the doorway and turned to Millie. "I haven't had the chance to ask if you're getting along okay at Carol's."

"The peace and quiet is certainly nice. It's given me plenty of time to think about my relationships with Lou and Mother." She watched the heavy rain hit the front window.

"What have you decided?"

"As far as Lou goes, it's been over a week, and he hasn't made an effort to contact me. I love him, but this feeling of rejection is killing me." Her shoulders rose in a half-hearted shrug. "If we make up, can I trust him not to run again?"

The love Stuart held for her was apparent in his expression. "I'm sorry, Princess. All we can do is trust the Lord and His timing." He came to her side and held out his arms.

Millie stepped into his protective embrace. She longed to assure her dad that everything would be okay. But in truth, she struggled with believing it herself. Her faith was lacking.

"What have you decided about your mother?"

Her words were muffled as she spoke into his

shoulder. "How do I keep her from meddling in my life?"

He kissed the top of her head, then released her. "If I had an answer for that, we wouldn't be in this mess."

"I feel like I'm the source of Mother's animosity."

"Don't ever feel that way. I want you to keep in mind that her anger isn't directed at any one person, she's mad at the entire world." He chuckled and patted her shoulder. "I guess that makes her an equal-opportunist. Since we live with her, we're constantly in the fallout."

Millie laughed at his attempt to lighten the conversation. "Exactly. The farther away Mother and I stay from each other, the better off we are."

"Does that mean you've come to a conclusion about an apartment?"

Her eyes met his. "I know you said you'd help me with the deposit, but I haven't found anything in my price range worth considering. Looks like I'll be returning home next week." Millie bit her bottom lip. "Did you ever get Mother in for those tests?"

"She went for a colonoscopy the day before yesterday. They were going to order an endoscopy and an ultrasound for later this week."

"How did you get her to agree to all of that?"

He grinned. "I had to bribe her with a new pink KitchenAid stand mixer. She's wanted a new one for a long time."

Another round of thunder drew their attention to the front window. "We'd better hurry, Stu." Max stepped into the showroom. "This is a bad storm, so let's not press our luck. It could take out our electricity any time."

"Be right there." He smiled at Millie. "I'm proud to be your dad, and will always be here for you."

"I love you. You always make me feel better."

Millie picked up a cleaning cloth and wiped the smears and smudges from the display items as he went to join

Max. She dusted the delicate sun catchers and smiled at the thought of Mrs. E's offer to find a dateable kosher man.

Her smile turned into a grimace. What would she do if Mrs. Eichenbaum and Mother decided to dig out their romantic muzzleloaders and snares to join forces? They'd be the matchmaker version of the Boone and Crockett club with every rich, eligible bachelor in their crosshairs.

Millie allowed her imagination to drift as she envisioned the two overzealous women with green and khaki hearts on their camo gear. They'd be sniffing out fresh bachelor tracks like Elmer Fudd.

As far as Millie was concerned, she'd already bagged Lou. Too bad he'd bolted. Instead of going after him Fudd-style with double barrels, maybe Mrs. Eichenbaum was right and she should go out with someone else, like Kent Sheridan. Lou needed something drastic to happen to open his eyes when he got home from the cruise.

Only one problem. Was his love strong enough that he would step up and try to win her back?

CHAPTER EIGHT

EVEN THOUGH THE TEMPERATURE FOR THE first weekend in August was cooler than average, Millie's nerves kept her a little too warm. She didn't want to attend the Chamber of Commerce dinner in the first place, but so many people had paid to put her name in the Dream Date raffle. The canasta club's tchotchke money was sure to have raised over a thousand dollars single-handedly. Millie's people-pleasing heart felt obligated to be there.

Light blue glass beads decorated the walls and ceiling of the banquet room. At the front, two large screens flanked the stage. Millie had never seen such impressive decor.

While her Uncle Max stopped to chat with friends, Millie followed her parents through a sea of round tables covered with white linen. Each of the six place settings had a crystal water goblet and a small bowl of salad.

The chairs were dressed in white slipcovers and embellished with gold bows draping down the back. The summer bouquets of pink hydrangea, lavender dahlias, and blue larkspur from Floral Scent-sations sat in the center of each table.

She stopped where her mother parked herself not far from the stage. Mother's shocking pink sequined gown and equally shocking tourmaline earrings shimmered under the bright lights. But it was her eccentric red bouffant hairdo that would attract the attention of onlookers.

A reserved sign for the Channel 2 celebrities rested on

the table next to theirs. Well played, Mother.

Millie glanced around the room and then hooked an arm through her dad's. "You and Uncle Max did a wonderful job on those centerpieces. What great publicity for the Floral Scent-sations."

"Thanks, Princess." He kissed her temple and held her chair. "By the way, I know your mother pushed you into coming tonight, but I'm glad you're here. It's nice to be sitting next to the prettiest lady in the room. That red dress is by far my favorite."

Millie's cheeks warmed. He always found a way to make her feel special. "Carol helped me pick it out for Valentine's Day." She scooted closer to the table and then straightened her skirt. Lou liked the dress too.

When Max came to their table, Millie leaned forward and spoke to him. "I'm sorry Aunt Syl wasn't able to come this evening. I miss her."

"Thanks, hon." Max smiled. "She always enjoyed going to the annual Chamber dinner. A few of our friends have asked about her already." He patted her shoulder. "I like your hair up like that. Makes you look as cool as a cucumber."

Penny pushed her red-rimmed glasses higher on her nose and nudged Millie. "Don't look now, Millicent, but that gorgeous Kent Sheridan is giving you the eye."

Millie glanced to the celebrity table. The handsome anchorman nodded, and winked, bringing a heated flush darting up her face. She quickly looked away and popped a cherry tomato into her mouth. The urge to look back at him was more than she could resist. One quick peek couldn't hurt.

He was still looking, with a teasing, reckless grin as he ran a finger around the lip of his water glass. Without a clue of how to react, she smiled back as anxiety jetted through her stomach. She cringed as memories of Lou sparked.

Her mother elbowed her side. "That's my girl. Keep flirting and you'll have him drooling and eating out of your hand in no time."

As the banquet room filled, the buzz grew to a loud chatter. Millie heard her name and turned to find Mrs. Eichenbaum sitting across the well-lit room with her canasta club friends. Much to Millie's horror, all three tables sent her a thumbs-up.

She looked at her mother. "You look pale. Are you feeling okay? Do you need to go home?"

Penny scowled and waved her off. "I'm fine. My stomach's a little queasy. It's probably because I'm excited for the drawing." Her cold hand grabbed Millie's wrist. "Oh, Millicent, look! They have television cameras here. We're going to be on the 11:00 news." Penny arched a brow, and her frown softened. "Pinch your cheeks, suck in your gut, and smile. Now, I expect you to act like you're having fun. You never know when the camera's going to be on us."

Millie winced at the hurtful comment, knowing the oft-repeated remark was to destroy any self-confidence that had taken root.

Her dad took Millie's hand and squeezed it before she had a chance to slither under the table to escape the embarrassment.

With the last of the seats filled, the houselights dimmed and a spotlight drew attention to the host on stage. The screens on either side lit up.

He took the mic. "Good evening. I'm Brad Kimball, president of Apache Pointe Chamber of Commerce. We'd like to thank everyone for coming to our twentieth annual banquet. You'll find our Chamber members represented in the pamphlets on the tables. Make sure to frequent and support these fine businesses. As usual, tonight's dinner comes to you from Catie's Catering Company and the honor students from Apache Pointe High School will be our servers."

Several teens at the kitchen entrance raised their school banner while the audience gave them a standing ovation.

A deep voice yelled from the back. "Go Braves!"

The president approached the microphone and laughed. "Okay, sit down Coach VanDerpelt." He sipped from his bottle of water. "In honor of the Chamber's twentieth anniversary, the news team from KAPP, Channel 2 has agreed to be raffled off as dream dates for two happy ladies and two lucky men. We appreciate their generosity."

The onlookers applauded.

"Our celebrity guests are at the table to the right of the stage. Will you please stand and wave as I call your name? First, we have KAPP's meteorologist, Will Scott."

Will got to his feet and waved to the crowd.

"And up next is our Noon News anchor, Miss Rhonda Robb."

The dark-haired beauty gracefully rose from her seat, curtseyed, and threw a kiss.

"And finally, put your hands together for the 6:00 and 11:00 News co-anchors, Kathy Rice and Kent Sheridan. Kathy was once first runner-up for Miss Arizona, and I'm sure many of you remember Kent as the teenage heartthrob in the TV sitcom, *Best Family Times*."

They both jumped to their feet. Kathy waved while Kent gave his famous two-fingered salute. Millie's mouth went dry and a sense of uneasiness took over.

"It appears our meal is ready. Everyone enjoy." President Kimball joined the celebrities as servers dressed in black slacks and blue polo shirts, passed out steaming plates of roast chicken, baked potatoes, and green beans.

With her nerves jangling, Millie eyeballed the

overloaded plate knowing her stomach wouldn't willingly accept a single bite. She took a gulp of water, hoping it would calm the queasiness.

It didn't.

Following dessert, the serving staff chatted as they cleared the dishes and refilled the empty coffee cups.

Raffle drawing time.

The president drew a name for Will Scott. Millie squirmed. Her nerves were like exposed wires. On one hand, she wanted to win the date with Kent Sheridan if only to make Lou jealous. On the other hand, playing with emotions was something Mother would do. And often did. It was childish and that kind of stunt could ruin any hope of getting back with him.

But, Lou had been on that stupid cruise for two weeks without any contact whatsoever. Millie licked her lips. By this time, he was probably crooning love ballads to little Miss Chiquita Banana in the moonlight.

Applause again filled the room as meteorologist Will Scott greeted his eager date. The host shared that the couple would enjoy an evening of dancing and dining at Pinto Pass Restaurant.

The emcee called the noon anchor, Rhonda Robb, to the front. She insisted on rotating the drum herself. "That's right, Rhonda. Spin it good. While she's doing that, I'll announce their date will be at Courtland Cornerstone Calliope where their fine dining experience will include dancing under the stars."

Rhonda reached in and pulled out the name of her date. "Vince VanDerpelt the third." She waved the card. "Where are you, Vince?"

One of the servers coughed and headed to the front. "Here I am!"

The coach's voice boomed from the back. "Way to go, Son."

The Chamber president laughed with the audience, then leaned closer to the mic. "Sit down, Coach VanDerpelt the second." While the laughter died down, he took a drink of water. "Now, are we ready for the final two drawings? Drumroll, please."

Tension pressed against Millie's lungs, sucking out the air as Kent's drawing drew nigh. Would she look like a frumpy klutz standing up there next to that perfect male specimen? What she wouldn't give for another layer of deodorant right about now. She took a deep breath and relaxed her shoulders. There was always a slight chance she wouldn't win.

Lou's face floated through her memory. Was she ready to let him go? But what did it matter now? It was too late to take her name out of the running since Mother, Mrs. Eichenbaum, and the canasta ladies had stuffed the ballot box. She closed her eyes and silently prayed for the Rapture.

The surrounding applause brought Millie back to earth. She blinked when the emcee called Kent Sheridan to the microphone. She'd missed the drawing for Kathy Rice.

"While he's making his way to the platform, I'd like to mention this good-looking guy has received more ballots than all the other members of the team put together. Someone has her heart set on a dream date with our wildly popular newscaster."

Millie was tempted to leave, but her curiosity kept her gaping at the anchorman. Her mouth went dry making it difficult to swallow. She reached for her water glass.

"And what you've all been waiting for, the winner of the dream date with Channel Two's own Kent Sheridan."

Kent waved before repeating his legendary two-fingered salute. High-pitched squeals came from all corners of the room. He cranked the raffle drum once, twice, and a third time before reaching in for the winning ticket. "My date is, Miss Nicole Sigman."

The canasta ladies released a chorus of moans while Penny slammed her fork on the table and half-stood.

Millie sighed and yanked on her mother's arm. "Sit down!"

There was a long pause as heads turned in all directions. "Nicole Sigman, are you here?"

The emcee went to the microphone. "Apparently Miss Sigman couldn't make it this evening. Our rules say you have to be present to win." He nodded to Kent. "You get to pick another name."

Kent cranked the raffle drum again. He opened the door, reached deep inside, and retrieved another ticket. After clearing his throat, he announced loudly, "Gwyneth Garroway."

Again, silence filled the hall.

"I'm feeling a bit rejected, President Kimball. Where-oh-where is Gwyn Garroway? Must be past her curfew." He threw his hands in the air before drawing another card. "They say the third time's a charm." He waved the paper and looked at Kimball. "Cross your fingers, folks. If this lady is MIA, then I'm going home."

A peal of laughter came from the audience.

Kent cleared his throat. "Miss Millicent Marie Drake."

"That's my daughter!" Penny shrieked. "Get up there, Millicent. Hurry."

The emcee leaned into the microphone and yelled over the standing ovation. "Will Miss Drake please come forward to claim her prize?"

From the side of the room, a choir of exuberant Canasta ladies yelled, "Mazel tov, Millie!"

The skin on Millie's forearms tingled as she slowly rose from the table. A menagerie of winged vermin flailed in her stomach. Her jelly-filled knees threatened to give out as she forced herself past the Canasta ladies, the red-eyed television camera, and then up to the platform.

The news anchor with light-brown hair and square jaw grew manlier, hunkier, and oh, so fine the closer she got to the stage. The glow of Kent's smile radiated as if the sun had risen across his face. Now would be a good time to get her hormones under control.

Kent stepped toward her, a take-charge air about him. He reached for her hand and pulled her into a side hug. Whistles and laughter came from the audience applauded when he kissed her hot cheek.

In her mind, amid a rousing rendition of Hava Nagila, her alter ego announced, 'May I now present Mrs. Kent Sheridan, no, Mrs. Millicent Marie Sheridan.' Millie clenched her teeth. She wouldn't allow her mind to venture in that direction. Mrs. Eichenbaum's suggestion of making Lou jealous was one thing, but losing him was quite another. Besides, Tawny Lamour had great success with this approach.

CHAPTER NINE

St. Lucia

WARM TRADE WINDS STIRRED DISTANT CUMULONIMBUS clouds, suggesting a brewing storm. Lou's heart accelerated as he sat at a remote outdoor table of St. Lucia's Beach and Brunch Café. With a gulp of orange-pineapple slurry for courage, he dialed Millie's phone number on the cheap cell he'd purchased on the island.

After several rings, someone picked up. "Hello."

Lou's breath wedged in his throat at the pugnacious tone of Millie's mother. "Hello, Mrs. Drake. This is Lou Blythe. May I please speak with Millie?"

"Millicent is not available. She has secured a new love interest and does not wish to hear from you again. Stop pestering my daughter. She only dated you because she felt sorry for you. Good day."

"Wait, Mrs. Drake. I haven't been gone that long. Who is she dating?" He wanted to throw up. How could Millie's feelings for him end so abruptly?

"Not that it is any of your business, but she is dating "the" Mr. Kent Sheridan."

His stomach dropped. "You mean that conceited guy on Channel 2 News?"

"The very same and they are head over heels about each other. She has finally met her soul mate, and you are not going to ruin it." Penny huffed. "Don't you think a Christian man, as you claim to be, would respect her wishes to be left alone? Of course you do."

"Can't I talk to her for one minute?"

"You may not! Should you dare to call again, I promise you will be blocked." With a click, the matter was final.

He gaped at the cheap cell. What just happened? His vision of regaining Millie's trust and love disintegrated in a two-minute span. Too bad the other numbers to reach Millie weren't loaded on this phone.

Lou unceremoniously dumped his melted slurry into a nearby trashcan. Sucker punched. He didn't want to face the other Warble-Heirs now. Fortunately, they were on a bus taking pictures of the Piton Mountains' twin peaks.

He needed to get away from the busy area to walk off tension. After handing the unwanted phone to a woman selling fruit at a booth, he dodged the guides and other vendors hawking their wares in the marketplace.

How did Millie happen to meet the newsman? Why did women always fall for the pretty boy? If he was competing with Kent Sheridan, he didn't stand a chance. Overwhelming inferiority haunted him all the way back to the Caribbean Breeze.

For the rest of the afternoon Lou had to work to put one foot in front of the other as he paced the main deck. In the depth of his soul, he knew Millie didn't date him out of pity. However, what his mind couldn't grasp was the sudden change in her heart. Didn't their love mean anything? Whether she admitted it or not, she needed him. His conscience made him face the truth. More than anything, he needed her.

A blast from the deep bass horn warned passengers to return to the ship. He looked at his watch. Their show would be starting in an hour, and he needed to get to his cabin to change clothes.

Thunderheads darkened the sky as the increasing wind sprayed salt water in his direction. The day had become as dreary as his mood. He hurried past the other tourists; their various conversations seemed to drone around him.

The complex layout of the Caribbean Breeze had him disoriented. He popped his knuckles as he walked. Each hall, door, elevator, and stairway looked exactly like the one before. Being lost on the rocking ship only echoed the confusion he felt in his heart.

A purser dressed in a white uniform and holding a clipboard strolled toward him. "May I help you, sir?"

Lou patted down his windblown mop. "I'm looking for my cabin on Baja Deck. Can you point me in the right direction?"

"I can do better than that. I'm headed for the same deck myself." The young man led him through the next door and up the wide stairs. "It took me a full month to learn my way around. By the way, aren't you in one of the gospel quartets?"

Lou nodded with a smile. "My group is the Warble-Heirs. We're supposed to sing in an hour, and I'm not ready."

"You guys are really good. I'll be in and out of the Neptune Grand Theater all evening, so I shouldn't miss much. The Breeze doesn't book Christian entertainers very often, so a lot of us are looking forward to tonight's show." The purser raised his clipboard. "I'd better warn you, a storm is going to hit later tonight, so be sure to get somewhere safe to ride it out."

Lou was encouraged that the knotted feeling in his stomach hadn't been noticeable while they sang. His mind had focused on worship instead of the problem with Millie.

The gospel concert was over at 11:00 pm. He followed the Chandlers out to the main deck and replaced the cap on his water bottle. "We had a great turnout tonight. I felt a sense of release as we were singing."

Lonnie stroked his white beard and stared straight ahead. "When you let go and let God take charge you get filled with a peace that only comes when you're in His hands." Lifting his wire-rimmed glasses, he rubbed his eye. "Did you notice the beefy guy on the far left? When we sang *Wonderful Grace of Jesus*, his face lit up and he tried to keep time with his fist. He almost had the right tempo."

"That whole side of the Neptune was certainly getting blessed." Dena's smile exposed the dimple in her cheek. "You know the Lord's there when the audience gets into the spirit."

"You're right, sweetheart." Lonnie pulled his wife closer. "And that's why we're here."

The Overton brothers caught up with them. Marv held up his hand. "Sorry you had to wait. Two little old ladies from Peoria stopped us on the way here."

Dooley grinned. "Yeah, and they claim we're all related to some guy named Elvin Weinmann from Indianapolis."

"He insists we're cousins. Go figure." Marv rubbed his hands together. "Dooley and I are going to hit the midnight buffet with Myrtle and Gertrude. Anyone want to go with us to hear the family history?"

"Not this time." Lou stifled a chuckle and waved at the twin octogenarians walking their way. "But thanks for asking. I'm going topside with the Chandlers to get a breath of fresh air before turning in."

Dena patted his shoulder. "Come on, it's getting late. We need to get our walk in before the weather gets any worse."

As they headed down the passageway, Lou pointed to a blue container filled with barf bags. "Looks like we're in for a rough walk."

Distant thunder greeted them as Lou opened the door and let the Chandlers go on deck ahead of him.

It wasn't long before the three of them had to shuffle arm-in-arm as the sea grew choppier.

Crew members gathered deck chairs, tables, and anything else that could be sent over the side. One man yelled at them. "Good grief! You don't have life preservers on. Get inside before we hit a swell and you're thrown overboard. The westerly front is on us."

Just as he finished his sentence, lightning flashed and a roll of thunder rumbled. The ship's whistle, followed by the captain's voice, echoed over the loudspeaker: "This is your captain speaking. The Caribbean Breeze will see rough weather for approximately two hours. Please remain calm and stay where you are or go to your cabin and enjoy the complimentary movies. I repeat, remain calm."

Once inside, Lou and the Chandlers scrambled to find the right passageway that would take them to the Baja Deck. The ship hit a wave and tossed them against the wall. Dena screamed as they stumbled to the opposite side of the hallway and into the path of tourists scrambling past them.

Orange-vested bodies collided. Arms and legs flailed. Sandals, flip-flops, and purse paraphernalia slid down the hall.

"Betsy, put your cell phone away," a strange voice yelled. "Don't you dare put my picture on Facebook."

"Why would I take your picture, Nadine? We see each other every day. I'm taking Lou's." A cackle ensued. "This is like playing Twister in an earthquake."

The great detangling began. People were on all fours groping for their personal belongings, swapping what they found with the rightful owners.

The Caribbean Breeze continued to bob like a cork in

the rough water. Lou and the Chandlers struggled to stay upright as they walked down the litter-strewn corridor.

Dena screamed as the ship rocked side-to-side and froze at a forty-five degree angle longer than what seemed safe. Loud noises came from within the shaking vessel as it tried to maintain its course. Crew members ran shouting through the hallway.

"Take my hand, sweetie." Lonnie held out his arm. "I've got ya. Now grab on to the railing with your other hand." He began to shepherd his wife down the tilting hall.

Relief filled Lou when Chandlers' room finally came into view. He kicked a stray bottle of sunscreen aside, took the key from Lonnie and rushed ahead to unlock the couple's cabin. Inside, he retrieved two overturned desk chairs that had collided against the bed.

Dena and Lonnie hurried into the room to wait out the storm.

"We're safe now." Lonnie held his wife close. "How ya doin', honey?"

Visibly shaken, Dena sat on the bed. "I've never been so scared in my life. If this boat sinks, at least I'm ready to meet my Savior." She groaned and her features contorted into a mass of creases. "I'm getting nauseated."

"Lie down until the rocking motion is over." Lou turned to Lonnie. "Why don't you get a wet cloth for her forehead? Oh, and better grab a bucket."

Lonnie returned with a glass of water and held up a small box. "I remembered we had Dramamine in our carry-on." He handed the medicine to Lou. "Will you give this to her while I get the wet cloth and wastebasket?"

"Glad you thought of that. Her stomach will settle quicker." He grinned at Dena and spoke in a soothing tone. "The only other time I've administered pills was to my dog. He likes his wrapped in peanut butter."

Dena sat up, scooted to the edge of the bed, and gave

him a playful punch. "I think I'll pass on the Skippy, thank you very much." She took the pill and water from him, then rested her head on the pillow.

Lonnie placed the wet cloth on her brow and looked out the porthole. "It feels like the storm might be calming a bit." He joined Lou at a small table as something in the hallway crashed against the cabin door. "Guess I spoke too soon."

The two men talked in hushed tones, allowing Dena to doze. Lonnie turned on the TV.

In spite of the raging storm outside, the signal came in loud and clear. They checked out a free movie, but every few minutes, switched back to a channel telling the ship's position and current wind speed.

Outside, the ocean churned wildly. Foaming water crashed against cabin porthole which reminded Lou of the glass on a front-loading washer.

A short time later, a whistle sounded and the captain's voice boomed through the loud speaker. "Your safety is our top priority. I want to assure you the Caribbean Breeze is designed to withstand even more extreme circumstances than we've encountered." He concluded by telling guests they were welcome to take anything from their mini-bars, free of charge.

Lonnie took the opportunity to grab candy bars, potato chips, and two cans of Bertie's Root Beer. He motioned to his wife. "That announcement didn't even wake her up." He chuckled.

"I'm awake." Dena's voice was weak. "I'm feeling better, but don't want to move, yet."

"Take your time, hon." Lonnie turned and put his hand on Lou's shoulder. "By the way, did you ever get through to your girl?"

"Her mother answered. Millie warned me about her, but I thought it might have been an exaggeration." He licked his lips and cracked his knuckles. "Mrs. Drake said Millie's dating someone else now, and she threatened to block me if I called again."

Dena eventually sat up and headed for the bathroom.

"My girl's mobile. That's a good sign." Lonnie grinned, then his expression grew serious.

"Lou, if it doesn't work out with Millie, remember there are other decent gals out there. Think about it, in the short time we've been on this ship, two young ladies have been interested in you. You're not lacking anything, son."

Dena joined them and sat next to Lou. "Honey, your next step is to apologize to Millie for doubting her and walking out when she needed you. That will go a long way in healing your heart and your relationship." She patted his hand. "The wounds of love can only be mended by love itself."

"But, that's the whole point, Dena. Our boy, Lou, would apologize if he could get a call through to her."

Another whistle indicated the captain had an announcement. "Ladies and gentlemen, we've passed through the worst of the storm. Continue to use caution as you leave your safe place."

The sting of their comments only served to remind Lou that time was slipping away. The muscles in his neck grew tense. Would Millie still be available when he got home?

CHAPTER TEN

Mid-August

MILLIE RETRIEVED HER FAVORITE LITTLE BLACK dress from the closet and hurried to change. This was her first date with Kent Sheridan, the pretty boy of Channel 2 News. While she didn't have any unrealistic expectations of wowing him, tonight's outfit still needed to hold his attention.

She pivoted in front of the full-length mirror. Thanks to Carol, her wardrobe now held up-to-date clothing that fit her size eight frame. She had donated every baggy outfit Mother had chosen for her to the Ladies' League Quilt Society.

She waltzed to the bathroom mirror to rearrange the bangs on her forehead. A quick and disturbing thought came to mind as she primped. What would she and Kent talk about through dinner? Her cheeks turned bright pink. Oh, no! A reporter was going to interview them for the 11:00 news. There was never a time she opened her mouth in public and didn't appear dimwitted. Would she embarrass herself on local television?

She could see it now. All heads would turn as they entered the restaurant, television cameras with their bright lights capturing the event, and Kent introducing her to his hordes of admirers in TV-land. 'This is Kent Sheridan, Channel 2 News. I'm here with my lovely date, Millicent Marie Drake, the woman of my dreams—'

"Millicent."

Snapped from her thoughts by her mother's stern

voice, Millie jumped.

"What are you doing in that black mourning garment? You might as well be wearing sackcloth and ashes." She frowned and lightly pushed Millie's shoulder. "You're not going to a wake you know. He's going to be here any minute and you're not presentable."

"Carol said this cocktail dress was perfect for tonight." She cringed, knowing the mere mention of her cousin's name would have her mother trying to wear her down. Any other time she'd change clothes to shut Mother up.

"Why must you bring up that woman's name?" She leveled Millie with a severe, maternal glare. "What does she know about fashion anyway? That dress makes you look as flat-chested as Olive Oyl."

The doorbell rang, sparing Millie from verbalizing the pithy reply abuzz in her thoughts. She breathed a sigh of relief.

Her mother peered through the vertical blinds. "He's here." She turned abruptly, ran to the top of the stairs, looked down, then returned to Millie's bedroom, hands on hips. "Your father's getting the door. I'll hold Kent off while you change into something more fetching." She took Millie's elbow and dragged her to the closet. "You need something to make you look curvier. Try the pink frock with the button-up collar. Men like their ladies in pink. It's the epitome of femininity."

Millie didn't have the nerve to tell her that particular dress was now part of a crazy quilt. "Why don't you offer him something to drink?"

"What a good idea. He's sophisticated, so he'll like my espresso." She turned to leave then stopped. "Oh, and I'll have him try a piece of my anise coffee cake."

Millie shuddered and forced her feet into the black patent leather heels, then wobbled down the stairs. Would Mother freak about the dress and end the date before it even started? She needed to get Kent out of the house as soon as possible.

His familiar news anchor voice projected from the living room. "I was born and bred in Los Angeles, Mrs. Drake. I entered show business at three-years-old. I did a lot of television commercials and bit parts before starring in *Best Family Times.*

"You were only three?" She smiled. "And please, call me Penny. What about your family? Are they movie stars?"

"My dad is a plastic surgeon in Hollywood, but he works on most of the super stars. I've met quite a few of them. As a matter of fact, I dated one of Kiki Lane's stepdaughters all through high school."

He dated Kiki's stepdaughter? Millie inched closer. She could never fill the shoes of the Hollywood upper class. How did she get into this predicament anyway? Oh, yeah. Mother, along with Mrs. Eichenbaum's canasta club, stuffed the raffle box. She smoothed the black skirt of her dress, took a breath, and dug deep for a smile.

Peeking into the room, Millie's heart caught. Kent was devastating in a white suit, light blue shirt, and white tie. The well-tailored outfit accentuated his natural good looks. However, her mother's eyes remained glued to his right hand. As Millie moved closer, his multi-faceted diamond ring sparkled from the lamp's bright light. Her borrowed chain necklace faded in comparison.

Millie hands gripped the handle of her leather purse. "Hello, Mr. Sheridan."

He stood and whistled his approval. "You look striking in black, Millicent. Are you ready to go?" He faced Penny and Stuart. "It was a pleasure to meet you both."

When they got to the door, her mother pulled her aside and whispered in her ear. "Pinch your cheeks, dear. Suck in that gut of yours and for heaven's sake, compliment the man." She instinctively waved her hand with a flourish, one of the grand moves she had perfected. "And whatever you do, don't let this one get away."

Millie rolled her eyes and cleared her throat. "Mother, please. He'll hear you."

"You finally landed a man who will get you somewhere. Fame and fortune, dear." She massaged her arm and sighed. "You will make us proud on television, right? Of course you will."

Her dad came from the living room and kissed her forehead. "You look beautiful, Princess. Have a good time."

"'Bye, Dad. Love you."

At last, Mother seemed pleased. Millie looked forward to the mundane shadows of her past morphing into a bright new future . . . either with Lou or with Kent. If Lou didn't come back for her, she'd still have someone.

She clutched Kent's arm in case Mother was watching. He drew her close as they headed for the shiny dark blue Corvette in the driveway. With a suave smile, he opened the door and helped her into the passenger seat. Her heart rate doubled with his firm, manly grip.

Millie's frustration with her mother eased as they turned on to the highway. For the next few hours, she determined to put the woman out of her thoughts. She was in a brand new Corvette with the most desirable man in town. Why not enjoy the ride?

The Sonoran Desert lay ahead in a blaze of beige and mauve. Sagebrush moved unpredictably over the sandy surface driven by an arid wind.

"This is such a nice car." She closed her eyes. Now what could she say? "Feels like it has a lot of power."

"Thanks." Kent pressed his foot harder to the accelerator and miles of steaming road vanished behind them.

The remainder of the drive was silent. Millie chewed on her pinky nail as they neared Phoenix. Thanks to Lou, this wasn't her first fine dining experience, and she knew what to expect. So why were knots forming in her stomach?

She glanced at Kent's debonair profile and admired the self-confidence the man exuded. He probably considered her a tough-luck date. How could she convince him she was more than a mere raffle winner? Not that she was personally interested in snagging the man, but what girl wanted to be thought of in anything but a positive light?

He glanced her way. "I like your dad. Are the two of you close?"

"Yes." Millie clenched her teeth. She could do better than a one-word answer. "My dad has always been loving and supportive." She closed her eyes. *Please don't ask about Mother.*

"I'm going to hazard a guess that your mom is the loquacious one in your family?"

"The what?" Great. He had to flaunt his Ivy League vocabulary.

He glanced her way. "You know, the official mouthpiece."

Millie laughed. "I have to admit, you're an excellent judge of character."

"My investigative reporter background shines through." He smiled and buffed his nails on his lapel. "Although it didn't take a background check to figure that out."

"I'm sure that's true." She racked her brain for another conversation ball to lob back. Nothing. It was easier to talk to Lou. He wasn't as intimidating as the number one news anchor in Apache Pointe. Would she ever outgrow her inferiority complex? The image of her mother had to be pushed out of her mind for that to happen.

The desert surroundings began to take on a thriving

urban quality as homes and businesses became more plentiful. Could her dry, empty life make a similar turnaround?

Once in Phoenix, they pulled up to the front of the ostentatious restaurant. The valet, wearing a dark red vest and bowtie, took Millie's hand to help extricate her from Kent's low-riding vehicle.

After the third attempt, Millie succeeded to maneuver herself from the front seat and still retain her femininity in the process. She stood slowly and brushed imaginary wrinkles from her little black dress.

Kent offered his arm and led her inside the building. Soft music, conversation, and laughter filled the room.

Dear Diary,

I stood up to Mother again this evening. She ordered me to change clothes for the date, but I chose not to bow. This feeling of independence is beginning to grow on me.

My date with Kent went well. He could easily sweep me away with his charm and good looks. He was funny and kept me laughing most of the evening.

The restaurant was beautiful with a view of the distant mountains. We ordered the skimpy vegetarian plate, which left a lot to be desired. Cauliflower couscous topped with two baby carrots, cherry tomato halves, and tofu crumbles didn't quite hit the spot. Kent declared it an epicurean delight. However, I was still hungry.

Several women came to our table and

asked him for his autograph. They asked me to take their pictures with him. There I was, pushed aside like a bargain basement reject.

Then came the dreaded moment, the interview with the Channel 2 news reporter. The cameraman hovering around was a distraction, and my doofus-ness was broadcast for the entire tri-state area to witness. Fortunately, Kent took the lead. I didn't say more than 'nice to meet you,' and I managed to repeat that same phrase to every one of his friends I met.

Tonight's raffle date was supposed to be a one-time thing, but he said I was a breath of fresh air and invited me to a ballet next Saturday. He's sure I'll like Coppelia because it's both funny and beautiful. We come from such different worlds. Too bad there isn't a connection between us like I have with Lou. He's down-to-earth and, unlike Kent, makes me feel like I'm the only woman in the world. I wonder if he's thinking about me tonight?

Dear Heavenly Father, for the first forty-two years of my life, no one loved me but family. Then Lou came, and now I've lost him. If I'm meant to be by myself, help me accept it. You know my heart's desire is to be with him, but more than that, I want to be in Your will.

And Lord, I'm concerned about Mother and Dad. They need Your help. He says a great deal of money is missing from their account. Meanwhile, Mother claims she hasn't felt like shopping in weeks. I'm leaving it in Your hands. In Jesus' name, Amen.

She closed her diary and rubbed her hands over the cover.

CHAPTER ELEVEN

Cruise—day 11

LOU SAT ON DECK WITH A pineapple-guava smoothie and wrote a few lines on a newly purchased 'Greetings from Aruba' postcard.

Dear Millie, our ship arrived in Aruba this morning. The guys are going ashore. If you don't snorkel or parasail there's little to do. I'm not into that. Miss you, Sweet Cheeks. Will write again in three days. Love, Lou.

Lou addressed and stamped the card and then handed it to Lonnie's wife, Dena, who promised to mail it in town. Folding his hands behind his head, he leaned back on the deck chair, and forced his mind onto the soothing ocean sounds around him.

A well-manicured hand rested on his shoulder. He flinched.

"I'm sorry. I didn't mean to startle ya." The tall, slender cruise director smiled and settled into the deck chair next to him. She wore a navy skirt and jacket with white piping on the lapels and pockets. A small package rested on her lap. "You're not going ashore with your group today, Mr. Blythe?"

"Not today, Miss Carr. I didn't sleep well last night. My bunkmates' snoring kept me awake. Then I heard someone rummaging around in the dark. I found all my socks soaking in the sink this morning."

"Sounds like you're in with a couple of jokesters." She laughed. "By the way, call me Gemma. My friends call me Gem."

"And I'm Lou. Mr. Blythe sounds like my grandpa." He picked up his smoothie and stirred it with the straw. "So far, those guys have slimed the doorknob, added salt to my water glass, and soaked my socks."

"You, my friend, Lou, are in for a long cruise. At least it won't be a dull one." She held up the box. The morning sunshine caught the natural shine of her curly blonde hair and turned it into a soft aura that encircled her face. "I have a few errands to run in Oranjestad. I could use the company if ya want to go with."

"Our group has been pretty busy, so I thought this would be a good time to chill without the pesky cowgirl hovering over me."

"It's a shame to waste a beautiful day like this. Nobody should miss going into Oranjestad." She nudged his shoulder. "And I'd appreciate the company, going without an escort makes me uncomfortable."

"Okay, I'll go with you." Did Dooley and Marv set up this "chance" meeting? He stood and glanced around the deck, looking for any signs of the mischievous Overton brothers.

"Good!" Gemma pointed down the walkway and waved. "Luuk and his ten-thirty trolley are still waiting for us. Let's hurry."

Once they made it to the trolley, she stopped to speak with the operator, a good-looking man with hair the color of ripened wheat. He wondered if a barber used a combine to harvest Luuk's choppy haircut.

Lou boarded and sat on the long bench close to the front. Off to the side, tourists were busy taking pictures of the flamingos standing on stilt-like legs in the shallow water. The winged creatures bent their S-shaped necks down to scoop up algae and small fish with their strongly hooked bills. A toddler with red pigtails and a yellow sundress attracted a lot of attention as she tried to feed her ice cream cone to one of the bright pink birds.

Gemma soon joined him. "I love Luuk and his wife. Marta's one of my best friends from my hometown. We went to school together. This package is for her twenty-seventh birthday." She held out the box. "Now we're both the same age."

"Where is your home?"

Her light blue eyes sparkled in the sunlight. "I come from the southern part of Moose Jaw, Minnesota. The locals call it the lower mandible, don't ya know."

Lou's deep belly laugh made her smile. "I don't live any place as fancy as the lower mandible of Moose Jaw. I'm from a small Arizona city called Apache Pointe."

"Are you near any reservations?"

"There's a large Native American community about twenty miles south of us. I've never been there before, but people tell me it's a very interesting place to visit. You can eat local cuisine and buy handmade items."

"Sounds fascinating. We have a lot of Chippewa and Sioux culture back where I come from." Gemma nudged him. "The next stop is where we get off."

Lou and Gemma delivered the package to her friend and following introductions, they visited for nearly a half hour. After the first fifteen minutes of their tittering laughter and Minnesota don't ya know, ya betcha, and okay then, Lou was more than ready to leave.

Eventually, the laughter subsided. "Okay then, we'd better be going. See ya next time. Have a happy birthday." Gemma stood and hugged her friend.

Marta's freckled cheeks took on light rosy splotches, which complimented her strawberry blonde hair. "Okey-dokey, Gem. Have fun shoppin'."

Lou hurried to the door and held it open for Gemma, hoping she'd take the less than subtle hint.

"'Bye then, Lou." Marta stood at the door as they left. "Nice to meet ya. Be sure and stop in when ya come through again."

Gemma took his arm. "Since we have an hour before lunch, let's go to the local shops and look around. Ya wanted to buy a gift for your girlfriend. Maybe ya can find something at Filomena's. She has lots of handcrafted jewelry, don't ya know."

It only took twenty minutes of futile searching in the small shop before Lou finally asked for Gemma's help. She immediately led him to a heart-shaped locket for Millie.

"I'll take your picture and you can put it inside." She opened the delicate locket. "A girl likes to have her sweetheart's handsome mug next to her heart."

"Thanks for your help. I never would've thought of that."

"Sure, ya betcha. Why don't ya pay for that, and we'll go for lunch."

With their shopping done, Lou and Gemma caught a cab to the popular West Deck Restaurant.

There were still two tables available on the open deck facing the ocean. They ordered their appetizers and meals, then sat back to enjoy the warm breeze and relaxed atmosphere while tropical beach music filled the air.

At the next table sat a young man with thick hair the shade of ripe pumpkins. With his head lowered in concentration, he pecked on the keys of his laptop with a steady rhythm.

Gemma removed her sunglasses and rubbed her bright blue eyes. "The view, great food, and casual mood make this my favorite place to eat in Oranjestad."

"I can see why." Lou leaned back in his chair as the server placed a goblet of shrimp cocktail on the table.

"This is huge. Thank you." He looked at Gemma. "Mind if I say a quick prayer first?"

"Please do." Her smile was warm and happy.

He bowed his head and asked the Lord to bless their time together and the food.

"Some believers don't like to pray in restaurants, but it shows me ya live your faith." Her eyes widened. "I hafta respect ya for that, Lou."

"The way I look at it, God continuously provides for me. Thanking Him is the least I can do." He dipped a jumbo shrimp into the tangy red sauce and tasted it.

Gemma laced her fingers together and leaned forward. "Good, huh?"

"Delicious!"

"Told ya so." She grinned. "Might want to wipe the sauce off your face."

With a shaky hand, Lou dabbed his chin with the napkin. It was impossible to ignore her mesmerizing smile. Maybe she hadn't noticed the awkward reaction. He turned his attention back to the appetizer and poked at a prawn. For some reason, he felt like a jumbo shrimp snagged in the cruise director's snare.

Gemma's quiet presence and genuine kindness reminded him of Millie and made him look forward to seeing the cruise director each day. She was beautiful and her skin appeared so incredibly soft, he was tempted to caress it.

The notion stung his conscience. Millie won his heart the first time he saw her in the church office. He loved her and hoped she still loved him, in spite of what her mother said. Never once had he considered God might have another woman for him.

Before he knew it, their large portions of grilled red snapper arrived. Lou quickly crammed the last bite of shrimp cocktail into his mouth, licked his lips, and eagerly rubbed his hands together. "I can't wait to dig into this."

Millie took a sip of hot tea, then sat against the pillow on her bed and opened the small book. She chewed the end of her pen while contemplating the journal entry.

> Dear Diary,
> Kent and I had a mind-numbing third date this evening. We went to the Japanese Cultural Festival where they performed Puccini's Madame Butterfly. Kent thought the singing was spectacular. I discovered a three-hour opera isn't my thing. I'd rather hear Lou sing our song, *Can't Help Falling in Love.* I miss the sound of his deep bass voice.
> Kent was quite the charmer this evening and tried to make me feel special. Up until now, he's been a perfect gentleman, but there's no chemistry like Lou and I have. Tonight he held my hand for the first time. There was no thrill, but I found myself wondering when he'll kiss me. What am I thinking? I want to remain true to my sweetheart, Lord, but if our romance isn't in Your will, could Kent Sheridan be my destiny? I'm so confused.

With that thought in mind, Millie scribbled in the margin. Kent and Millicent Sheridan. With a sigh, she crossed it out and wrote Mrs. Lou Blythe, then laid her pen down and closed the diary.

She had to admit, life would be exciting with Kent. Money would be no object. And the bonus: they could live miles away from Mother. With that thought, a warm aura surrounded her as she rested against her pillow and allowed herself to melt into the realm of possibilities.

Kent would take her in his arms and whisper in her ear. "Oh, my darling Millicent. I must tell you, I've been nominated for the News and Documentary Emmy Award."

"That's wonderful, my love." She threw her arms around him and snuggled against his chest. Suddenly, his trim physique morphed into a more muscular form and once again, she was wrapped in Lou's arms.

Millie flipped the pillow over and gave it a full-fisted punch. How was a girl supposed to get over someone when he kept barging in on her daydreams? She hadn't heard from him since the disastrous birthday cookout. Why hadn't Lou called? If he cared, wouldn't he have contacted her by now? The ache in her heart deepened and hot tears trembled on her lashes. Would she have to settle for Kent instead of the love Lou could offer?

The full moon flooded through the bedroom window as she reached for the teacup and took the last sip. Maybe she could sand off Kent's rough edges and learn to love him. With a deep sigh, she wiped her face and pushed a lock of dark hair away, allowing her imagination to drift.

"The best part is we'll be interviewed on the red carpet with all the national nominees. I'll buy you a sparkly new gown with shoes to match." He wiggled his eyebrows. "Be sure to brush up on your loquaciousness, babe. You're going to need it."

"Loquaciousness?" Millie's brain short-circuited as she bounced back to reality. Not an iceberg's chance in a Phoenix heat wave would she agree to an interview on any red carpet.

"Millicent." Her mother entered her room and sat on the bed. "So tell me all about your date with Kent. Was he a gentleman? Oh, of course he was, that man has class."

She scowled. "Unlike others who bring their wormy dogs into another person's home. But I digress. Let's get back to Kent. Where did he take you? Give me the details."

Millie tried to avoid eye contact as she nonchalantly slid the diary under the pillow behind her. "We went to the Japanese Cultural Festival. He held my hand during most of the opera."

"An opera? How exciting. First a ballet, now the opera. He's introducing you into his world of culture." She shook her finger. "Didn't I tell you Kent Sheridan was a good catch? Of course I did."

"Hate to tell you this, Mother, but I really didn't enjoy either one. They're a little too sophisticated and ritzy for me. I couldn't relax."

"You'll learn." Penny grimaced and leaned over, holding her stomach.

"Are you okay, Mother?" Millie touched her arm.

"I'm fine. Tell me about your date."

"They sang in Japanese tonight." She shook her head and sniffed. "And who understands ballet?"

"Millicent Marie! Let me try to explain. It has nothing to do with understanding. Just smile and walk the red carpet holding a handsome man's arm. You know like Kitty Mayfield in *Paris Fever*." She stiffened her shoulders. "Do you think she wanted to wear that whalebone corset all night? Of course she didn't. But it was a necessity to get her man and take her place in society."

"But, Mother . . ."

"Hush. I know what I'm talking about." Besides, Kent held your hand."

"I didn't feel any spark, though."

"So what? I've never felt a spark in my life, and I managed to stay married for forty-four years." Her mother shook her head. "If you want sparks, stick a wet finger in a socket."

Great maternal advice. Millie closed her eyes. How was it possible she had this woman's blood coursing through her veins?

Her mother headed across the room and stopped. She moaned and leaned on the dresser for support.

"Tell me what's wrong." Millie jumped up and hurried to her side. Was this another one of her cons?

"My stomach hurts, okay? Leave me alone."

"You haven't had those tests run, have you?" You probably have an ulcer or something. They can give you medicine to make you feel better."

Penny clenched her teeth, "Get off my back, Millicent. Do you think I want some prepubescent rookie touching me? Of course I don't." She reached in her pocket, pulled out antacid tablets, and popped two in her mouth. "These work perfectly well."

She recognized the stubborn set of her mother's jaw. "You're sick. I'm going to get Dad." She hurried to her bedroom door.

"Millicent Marie!" Mother's oppressive glare zeroed in on her like a vulture targeting her prey. She grabbed a cell phone from the dresser and pitched it across the room. "Don't argue with me. I'm your mother." Her knees buckled, and she grabbed the dresser.

"But you obviously need help." Millie took her arm and guided her to the bed.

Pain etched the older woman's ashen face. When she spoke again, it was in a whisper. "I am not going for tests, and I do not want to hear any more about it."

CHAPTER TWELVE

Late August

IT HAD BEEN FOUR WEEKS SINCE Lou left on his cruise, and still no word from him. As difficult as it was, Millie resigned herself to life without him and finding something positive about her connection with Kent. Anything besides Mother approved of him.

She sat motionless in the front seat of Kent's Corvette with her arms crossed. This was their fourth date and the events were getting progressively worse. Dinner with a TV camera in her face. Ballet. Opera. And now a repulsive movie. Did she want to chance going out with him a fifth time?

His cell phone rang as they pulled into the Drakes' driveway. He threw the gearshift into park and answered the call. "Uncle Reggie! Yeah, we saw it tonight. I think it's your best movie yet." He shifted in the bucket seat, phone to his ear. "Can I call you back in a few? I brought my girl home and I want to walk her to the door."

Did he really think of her as his girl? Would he try to kiss her in the moonlight? Talk about romantic. Just like Adrian Rothchild in her favorite show, *Squire of Dames.* Okay, maybe there was as chance for them after all. Millie instinctively glanced to the front window for prying eyes. The house was dark, so Mother's pain pills must have put her to sleep early.

Kent ended the call and shoved his phone in his back pocket. He climbed out of the car and headed for her side.

She nervously popped a Sassy Lassie breath mint into her mouth, just in case, and then unbuckled the seatbelt.

Kent's distinctive smile stretched across his chiseled features as he opened the Corvette's door. The interior light came on to illuminate her awkward exit. He bent slightly and held out his hand.

Before she reached up, Millie paused. Getting out of this car was a pain. There had to be an easy way to do it. She pivoted in her seat, straightened her dress, and took Kent's hand.

He pulled her to a standing position and closed the car door. His expression grew serious as he inched closer, and his arms went around her. Millie's heart melted like one of Mother's chocolate truffles.

Breathe, girl, breathe!

She closed her eyes and without warning, found herself returning the irresistible affection.

In an instant, his gentle kisses turned demanding. Her mouth ached as he held her tighter against him. A shockwave charged through her. His low groan was like an alarm reverberating in her head.

Lou would never do this. Millie gasped and jerked away, covering her mouth. Tears of remorse welled. What kind of woman kisses one man while in love with another?

"What's wrong?" A frown creased his brow.

She lowered her head as heat rose in her cheeks. "I'm not ready for this." She hoped he'd understand and back off.

Silence loomed between them.

"You're right. I'm sorry, but I've never met anyone as delightful as you, Millicent." His index finger gently lifted her chin until their eyes connected. He stroked her arms. "You really are sweet and innocent. I won't try that again."

She searched his face, trying to determine if his remark held sarcasm or sincerity.

"It's getting late. You'd better go inside." With a sigh, Kent led her to the front door. He placed a quick kiss on her forehead then trudged to his Corvette without looking back.

As Millie stepped into the entryway and closed the door, the heavy scent of a cinnamon candle and music from *The Love Story* greeted her. She peeked inside the living room where her mother was snoring in front of the flickering TV screen.

Removing her shoes, she tiptoed up the stairs so Mother wouldn't hear. Who wanted to spend the rest of the night trying to explain her dithering mindset about Kent Sheridan?

Millie schlepped to her room and tossed the shoes into the closet. She collapsed face down on the bed and shivered. How close had she come to letting Kent take over? The thought of it was unnerving. She groaned and flung herself onto the bed exactly like Giselle on *Squire of Dames*. With a huff, Millie sat up. Giselle definitely wasn't the role model she planned to follow.

Mother had high hopes for this dating experience to come to fruition and would go ballistic when she found out about her wavering feelings for Kent. Millie was tired of being wimpy. She rubbed her forehead. The woman demanded to have a say in who she liked, dated, or married. It was time to let Penelope Joy Drake know this is where her control ends.

Millie pulled a clean nightgown from her drawer, and drew a hot bath. Her mind relaxed as she lounged in the bubbles, until Kent's puckered platypus lips came to mind. She didn't want to sit there and dwell on his questionable intentions. Maybe entering tonight's date in her diary would help put everything into perspective.

After donning the pink gown, Millie made her way to the closet. Mother hadn't been feeling well the last couple of days and apparently had fallen asleep early. Therefore, it was safe to retrieve the diary from its hiding place. Years ago, she discovered the top of the hollow core door was open and inside the cavity hung an empty file holder. It was the perfect place to keep her genuine diary and private thoughts away from Mother.

Dear Diary,

Tonight's date with Kent was confusing. The movie we saw made me uncomfortable. Since his godfather, Uncle Reggie, was the producer, Kent insisted we stay through the whole thing.

The language and violence got very rough in several places, and I covered my eyes through the provocative scenes. After years of reading Mother's torrid romance novels, it would be too easy to get hooked on the pursuit of sensuality again. It's been a relief to be free of those chains.

As we left the theater, people from our church were leaving family friendly movies. I was embarrassed when they looked at the marquee of the one we were leaving. I tried to hide my face, but someone hollered, "Hi, Millie."

The rest of the evening, Kent talked about how great the flick was, but I was miserable. When we got home, he pulled me into his arms and it shook me up. Sure, he's more skilled in the romance department, but his kisses turned demanding. In his defense, he did stop when I told him to. I also said we couldn't go to any more racy movies. It made me feel good to take charge for once. Looks like we'll only be lunching for a while.

> It's confusing because I still have feelings for Lou. His warmth and honesty captivates me. He never would've taken me to such an offensive movie. He's sweet and tender and there's no awkwardness between us. I miss him, but I may have lost him. My biggest fear is to end up utterly alone.
>
> Why can't I find the right guy to love me?

Her throat constricted as she contemplated the last question. It wouldn't even be an issue if Lou were still in her life, but his silence made it clear that wasn't the case. She grew annoyed with the failure to tear her mind from the one who got away.

Moonlight streamed through the bedroom window as Millie locked her private diary and returned it to the hollow hiding place. After moving the chair back, she reached under her pillow for the counterfeit journal. It was no secret that Mother faithfully read each bland report of encounters with Kent. Satisfying the woman's curiosity would keep her from arranging any more undesirable blind dates or signing her up for some online singles group.

> Dearest Diary
>
> Here's another secret for you. This was movie night with Kent. He bought me popcorn, candy, and a Colossal Slurp. He kissed me in our driveway. I like him, but unfortunately, no fireworks to report at this time.

With less than a week until the cruise was over, Lou

marked the days off the calendar like a prisoner waiting for parole. He couldn't wait to get home on Labor Day so he could find Millie and set things right. The only bright spot during the cruise was singing for the Lord and getting to know Gemma Carr. Her bubbly personality and flowing chitchat took the pressure off his introverted and conversation-challenged nature. At any rate, her friendship and advice had helped him get through the last month.

He hurried to their usual meeting spot at the gangway. With Gemma's schedule as cruise director, today's excursion to St. Johns might be the last time she'd be free to go ashore with him. He'd miss their time together.

The air had a briny tang as Lou leaned on the ship's railing to watch seabirds swoop above the wooden piles connecting small boats to their moorings. Tourists wandered from shop to shop along Heritage Pier.

A melodious giggle behind him broke into his trance. He looked up as Gemma's arm linked with his.

"Here I am, Lou. Are ya ready to go?" She led him off the Caribbean Breeze and onto Heritage Pier. "We don't have a lot of time, don't ya know, but ya might enjoy one of the museums. After that, maybe we can take a leisurely stroll along Dickenson Bay."

"That's great. You're a good tour guide, Gem." He smiled at the willowy young woman. If his romance with Millie was over, would Gemma be open to a deeper friendship? The random thought shocked him. Perspiration beaded on his forehead as he followed her into the Museum of Antigua and Barbuda.

The once irritating accent of his private tour guide now charmed him, and Lou struggled to keep his focus on the museum's basketry and pottery exhibits.

Gemma stopped and took his hand. "This doesn't seem to be holding your interest, Lou. I think it's time to walk along the shore."

Was he that obvious? Distinct warmth settled in his ears. "It's a pretty day. The beach sounds good to me."

As Lou and Gemma stepped out of the building and into the sunshine, a gentle breeze ruffled his hair. Within a few minutes, they arrived at Dickenson Bay where seagulls flew overhead, squawking for a handout.

They carried their shoes and walked in the damp sand of the crescent-shaped coastline. With every step, their footprints stayed behind, waiting to wash out to sea.

As they reached the water, Gemma stood with her arms held wide, her light blonde hair tousled and tangled in the wind. She stepped into the tide and peaceful waves washed over her feet, soaking the bottom of her jeans.

Her face took on a delicate glow that drew him in. Gemma glanced his way, and a vague attraction passed between them. She moved closer.

"Spending the last five weeks with ya has been wonderful for sure, Lou." She looked at the sand. "I hate for our time to end so soon. Will I ever see ya again?"

"I don't know, Gemma." He turned his head, struggling against the urge to gaze into her light blue eyes. "I made a commitment to Millie."

"But I thought ya said your relationship was over."

"She hasn't talked to me since before the cruise." He glanced away. "My attitude was way off and I shouldn't have left her the way I did. No one would blame her if she doesn't want to get back with me."

She wrapped her slender arms around his middle. "I thought maybe you and I . . ."

"I need to see where things stand with her, first." Lou's throat ached as Gemma kissed his lips. The temptation to pull her close was overwhelming. He shut his eyes, placed his large hands on her shoulders, and lightly kissed the top of her head. He struggled with letting her go.

Lord, help me not to act on impulse. She's ignited a feeling I thought only belonged to Millie.

Labor Day

Lou shouldered his backpack and grabbed his suitcase. Before he spun on his heel to leave, he couldn't help but steal one last glance at the Caribbean Breeze that had been the Warble-Heirs' home for the last month and a half.

Lonnie patted his back. "Are you going to miss Gemma?"

His shoulders went up in a half-hearted shrug in reply to the question. "But I'm eager to get back to Apache Pointe. Mom will be moving in with me until she finds her own place."

"I can't wait to meet your mom." Dena's dark eyes shone as she adjusted her floppy brimmed hat and slipped on her bone-colored sunglasses. "If she's as sweet as you are, we're in for a good time."

"Mom's so sweet; you might need to stock up on insulin. She's an extrovert and a real livewire who's planning to go skydiving and bungee jumping on her ninetieth birthday. That's fifteen years away, but it's in her itinerary. Something you have in common, she likes to shop, so I know you'll get along fine." He switched his suitcase to the other hand. "I'm hoping she'll help me win Millie back."

Lonnie looked around. "Have you seen Dooley and Marv lately?"

"I think they jumped ship to escape Gertrude and Myrtle. Those gals wanted to set up a family reunion with the Weinmann cousins." Lou laughed. "They've heard enough ancestry to last them till the next cruise."

Lou lingered at the edge of the thinning crowd. Would he ever see Gemma Carr again? He checked his shirt pocket to make sure the note with her e-mail address and phone number was still there. Did he have the nerve to contact her if things with Millie fell through? He pulled out his cell and dialed Millie's number.

On the third ring, a male voice answered. "Yeah?"

"May I speak with Millie Drake?"

"Who's calling?"

"Lou Blythe. Who am I talking to?"

"This is Kent Sheridan. Millicent is done with you, pal. She said you're dead to her after what you did. Don't you have any pride?" A click indicated the call was over. Irked by the self-righteous attitude, Lou's breathing quickened as humiliation and anger grew. He crammed the cell into his pocket and marched down the gangplank. It looked as if his hopes of seeing her washed away with the tide.

CHAPTER THIRTEEN

Mid-September

THE BELL OVER THE DOOR JINGLED when Millie entered Floral Scent-sations. The flower shop was filled with planters and gift displays in the rich colors of autumn.

She approached the service desk. "Hi, Carol. Can you spare a few minutes?"

Carol looked up and smiled. "Mills! Good to see you. It's been a while. The shop isn't busy right now so I have time for a visit. What's up, Cuz?"

"I need your advice about dating." Millie propped her elbow on the waist-high showcase knowing Carol would give her an honest answer. "Kent's taken me to expensive places like the ballet and an opera."

"That's impressive. Did you have a good time?"

"Not really. But I always wondered what it would be like to go. The ballet was pretty, but I had a difficult time sitting through the opera." Millie rested her chin in her hand. "Kent's been very sweet and attentive."

"So, what's your problem?"

"A couple of weeks ago he kissed me. It made me uncomfortable. Carol, what's wrong with me?" Her eyes widened as she stood. "I feel like a starry-eyed, romantic simpleton."

"Don't say that, Mills. Did you kiss him back?"

"I did at first. I couldn't help myself. But when he got too passionate, I thought of Lou and pushed Kent away."

Carol hugged her. "You did the right thing. No doubt,

your Mr. Sheridan is used to more aggressive women and doesn't know how to respect a lady." The store phone rang, and she answered it. "Yes, Mr. Wingate, your order is ready for pickup any time. Thank you." She turned to Millie. "Your mind went to Lou when you were kissing someone else. What does that tell you?"

"It means I love the man, and I admit it." Millie hung her head. "Going out with Kent the last couple of months has helped me deal with losing Lou. Dating a celebrity opened up a bright, new world for me. He knows a lot of famous people, Carol, and that's exciting." She raised her index finger to make a point. "And besides, Mother adores him, so it makes it easier to live with her."

"I understand your attraction to his lifestyle, but what about Lou?"

"That's where I'm confused. I still love Lou and thought we'd be together forever, but he hasn't called me since my birthday back in July. That's almost two months!"

"Maybe he's tried to contact you. Meanwhile, as I've said before, you should probably call him. You know how backward he is."

Millie crossed her arms and frowned. "Don't you think he should apologize for walking out on me?" Her eyes flashed. "On my birthday?"

"Let me ask you this, Mills, why do you think Lou left?"

"I've already told you he heard me fighting with Mother. I was standing up for him, so he should've stayed to protect me. How can I trust him not to leave again if things get rocky? And you know with Mother it's gonna happen."

A customer entered the shop. He stopped at a rack of colorful throws with scripture written on them.

Carol lowered her voice. "Think about it, Mills. He

witnessed the worst of your mother's tantrums. What was your reaction?" She left to help the shopper.

The shame of yelling at her mother cut into her conscience. Millie moaned. If only Lou hadn't seen their ghastly outbursts. How many times had she promised him she would never be like her mother? No wonder he slammed the door in his haste to get away.

A few minutes later, Carol returned and put an arm around Millie's shoulder. "Are you okay?"

Millie shook her head. "I've been blaming Lou the whole time, and it's my fault. I screamed at Mother." Her eyes widened. "Oh, no! He might've heard me call him a Neanderthal."

"A what?"

"She thinks he looks like a caveman and calls him awful names. As I yelled, 'I love that Neanderthal,' Lou was at the bottom of the stairs looking totally disgusted."

Carol led her behind the counter and had her sit on a stool. "Here's a tissue. I'm proud of you for taking a stand. Normally that's not in our DNA. We come from a long line of docile Drakes."

"Yeah, and look where my backbone got me."

"Grandpa Drake always said life is more peaceful when we keep our big bazoo shut. But, in this case you did the right thing. Aunt Penny's been a bully for way too long. You don't want her mingling into your personal affairs for the rest of your life, do you?"

"Absolutely not." Millie stood and waved her hand over her head. "I've had the mama drama up to here."

"Now, how are you going to rectify this problem with Lou?"

"That Neanderthal comment had to hurt his feelings, so I should be the one to apologize first. I'm also guilty for kissing Kent on the rebound. No wonder it feels like I cheated on Lou."

"Sounds like you've made a decision, but it may not be the right time to mention kissing Kent."

Millie nodded. "But if Lou doesn't want to come back, I'll be alone."

"Which is it? You don't want to be lonely, or you don't want to be without Lou? There's a big difference. Fear of being alone can lead to bad choices."

"I guess it's both, but mostly I don't want to be without Lou. Since he's been gone, something is missing in my life. Kent's nice and I like him, but he isn't Lou."

"Think about this, Mills. Kent's been calling all the shots since you've been going out. Do you really want to go from one controlling person to another? I'm afraid that will happen if your relationship continues."

"I never thought about it from that angle." Freedom from Mother just crumbled in front of her like an old, dry cracker.

"Let me ask you one more thing. Do you feel Kent knows the Lord? Has he gone to church with you? Are you able to talk about spiritual things?"

A flashback of the suggestive movie hit Millie between the eyes. She lowered her head. "No. In fact he changes the subject whenever I bring it up."

"If he's changing the subject, then he's not going to talk about it. Remember the Bible says to not be unequally yoked with unbelievers."

"I've thought a lot about that since Dad mentioned it a while back. Kent's taking me out later this week, so I'll ask him straight out about his beliefs then."

"How un-Drake-like."

"Touché." Millie's attempt to smile wavered. Surely she could do it with God's help. *Please, Father give me the words.* "Some of the best talks Lou and I have had were about the Lord and His love for us."

"Kent's a player, Mills. Don't let him mislead you."

"I'll be careful, but people can change, can't they?"

Lou flipped the calendar page to October. After being home from the cruise for a month, he had yet to contact Millie. She'd conveniently managed to avoid him at every turn. Her mother and Kent saw to that.

Letters, post cards, voice mail. He gave up. It was Millie's turn to reach out. She owed him that much. He needed closure to move on with his life, or at least try. He ran his fingers through his dark hair. What could he say to the woman who no longer wanted him in her life? It took her less than two weeks to move on and date someone else. Besides, how could he possibly compete with Kent Sheridan and his fame, good looks, and wealth?

After work, Lou checked his mailbox hoping to find a note from Millie, or maybe a postcard from Gemma. Instead, he counted two bills for himself, along with four letters and two pieces of junk mail addressed to Mrs. Gabby Blythe. Mom hadn't moved in yet and she was already getting more mail than he was. He glanced back into the mailbox in case he missed something.

Laying the envelopes aside, Lou picked up the remote, and sat on the couch next to his basset hound. He opened a bag of potato chips and tossed one to his dog.

"Let's get the weather report on and see how hot it's going to be when we go to the airport to get your grandma tomorrow." He groaned when Kent Sheridan's grinning mug appeared onscreen.

The sandy-haired anchorman looked directly into the camera and flashed his award-winning smile. "And now here's Will Scott with your weather forecast."

"Sheridan. Look at that smug face, Farfel." He crumbled a furniture sales flyer and threw it into a nearby waste can. "Why can't Millie see through that plastic facade?" He crossed his arms and glared at the large TV screen.

Lou's phone rang. He muted the audio on the TV and retrieved the cell from his pocket.

"Hi, Lou, it's Momma. I'm back in Seattle with Bart and his family."

"Hey, there, good lookin'. It's great to hear your voice after all these months. What have you been up to?"

"I worked on my speeches for several weeks, flew to London for the symposium, and then met up with Flo Smythe. You remember her; she was our foreign exchange student when you were about ten."

"Oh, yeah. I haven't thought about her in years." He chuckled. "She waited until you left for work and then juggled oranges and fresh eggs for us at breakfast. How is she?"

"That's the gal. Would you believe she married a fella from Northumberland. Guess what his name is?"

"Come on, just tell me."

"Eb. His name is Eb." She cackled. "Isn't that the funniest thing you've ever heard?"

"Okay, Momma." Lou held his phone closer to his ear. "What's so funny about some man named Eb? Am I missing something?"

"Honey, think about it." She paused. "Her husband's name is Eb. Her name is Flo. Now do you get it?"

"Eb and Flo?" He pulled the cell away, stared at it, and then returned it to his ear. "Are you kidding me?"

"It's true, Squishy."

"Please promise you won't call me that name in public."

"On my word of honor, but I can't promise your brothers won't give it away." Gabby's rich laughter resonated over the phone. "Enough about your nickname and my adventures."

"Yeah, about those adventures. You're in your mid-seventies, Momma. When do you plan to slow down?"

"Haven't you heard? Seventy-five is the new sixty. I have no intention of slowing down. Let's can the old lady jabber. We haven't had a chance to talk since before you left for your cruise. How did it go?"

"We had a great time, and the Overton brothers managed to behave themselves for the most part. We received several compliments on our performances. The new songs Lonnie wrote seemed to touch a lot of people."

"That's wonderful. Sounds like the Lord is using your group more all the time. I pray daily that souls are saved through your musical gift." Gabby cleared her throat. "I'm calling to remind you that I'll arrive tomorrow afternoon."

"You've sent six text messages, Momma. How could I possibly forget?" Lou laughed. "I can't wait for one of your famous fried chicken dinners. I even have your room ready."

"Let me guess, my bed's probably strategically placed next to the stove, isn't it?" She giggled. "You boys and your food."

"Absolutely. We've tasted the best, why try the rest?"

"I'll be waiting for you to pick me up at the airport around 2:30. You have the flight schedule, right?"

"You left it six times on my phone, remember? My plan is to leave a half an hour early in case the traffic's bad."

"One more thing, Son, the moving van is scheduled to be at the storage unit you rented for me in a day or so."

"I'm glad you finally agreed to move to Apache Pointe, and not only for your stellar cooking abilities." He took a long drink of his Mountain Dew.

"Are you ready to put up with an old lady living with you for a while?"

"It'll be nice to have you around. But don't be hanging

your skivvies in my bathroom or leaving your teeth on the kitchen counter."

"No guarantees. By the way, have you gotten any news from your girl, lately? I can't wait to meet her."

Lou shook his head as his insides crumbled. He struggled to keep his reply from sounding emotional. "She has a bad habit of forgetting her phone, so I haven't been able to get through to her since before the cruise."

"That's a shame, son. What on earth happened?" Her voice held a hint of regret. "I thought the two of you were getting serious."

"We'll go deeper into it when you get here in a few days, Momma. Maybe by then I'll have heard from her." He coughed to keep from saying anything more.

"That's okay. Your brother just pulled into the drive. They're taking me out for a farewell dinner at the Space Needle Restaurant. I need to scurry before Mr. Cheapskate changes his mind and takes me to Burger Barn."

He laughed, relieved the awkward topic of Millie had been changed. "SkyCity is the best place in Seattle. Eat some shrimp for me and say "hi" to Bart, Tara, and the kids. Have a safe trip, and I'll see you tomorrow."

Lou hung up, kicked his shoes off, and pushed the TV's mute button in time for Sheridan's cheesy sign-off salute. He was happy his mom was moving nearby. She would keep his mind off the Millie and Kent situation.

CHAPTER FOURTEEN

MILLIE FINISHED APPLYING THE MUDPACK ON her face. She turned on the desk light. Thoughts of Kent and Lou brought up many questions in her mind and absolutely no answers. All she knew was Kent Sheridan had become an irksome reminder that her mother was still playing her like a puppet on a string. Time for Howdy Doody to sever those binding cords and hog-tie Mother with them. Maybe there was a simpler solution and writing it out would help her find it. She opened her private diary. With pen poised, she mulled over her next entry.

Dear Diary,

Kent and I are going out this evening. Talking to Carol last week has me thinking deeper about my relationship with him. She mentioned the drawbacks of dating someone who doesn't believe in God the way I do.

Kent has many good qualities. He is handsome to a fault, has a lucrative career with a bright future, and an edgy sense of humor.

On the flip side, he is a skilled kisser, but overzealous in my opinion, which is a major turnoff. His taste in movies is severely lacking too. Socially, I feel awkward since he treats me more like a companion than a possible sweetheart. I've had my fill of his fans constantly interrupting our dates. Lady fans. Pretty, buxom lady fans, throwing themselves all over him.

Up until ten months ago when Lou came along, I'd never had a date. Kent, on the other hand, has dated many models and actresses through the years. What do we have in common? Nothing, really, but, I don't want to hurt anymore.

I feel safe and special with Lou. He's kind, considerate, compassionate, and likes to please me. I love his deep voice.

However, Lou tours with his group a lot. I worry about his safety while they're traveling. He has lady fans too, but I don't have to worry about them. They only want to mother him with cookies, brownies, and other goodies.

Millie closed her journal and answered her ringing cell phone. "Hello?"

"Hey, Mills. Just called to see if you wanted to watch a chick flick with me. Frank has to go to a meeting and Andy said he could find better things to do. So here I am sitting by myself with a big bowl of popcorn."

"I'd love to, but I'm going out with Kent tonight."

"Oh."

The tone of Carol's remark was one of disappointment.

"Don't worry. I still plan to ask him where he stands with the Lord as promised."

"Do you think he'll break up with you?"

Millie thought about the possibility of Kent's rejection. "I don't know. If we aren't officially a couple, can we still break up?"

"Good question." Carol laughed. "Will you be okay if he doesn't ask you out again? I know he's taken your mind off Lou's absence."

Her shoulders lifted as she drew a deep breath. "I've

decided I can handle not dating Kent."

"High five, girl. A step in the right direction." She paused. "Can you say the same about Lou?"

"My problem with Lou is that he walked out and may never come back. I don't have a choice." She blinked back tears, glad that Carol couldn't see her. "I have to be willing to let go of him too, don't I?"

She longed for Lou's hugs and kisses. No way to deny that! More importantly, she knew he loved God and was a man of integrity. She wanted to marry someone who could be the spiritual leader of their home. Kent sure didn't fit that role.

"So you're not hung up on Kent Sheridan?"

"No. He comes on too strong for my taste. His overbearing feminine following drives me crazy. No matter where we are."

"I'm glad you're seeing Kent for what he is."

Millie toyed with her pen. "Look how long I've worked two jobs and still don't have the money to move out. I've been in this rut forever. No one else wants to date me. Going out gives me a break from you-know-who."

Carol laughed. "I can't imagine who you're talking about." She paused. "Meanwhile, let's not give up on Lou yet. And remember, Mills, I'm always here for you."

"Will you help me to pray about something? You've convinced me to tell Kent this is our last date." She took a deep breath. "I've got to be strong and do it."

"Good for you, and you'll be fine,"

"I don't want fear and doubt to come in and have me second guessing myself."

"I promise I'll pray for you tonight."

Millie could almost hear Carol's smile. "Thanks. I have to go now and get ready for my final date with Kent. Thanks for calling. I'll let you know how it works out. 'Bye."

Millie set her fork on the plate and wiped her lips. "The Arroz con pollo was delicious, Kent. Thank you for the suggestion. I've never had it before."

He pushed his plate to the side. "It's one of my favorite dishes. Did you save room for their Tarta de Queso dessert?"

A bleached blonde cut into their conversation and put a hand on his shoulder. "Hey there, Kent, baby."

He slid his arm around her waist and grinned. "Well, hello."

Catching the woman giving her the once-over, Millie squirmed and crossed her arms, trying to maintain a calm veneer. He was enjoying this a little too much, and she was definitely getting tired of the blatant flirting. Kent was still her date, and this shameless hussy was taking over.

The top-heavy woman leaned down. "I watch the news every night just to see you. You were my crush when you played Buster on *Best Family Times*, Can I have your autograph, gorgeous?" She placed a spiral notepad in front of him and kissed his cheek. "Ooh, you smell as good as I thought you would."

Millie clenched her fist and wondered if the flirt could smell with a broken nose. *Careful Millicent Marie. You'll end up like your mother.*

An older woman came up behind them, giggled, and nudged Blondie out of the way with her hip. "The girls at work aren't going to believe I talked to you, so let me take a selfie of us, honey. They're going to die." She set her empty wine glass by Kent's plate and raised her phone. "Flash that million-dollar smile, sweetie. Good. Now I want one with your cute little sign-off salute."

The anchorman complied with the request and raised

his chin with a little too much chauvinistic arrogance. He sent a proud glance toward Millie.

She swallowed hard and directed her eyes from the scene. She'd had enough. Time to dismiss herself from the spontaneous photo op. She grabbed her purse. "Kent, why don't you go ahead and order the special cheesecake for the two of us. I'm going to the powder room and freshen up."

The older woman rolled her eyes and nudged Kent's shoulder. "Isn't she a bossy little thing?"

Needing a few moments to regain her composure, Millie entered the posh ladies room and forced a smile at the matron. So much for privacy. She sighed, went into the last stall, and closed the door. The sneer on Blondie's face still stuck in her mind.

She never got used to the hordes of women buzzing around Kent. Did he brush them off? Nooo! In fact, his disgusting reaction to their flirting was straight out of Mother's romance novels. If she continued to see him, she'd have to accept all of it. Her eyes narrowed. Either that or punch him in the snout.

A sultry voice, much like Blondie's, interrupted her thoughts. "Hey, Brandee. Guess who I'm going out with later tonight? None other than Kent Sheridan, himself!"

Millie sat very still on the edge of the stool and listened intently. She slanted her head and tried to get a peek through the crack between the door.

Another woman answered. "Really? That's awesome. But isn't he here with some middle-aged brunette? Honestly, what's the attraction? She has to be in her face-lift years."

"I know. A jowl reduction would do wonders."

Millie felt for a turkey neck as they continued to jeer.

"He's going to dump that loser and take me dancing. Wanna hear something hilarious? Her old lady is actually paying him to date her. How pathetic is that?"

Their mocking laughter echoed off the tile walls.

Blood began to pound in Millie's temples as the heat of humiliation rose from her chest. Blondie had been at the table and knew she was going to the powder room. Why couldn't she fling the stall door open with gusto, and get in their faces? Mother certainly would. She rolled her eyes. Question answered.

She swallowed as her stomach tied into a firm knot. Not wanting to face her rivals, she remained quiet and waited for them to leave. Blinking back tears, she peeked out to make sure they were gone. Her first instinct was to march from the restroom to the table and smack the arrogant look off Kent's face. But why give those hateful women any more ammunition for ridicule?

Millie rooted in her purse for her phone. *Please, Lord, help me to have remembered to bring it this time.* Her fingers grasped the cell and she breathed a sigh of relief. After calling a cab, she left the stall and washed her hands.

"Are you okay, miss?" The matron offered her a hand towel and pushed the tip jar closer to Millie.

"No, I'm not." Millie blotted her eyes with a tissue and added a dollar to the jar. Then, with one last swipe to her nose, she opened the powder room door and entered the hall. Her thoughts screeched like a howler monkey as she pushed past a small group of people in the foyer and ran out the restaurant door.

She took deep breaths, almost hyperventilating to keep from crying as she climbed into the waiting taxi.

Pulling out her cell, she spoke into it. "Call Carol." A few seconds later, her cousin answered. "Hi Carol. Is it okay if I drop by? I need to talk."

"Sure, what's up, Mills?"

"Mother would stoop at nothing to keep me from Lou.

I can now add bribery to her growing list of atrocities. I've had it with that woman." She glanced at the back of the driver's head and lowered her voice. "May I stay with you for a little while?"

"You're always welcome. I won't be home for a couple of hours, but you have a key. Grizzly Bars are in the freezer. Will you be all right until we get back?"

"I think so. Thanks, Carol." Millie closed her burning eyes and sniffed. "Talk to you later."

She huffed and leaned her shoulder against the taxi door. Had Mother ever cared or showed a hint of maternal compassion? She'd been Penelope Drake's lifelong doormat, and Kent was no better. He ignored her feelings while those obnoxious, well-cleavaged broads openly flirted with him. The cad even had the audacity to accept Mother's bribe.

"I bet I can pull you out of that blue funk, baby doll." The cab driver wiggled his furry unibrow and bared his snaggle-toothed smirk in the rearview mirror. "You're my last fare. How about me and you go out for a drink?"

"Just take me to 1507 Night Hawk Drive." Millie's gut burned as she pulled a tissue from purse and broke down. Was this slob on Mother's payroll too?

In the restaurant foyer, Lou and his mother patiently waited for Lonnie and Dena Chandler to join them. They were usually a bit late, and tonight was no different.

Someone raced past their seats and headed outside.

Lou jumped to his feet. That was Millie! With heart pounding, he ran out the door, hoping for a chance to speak to her. By the time he made it to the curb, the taxi door slammed shut, and the cab sped off. A thick sense of defeat hovered overhead as he went back inside.

"Lou? What's wrong?"

Disregarding his mother's question, he hurried to the nearby dining room Millie had come from. A redheaded lady was taking a picture with Kent Sheridan. Lou clenched his jaw and stomped to the table. "I want a word with you."

Kent ignored him and continued to smile for the woman's camera.

"One more, Kent." She leaned over and put her cheek next to his.

When the redhead finally left, Lou stepped closer and prayed Kent wasn't a black belt. He placed his hand firmly on the man's shoulder.

Kent knocked it off and sprang from his chair. "What's your problem, man?"

"Millie left the restaurant crying." Lou grabbed the cocky newsman's lapels and stared him down. "I don't know what you did to her, but I don't like it."

"What? Who's Millie?"

"Drake. Millie Drake. Wasn't she your date tonight?"

"Oh, you mean Millicent." He laughed, turned in his seat, and pointed down the hall. "She's probably still in the ladies' room."

Anger twisted in Lou's throat at the glib reply. Without hesitation, he formed a tight fist and shoved it under Kent's nose.

"Hey! Wait, man." He grabbed Lou's wrist. "Don't hit the face. I have to be on TV in a couple of hours."

Hot, angry prickles enveloped Lou. He released his hold. Slugging this moron wouldn't help Millie. "You're not worth it." He slammed Kent back into his chair and marched through the swarm of cell phones capturing the fierceness on his face.

When he reached the foyer, he approached his mother

and the Chandlers. "I'm sorry, but something's come up and I have to leave. Lonnie, will you take Mom home for me?" Without waiting for an answer, he hurried from the restaurant.

CHAPTER FIFTEEN

FOLLOWING A GOOD CRY, MILLIE MOVED her chair closer to Carol's kitchen table and reached for her third Grizzly Bar that night. "How is it possible to lose two, count 'em, two men in the span of a few weeks?"

"By dating Kent, you learned the kind of man you don't want. You made the right decision to dump him." Carol refilled Millie's glass with cold milk and patted her hand. "My sweet cousin, you're lovable and don't ever forget it."

"Mother insulted the only man that ever loved me, and chased him away. On top of that, she paid Channel 2's Romeo to date me."

"You're worthy of more respect than your mother can supply. Not only respect, but kindness, happiness, and dignity. You matter, Mills, and you deserve to be with the man you love too." Carol's eyebrows furrowed. "Sometimes manipulation can turn into abuse. Unfortunately, Aunt Penny's crossed the line many times."

Abuse? The last bite of Grizzly Bar seemed caught in Millie's throat. She sipped her milk, swallowed, and smacked the table. "I know I'm supposed to forgive Mother, but how can I?"

"Think of it this way, Mills. Forgiveness doesn't deny or justify the damage brought on by cruelty." Carol met her gaze. "We forgive because God forgave us, and it allows Him to heal us. Exactly like love; it's a choice, not a feeling."

The next morning Millie awoke to her cousin's gentle nudge. She yawned and propped herself up with her elbow. "What time is it?"

"It's after nine o'clock. Andy and I are about ready to leave for Sunday school. Do you still want me to take you home?" Carol handed her a steaming cup of coffee. "Were you able to get any sleep?"

"Not much, but I'm feeling a lot better after last night's chat. Thanks for helping me think things through."

"You've done the same for me." Carol grinned and shook her head. "I don't know how you managed to sleep through my son's racket this morning. He didn't realize you had stayed the night."

"I didn't even hear him." Millie threw the plush blanket aside and swung her feet to the floor. "Thanks for calling Mother last night. The last thing I needed was to get into an argument with her." She took a sip of the hot drink. "You watch. She'll come up with a grand attention-getting scheme to make me feel guilty."

"Don't worry about it, we all see through her tactics. You're welcome to have lunch with us today and stay as long as you like."

"Thanks, anyway, but I'll probably skip lunch. I'd better hurry so you're not late for Sunday school." Within a few minutes, she had gathered her belongings, set the half-emptied cup on the kitchen counter, and met them on the porch.

Carol stopped to lock the door. "Are you going to morning worship?" She followed Millie to the car.

"My plan is to hide out in the balcony and leave early. I'd rather not talk to anyone today." She buckled her seatbelt and glanced in the backseat. "Hi, Andy." She smiled politely at the teenager despite her pounding headache.

"Hey, Millie. Sorry if I woke you up this morning. I like to warm up for our praise band in a steamy shower. It helps to relax my vocal chords."

"It's okay. By the way, I didn't hear you today, but I think you have a nice voice." She reached into the back and gave him a high five.

Carol backed the car onto Night Hawk Drive. "When I don't feel like going to church but go anyway, the Lord usually speaks to my heart. Maybe today's message will help you begin the healing process."

"I could sure use it."

"My offer for you to stay with us for a while still stands." Carol pulled into the drive at Millie's house.

"Yeah, Millie." A sparkle came to Andy's eyes. "I promise to share my chocolate-caramel Toastee Tortz with you."

"That's something to look forward to." She laughed and turned to Carol. "I'll bring a few things over this afternoon."

"Sounds good. If we're not there, make yourself at home. See you later."

Millie climbed from the car and hurried inside. As she set her purse on the coffee table, her mother's current romance novel, *Confessions of a Conniving Contessa*, fell to the floor. She fought the urge to rip it apart . . . page by scorching page. With one swift kick, it was under the pink floral couch.

She attempted to straighten her tense shoulders and marched upstairs. Maybe Andy's idea of a steaming shower would help her muscles relax. In a few minutes, she closed the shower curtain and hoped the hot water would rinse her stress down the drain.

Surely Dad wasn't aware of Mother's pity-date

schemes. Now he was going to find out his missing money ended up lining Kent Sheridan's pocket. She'd love to be a fly on the wall and witness that scenario unfold.

She could see it now. Dad would turn into an international spy like Antoine le Bond in *The Jackal's Cackle.* He'd wring Mother's flaccid turkey neck, and the loud squawk coming out of her mouth would echo throughout the neighborhood. "I did this for you, Millicent." Millie almost felt sorry for the woman. Almost. Poor Dad would have to fork out more money for her psychotherapy sessions. Maybe it would work this time.

She got ready in record time and packed the necessities to take a maternal reprieve at Carol's house. Time to make a quick entry in her false diary, first.

> Mother,
>
> I know you're reading this. I was appalled to learn about your wicked plot in my love life. My wonderful romance with Lou Blythe is beyond repair, and now you've made me a laughing stock by paying Kent Sheridan to date me. I hope you're happy now. Thanks to your interference, I have no one to love me.

Millie didn't bother to hide the open book.

She checked her watch. Sunday school was over and everyone would be chatting and having coffee and snacks for another twenty minutes. Millie tossed her real diary in with her clothes, mashed down the lid of her suitcase, and zipped it. Grabbing her Bible, she wheeled the luggage to the door.

After putting her belongings in the trunk of her car, Millie headed for the church. She parked behind the office in case her mother's radar would be tracking her.

The congregation was singing as she entered the

vestibule. The tall and lanky greeter handed her a bulletin.

"Good morning, Mr. Kerrigan." Millie put the car keys in her purse and shook the old man's hand. "Is anyone in the balcony today?"

"No ma'am, but I think your young man is sitting near the back of the sanctuary with his mother and Carol." He pointed to the left section where Lou was sitting with his arm draped on the shoulder of a silver-haired woman. "That Mrs. Blythe is such a friendly lady. I don't think she's ever met a stranger."

Mr. Kerrigan was still holding her hand. Millie inwardly grimaced. If she didn't get away from him now, he'd talk to the end of the service. "It's late, so I'm going to slip upstairs." Moments ticked by before she succeeded in extracting her hand from the greeter's death grip. She hurried to the balcony to sit out of sight. Apologizing to Lou in a public place would be awkward, especially in front of his mother. Some things need to remain private.

The smell of seldom-used hymnals greeted her as she dropped into the back pew next to the wall. A heavy sense of emptiness and penetrating regrets bombarded her already wounded soul. Millie lowered her head and fought back tears. Carol was right. She needed to hear from the Lord.

Pastor Frank Bailey walked to the pulpit following the last worship song. The congregation bowed their heads as his baritone voice led them in prayer.

"Our dear and gracious Heavenly Father, we gather this morning in the name of Jesus to lay before You our many needs and concerns. Help us put aside the cares of life, since those thoughts drown out Your voice and Your message. For some, today is filled with disappointment and heartache. Their circumstances may be dreadful and filled with sadness and sorrow. They need the comfort of being in fellowship with You and with each other. Your compassion never fails. Enable us to hear the word You have for us today and consider it in our hearts. In Christ's name we pray, Amen."

Frank took a drink of water before he began. "Sometimes things are not as we want them to be. In spite of our best efforts, our circumstances aren't user friendly. Our message today focuses on a verse filled with the promise of God's faithfulness.

"Please turn in your Bibles to Jeremiah 29:11. Here we read a favorite verse of many believers. "For I know the plans I have for you," declares the LORD, "plans to prosper you and not to harm you, plans to give you hope and a future."

Millie closed her eyes. *Lord, I trust Your plans for my life. It may look terrible now, but You promised a hope and a future, so I'll rely on You no matter what.*

CHAPTER SIXTEEN

LOU'S PULSE ACCELERATED. EVEN IN THE large sanctuary, he felt claustrophobic. He had memorized the verse in Jeremiah many years ago, but the promise never held so much meaning before. With or without Millie Drake, the Lord still had plans for his life. Surrendering his love for her was the hard part, but if God wanted her to be in his life, He'd work out all the details.

His mouth was dry. He leaned over and whispered between his mother and Carol. "I need a drink of water. I'll be back."

They nodded.

Lou walked down the hall to a water fountain near the kitchen. He bent his long frame and took a cool, refreshing drink.

The white-haired usher touched his arm. "If you're looking for your girl, she came in late and went to the balcony."

Lou stood, wiped the water dribbling from his chin, and stared at the man. "You mean Millie's here?"

"Bless her heart. Guess she didn't want to distract anyone. She's such a thoughtful little gal. Reminds me of—"

Lou didn't wait for the man to finish his rambling sentence. "Thanks, Mr. Kerrigan. I have to go." He ran to the stairway and, despite his mounting anxiety, managed to climb the steps two at a time. Thanks to Penny Drake and Kent Sheridan's interference, the long days of waiting to talk with Millie had been filled with painful anticipation that tried his patience.

As he entered, the balcony seemed empty until his eyes adjusted to the dim surroundings. Millie was nestled in the corner. She still possessed a certain attraction that went beyond physical beauty. His love for her had continued to intensify from the first time he saw her. A powerful surge of passion clutched his heart. Would he ever get over her? Another glance told him she was crying.

Lou bowed his head and prayed in earnest. *Thank You for this opportunity, Lord. Thy will be done.* Taking a deep breath, he hurried to the top row, and gently slid in beside her. "Honey." He gazed at her, reading total surprise in her expression. The dark circles under her puffy eyes were evidence of how little she had slept.

She turned her head and pushed a wayward lock of hair from her face. A questioning smile tugged at her lips. "Lou?"

In one quick move, his arm went to the back of the pew. Mindful of being quiet, he spoke softly into her ear. "I can't live without you, Millie." He paused, conscious of the still strong connection between them. His heart constricted. Was it enough? There was not a seed of doubt in his mind, but how did she feel? "Is there still a chance for us?"

A tear rolled down Millie's cheek. She nodded in reply and rested her head in the hollow between his shoulder and neck.

Thank You, Lord. With fresh hope in his heart, Lou held her hand and stared at her in silence. It took him a few seconds to regain his composure. "Would you mind if we went somewhere private to talk?" Resolve filled his voice.

Without hesitation, a glint of wonder filled her dark brown eyes, and the smile he'd come to admire tugged at her lips. She gave his hand a gentle squeeze.

Lou's heart skipped a beat as he interlaced his fingers with hers. Hand-in-hand the two hurried out of the balcony, down the stairs, and past old Mr. Kerrigan.

Once they found an empty Sunday school room, Lou swept Millie into a hug that lifted her off the floor. He lowered her onto the long classroom table and cupped her face. "You're the most precious person in my life. I've missed you so much."

Millie's eyes narrowed as she edged off the table. "Then why didn't you write or call me on your cruise? Or contact me when you got back?" Her hand covered her quivering mouth as she looked away.

Lou frowned as his mind burned with questions. "I called and left messages several times." He took her hand. "And I also sent at least a dozen letters and postcards."

"Wait a minute, I never received any of them."

"I tried my best to call at every port when we stopped, until your mother said you were dating someone else and wanted nothing more to do with me."

Millie sat on the corner of the table. "My mother, the great manipulator. She's determined to control every aspect of my life. That's how the other man got into the picture."

Lou offered a barely noticeable nod, lifted her chin, and looked directly into her eyes. "Let's forget about all that and move on. You made a difference in my life, and I've been miserable without you, Millie."

"I missed you, too, but I need to explain something. Mother's attitude toward you is exactly why we were fighting on my birthday. I was trying to defend you. There was never a good reason to stand up to her until then. You shouldn't have had to hear the terrible things that were said."

Lou's forehead touched hers and a surge of awkwardness loomed over him. "I didn't know the reason at the time, but the screaming and yelling threw me off. Even so, there was no excuse for walking out on you, and I apologize."

"I'm sorry too." She took a deep breath. "I need to get something else off my chest. Thanks to Mother's ingenuity and Mrs. Eichenbaum's canasta club, I won a raffle date with Kent Sheridan. You know, the anchorman from Channel 2 news?" She gave Kent's famous two-fingered salute.

Lou gave a low moan. "I've heard of him. Do you like him?"

"No." She waved him off. "Trust me, Lou; we didn't connect on any level. He was simply someone to go out with because I was lonely and thought you'd left me for good."

He licked his lips. Should he mention his friendship with the ship's cruise director? This would be the time, but it could haunt Millie with doubts of his fidelity. It was on the tip of his tongue to admit it, but he couldn't stand to hurt her. Besides, nothing happened. "I was lonesome too." Lou's voice softened. "I shouldn't have left when you were vulnerable, but that amount of hostility upset me. Will you forgive me?"

Millie stood on tiptoe, linked her fingers behind his neck, and pressed her lips to Lou's in a lingering kiss. Pulling away, she searched his eyes. "Does that answer your question?"

"That reply was not only enlightening, but highly rewarding as well." Lou enjoyed the sparkle in her eyes as he reached into his pocket and handed her the tiny box. "I bought you something while I was in Oranjestad, Aruba. Hope you like it."

He chuckled at her childlike enthusiasm as she opened the gift. A gleam shot through her eyes. She held up the heart-shaped necklace and peered into his face.

"It's beautiful." She fell into his arms and pulled back. "Would you put it on me?"

Joy and relief swelled in Lou's chest as he fastened the locket around her smooth neck. He held her in a snug embrace and stroked her hair. "I love you, Millie Drake."

A soft tap sounded on the classroom door. Millie pried herself from Lou's arms as Mr. Kerrigan's thin face appeared.

He scrubbed a hand over his chin. "Hate to interrupt your little rendezvous, but I wanted to warn you lovebirds that the service is almost over. You might want to go out to the vestibule so folks won't talk."

"Thanks for the warning." Once the rheumy-eyed usher left the room, Lou turned to her, bright pink inching up his face. "As much as I hate to say this, we'd better get out there."

"You're right. We don't want Mother to make a scene."

"Now, where'd I put my keys?" Lou snatched his jacket from the chair and frisked the pockets. He took her hand. "Would you like to go to the Hollow Coyote Buffet with Mom and me? She can't wait to meet you."

"I'd love to. Go find your mom, and I'll join you in a minute." Suddenly, the realization hit her full force. She was about to meet his mother with a tear-tracked face and puffy just-been–kissed lips. A wave of adrenaline pushed her like wind in a sail as she crossed the still-empty lobby to the ladies' room.

Glad to be alone in the quiet bathroom, Millie hurried to the middle sink and gasped when she looked into the mirror. All the tears she'd been holding back had wreaked havoc on her face. "I looked like this and he still kissed me?" She dampened a paper towel and wiped at the mascara streaks. Note to self: buy waterproof mascara next time.

A flush came from the third stall from the right. Oh, great. Someone was in there! Millie's cheeks grew warm as a woman in a navy-blue outfit walked to the sink beside her. The wrinkles in the corners of her blue-gray eyes were hardly noticeable, so it was difficult to guess her age.

"Hello, dear." The older lady spoke kindly as she washed her hands.

"Hi." Millie continued to wipe at the black lines, determined to keep Lou's mother from seeing her this way. First impressions went a long way.

The bathroom door squeaked open and three teens came in. The tallest one looked over her shoulder on her way to the stall and gave Millie a weak smile.

The woman at the sink searched through her purse and pulled out a small tube. "I think this moisturizer might help your situation. Let me put a smidgen on your finger and you can rub it in. Oh, and here's a tissue. It'll be gentler for your face."

"Thanks so much. You saved the day." Millie dabbed the cream around her eyes and carefully wiped away all traces of the makeup. Then, reaching for her compact, she brushed on a generous amount of powder and smiled at the results.

"Now your face is glowing. Looks like you're in good spirits, today."

"I am. My sweetheart and I finally made up following a long misunderstanding." After Millie ran a comb through her hair, she pulled lipstick from her purse. "I'm so in love with him."

"I see. Sounds like wedding bells are in your future." She pointed in the mirror. "That's a pretty lip color. It goes well with your peaches and cream complexion."

"Thanks. They call it Pink-Pucker Phrost." Millie blotted her lips on the tissue. "I'd better go. He's waiting on me."

"I'll walk out with you."

"Okay. I don't remember seeing you before." Millie held the door open for her new friend and followed her into the vestibule. "Is this your first Sunday here?"

"It is. Pastor Bailey is wonderful. He's good at weaving humor into his sermon." Her giggle was infectious. "I like that in a man."

Lou joined them by the water cooler. "I'm glad to see my two favorite women have already met."

Mortified that she had let her guard down, heat percolated through Millie's veins. How could she have been so transparent? "Wait. Are you Lou's momma?"

The wide-eyed woman next to her smiled proudly. "Yes, and you must be Sweet Cheeks." Deep dimples joined her charming giggle.

"Aww, Momma." Lou's face colored as he glanced around. "That's my personal pet name for her. I don't want anyone else to know."

"Don't worry about it, no one heard me." She patted his arm then turned and gave Millie a motherly hug. "I'm so glad to finally meet you. I know we're going to have a great relationship."

The warm greeting made Millie's heart bubble with joy.

"We need to get to the restaurant, ladies." Lou tapped his watch.

His mother poked his stomach. "Meanwhile, did you ask Miss Cheeks to have Sunday dinner with us?"

"Millie," he emphasized the name, "is joining us. But only if you behave yourself."

"That's wonderful." She gave Millie another hug. "Let's all go in my car and you and Lou can come back for yours later."

Lou ran ahead while they walked to the parking lot arm-in-arm.

Blinking back happy tears, Millie caught herself gazing at the remarkable lady. So this is how normal mothers were supposed to be. Her warm embrace was genuine and natural. They'd barely met and already Gabby's hugged her a hundred percent more than her own mother ever did.

Sunday dinner at the Hollow Coyote Buffet with Lou and his mother lasted almost two hours, but to Millie, it seemed to go by in a flash. It was as if she'd known Gabby her whole life.

While waiting outside for Lou to bring the car around, Gabby held on to Millie's arm. "Let's plan to get together soon." Her dimples emerged and gave her an endearing quality.

Lou pulled up in the car. He jumped out, helped his mom into the backseat, and shut the door. With a playful grin, he spun on his heel and opened the front passenger door. "You're next, Sweet Cheeks."

Millie playfully punched his shoulder and settled into her seat. She buckled the seatbelt and waited for Lou to get behind the wheel. "I hate for this afternoon to end. It's been wonderful."

"I agree." Gabby leaned forward. "Does your mother like coffee? Lou's always talking about Java Joe's. Maybe she could join us there this week."

In an instant, Millie's eyes pleaded with Lou's. Mother could, and probably would, crush Gabby with one quick glare.

"That might not be possible this week, Momma. Millie's schedule gets pretty hectic sometimes." He made a right-hand turn at the light. "We'll be home in a few minutes, so you might want to get your house key out."

Gabby held up her key ring and jiggled it. "Have it

right here. I'll be glad to get out of these tight shoes. Whatever possessed me to buy pointy toes?"

Lou drove to the front of his small bungalow. "Millie and I are going back to the church to get her car. I'll be home in a little bit."

"I'm going to need help finding my way around Apache Pointe. Maybe you can direct me to a good shoe store, Millie. Give me a call when you have free time." She got out of the car, closed the door, and tapped on the window.

Millie smiled and rolled her window down.

"Why don't we take your mother along with us when we go shoe shopping? Then the three of us can go out to eat too."

"That might work." Millie's stomach knotted. After last night, she didn't even want to speak to her mother let alone go out to eat with her. "Thanks, Gabby, goodbye."

Gabby stuck her head in the window. "You two have some catching up to do, so take your time, Son. 'Bye." She went to the front door, turned, and waved before going inside.

"Your mom is so fun and bubbly. Has she always been like that?"

"As long as I've known her." Lou pulled away from the curb and headed for Apache Pointe Community Church. "You don't have to worry about our mothers meeting any time soon. Remember, Mom is a trained psychologist. She has a way of drawing people in."

Millie adjusted her seatbelt. Trained psychologist or not, the last thing she wanted was for Gabby to witness one of her mother's rants. "You must have had a wonderful family life. Was your dad like that too?"

"His personality was a lot like your dad's. He was a man of integrity and taught his boys to be the same." He fixed his eyes on her. "I respected him."

"You're very fortunate to be blessed with two great

parents."

"I know. The guys in my quartet have told me that many times." Lou cleared his throat. "Speaking of the quartet, the Warble-Heirs will be singing at the Armadillo Gorge Gospel Convention at the end of the month. Would you like to go with me?"

"I'd love to."

"It's a two-hour drive from Apache Pointe. Will that upset your mother?"

"Who cares? I've made plans to leave home so she'll never find out about it." Millie glanced out the window and turned back to him. "I need to tell you what happened between Mother and me before you hear it from someone else."

Lou pulled into the church parking lot and turned off the ignition. "Sounds serious. What did she do this time?"

"I found out last night that Mother has been paying Kent to date me." The air around Millie grew heavy and warm. She closed her eyes to ward off tears. "Carol is letting me stay with her for now. I don't know if I'll ever go home."

Lou reached over to gently massage the back of her neck. "I'm sorry, honey. She's made your life unbearable. Let's pray Mom can help her. What else can I do for you?"

She tilted her head to one side and studied his straightforward expression. "Just be here for me. I need you now more than ever."

"I'll never leave your side again." He wiped tears from her face, lifted her chin, and drew her close.

A harsh ring came from her purse. Why hadn't she turned the thing off? Millie retrieved the phone. "I'd better take this, it's Dad. He's probably calling to see if I'm okay." She cleared her throat. "Hello?"

"Hey, Princess, sorry to interrupt you, but I'm in the emergency room at Apache Pointe Hospital with your mother."

"What's wrong?" Millie clenched her teeth. Did Mother see her in the balcony with Lou? This could be another tactic to break them up again. "Things like this happen all the time, Dad. Is she faking an illness again?" The accusation slipped out a little harsher than she intended.

"I know what you mean, but this time she really is sick." His voice sounded troubled.

"What's going on?"

"Your mother didn't feel like cooking today, so we went out to eat after church. About an hour later, she lost what little she did eat. She threw up blood."

Millie clutched Lou's hand and noticed he was leaning in to listen. "Wait a minute, Dad. Lou's here. I'm going to put you on speaker so we can both hear. She threw up blood? That sounds serious."

"Hi, Lou." He cleared his throat. "My first thought was that Penny had the flu or maybe food poisoning, so I brought her here to the emergency room right away."

"How did you convince her to go?"

"She was feeling too bad to fight me." He chuckled. "Anyway, her numbers are all off, so they put her on an IV."

Millie's gaze drifted out the windshield. She pulled down the visor to shade her eyes from the sun's glare. "Have they given a diagnosis, yet?"

"The doctor thinks it might be a gastrointestinal bleed or something like that. Tomorrow they'll give her an endoscopy and run a few more tests."

Lou lowered his window. The cool breeze sent relief to her hot cheeks.

Millie straightened in the seat and pushed the hair from her eyes. "Have they said how long they're going to keep her?"

"We're probably looking at a few days. It'll depend on

the test results." Her dad released a lengthy sigh. "That's all I know for now. I'll keep you updated."

She glanced at Lou. "I'll be there right away, Dad. Is there anything you want me to bring for either of you?"

"Wait, Princess. They gave her something to sleep. Why don't you come tomorrow when she has the tests? I'm sure she'll be fine."

"Don't you want somebody up there with you?"

"I'm going home after I check on her one more time. Meanwhile, Pastor Frank is keeping me company here in the cafeteria."

"I guess I'll see you at home, then. Call me if there are any changes. 'Bye, Dad."

In spite of their dismal connection, Millie was shocked to learn she honestly cared about her mother's future.

CHAPTER SEVENTEEN

Two weeks later - Late October

MILLIE STOOD GUARD AT HER OFFICE window watching for Lou. Since she'd moved back home to care for Mother, escaping the irritable woman's wrath was a minute-by-minute mission. Millie and Lou had to meet at the church to spare him the harsh words and arguments that were bound to occur.

She couldn't hold back a smile as he rounded the corner in the clunky red van, which he'd aptly named Ruby. The unreliable engine might belch oil and gas fumes, but at least its driver could be trusted.

Millie stepped out of the church office as Lou jumped from the van. She was thankful he now understood the relentlessness of her mother's biting temper.

He took her hand in his and led her to the chugging Ruby. "You sure look pretty today, Sweet Cheeks." He winked and yanked on the passenger door.

She shot him a brilliant smile. "Thank you." With his help, she climbed into the front seat and buckled up.

Once he settled behind the steering wheel, he tested the engine with a mighty rev before slipping it into gear. He glanced her way. "How's your mother doing?"

"After two weeks, she absolutely refuses to go to her doctor. Last time Dad mentioned it, she threw her Prince Charles and Lady Di commemorative teapot at him. He ducked, but the royal teapot bit the dust. Her excuse is that she doesn't want to undergo any more disgusting tests." She shrugged. "I really can't blame her. Those tests are invasive, but I think she's more afraid that the results might show something serious."

"I can understand that too. It's human nature to think if we don't acknowledge something, it doesn't exist." He turned the corner. "How's your dad getting along with her?"

"Mother constantly bites his head off, poor guy." Millie shook her head. "She isolates herself to read her books, drink coffee, and eat chocolate. Unfortunately, the coffee and chocolate make her sick."

"What does she do when your dad is at work?"

"She can be up and around. They don't want her to lift anything heavier than a coffee cup or climb stairs until they know what's going on."

Lou scratched his chin with his thumb. "And without tests that means the doctors aren't going to find out what's wrong."

"You got it." She leaned against the headrest and desperately searched for another conversation ball to lob back. For miles, they rode in silence, her tongue Velcroed to the roof of her mouth. Inspiration hit. "I'd like to invite you and your mother to Thanksgiving dinner next month."

"As tempting as that might be . . ." Lou cleared his throat.

Millie couldn't help herself as she burst out laughing. "I promise it'll be better than my birthday cookout even if we have to sedate Mother."

Ruby veered slightly to the right as he released an uninhibited chuckle. "We'd love to have Thanksgiving dinner with you; however, Mom and I are going to spend the weekend at my brother, Bart's, house."

She stared at her hands. "I'm sorry you can't come, but maybe it's for the best. I'd hate for your mother to see how mine acts, especially now when she's not feeling well."

"I've told you before, that wouldn't bother her. She's experienced with people like your mother and won't hold her actions against you." Lou reached over and held her hand. "Mom absolutely adores you. She said you're not only pretty, but you have an inner elegance that goes beyond beauty."

"She said that about me?" Millie's pulse kicked into overdrive at the acceptance. Her own mother had never made her feel so loved.

Lou took her hand. "Yes, and I happen to agree with her." He stopped at a red light and cracked his knuckles, one at a time. "A little music might be nice. Why don't you put one of those CDs in?"

Millie reached for the plastic case on the console between their seats. The picture on it was of Lou's group, the Warble-Heirs. She slipped the CD into the player. "How did you get interested in singing?"

"Mom has a second doctorate in theater arts. She was our church soloist and choir director for years and taught all four of her sons to harmonize at an early age."

Great! Gabby had a double doctorate. She put her hand to her mouth. At least her mother was literate, thanks to romance novels. "Are you sure our average family is going to measure up to yours?"

"Wait until you meet my big brothers, Sweet Cheeks." Lou stopped at another red light. "You won't have to ask."

Millie envisioned little Lou and his brothers singing songs together in their short pants, suspenders, and little beanies, while a metronome relentlessly ticked on the piano.

His gentle nudge brought Millie out of her musical reverie. "We're here." He climbed from the van and hurried to open her door. "I hope you don't mind helping me take some of the lighter things in."

"Sure. I'd love to help." Millie could hear her mother

now. 'Do you think we sent you to Perdant Business College so you could be a lackey for some shabby band? Of course we didn't. Mark my word, he'll use you, abuse you, and lose you.' Millie clenched her teeth. *Get thee behind me, Mother.*

Lou opened the back of the van, moved a speaker aside, and pulled out a small box. "Here's one you can handle."

She took the box, happy to do anything for him—and to prove her mother's negative counsel wrong.

He grabbed a large case on rollers as the other quartet members, dressed in matching khakis and blue shirts, came to help. Following a quick introduction, they made their way into the convention center.

Millie was losing the battle to keep up with Lou's long strides as he pulled the squeaky-wheeled product case. The auditorium was a huge wide-opened space. Her heels clicked on the concrete floor and her breathing escalated. Good grief! She sounded like the obscene phone caller on *As the Willow Weeps.*

Around the perimeter, tables and folding chairs were waiting for the various groups. Adults swarmed like locusts on a mission as they carried their merchandise to the assigned areas. Millie stepped aside as unsupervised children, in their flashing sneakers, darted through the growing crowd.

Lou stopped at two empty tables, turned, and searched the area. When his eyes eventually locked with hers, he yelled, "Over here, honey! This is our booth."

He called her honey in public. An adrenaline rush sent her high-heeled feet into overdrive. Memo to self: wear flats to these things. Or roller skates.

Lou took the box from Millie's arms and opened his wheeled case. "Lonnie and Dooley will have the rest of our stuff here in a minute. I need to talk to someone in charge of the event. Wait here and I'll be right back." He held a chair for her.

Millie no sooner plopped into her seat before he loped across the expansive auditorium. She shrugged. At least there was time to quiet her wheeziness.

Marv, the shortest member of the group, joined Millie and handed her a dark blue tablecloth. "Would you mind helping me arrange the display? My wife was buying a Kum-ba-ya Chorale CD, and a chatty friend cornered her. This table needs a woman's touch." He wiggled his eyebrows. "Just like our boy, Lou."

She hid her smile behind the folded tablecloth. She liked this Marv person. Millie shook the covering open and let it fall in place on the table.

"Hello." The lilting female voice came from behind.

Millie turned and smiled at a woman with rich auburn hair. "Hi."

The woman wore a pencil skirt and sleeveless blouse, which accentuated the freckled skin of her upper arms. "You have to be Lou's girl. I'm Hope, Marv's wife." She pulled Millie into a tight hug, and then handed her a program. "You'll need this to keep up with the groups and learn your way around. Word of advice." She pointed to the schedule. "Right here, where the Rhettenmeyer Family sings? That's the best time for a bathroom break. You'll thank me later."

Millie gasped. Who would've guessed bubbly Hope for the judgmental type?

"Oh, dear." Hope giggled. "I didn't mean that the way it sounded. Their voices are fine, but they sing right before the scheduled break. If we don't go early, we'll stand in the bathroom line forever."

Relief settled over Millie. Hope wasn't like Mother after all. She glanced at the schedule. The Warble-Heirs were to perform early, right between Beulah and Her Glory-ettes and the Jovial Jubilees. Then Lou would be by her side during the rest of the concert. She didn't bother to read the rest of the line-up. Who cared?

The overhead lights dimmed. The spot in front of the microphone brightened. The lanky emcee introduced himself and shared a couple of old, recycled jokes to warm up the crowd.

Millie sighed. She couldn't wait until Lou finished singing and came to sit beside her. Would he be brave enough to put his arm around her in front of his friends?

Laughter erupted from the crowd, and Hope nudged her elbow. The one good joke and she missed it.

"Now, all you fathers will need to contain your daughters. We have a brand-new group of young men, all the way from Lizard Lick. Let's hear it for the Benton Brothers."

Whistles and cheers rose throughout the auditorium as the three red-faced teens came forward. The trio's close harmony and upbeat songs held Millie spellbound. This event was going to be more enjoyable than she'd thought, especially after Lou joined her. She smiled in anticipation and rested an arm on the back of her sweetheart's empty seat.

Two groups, and eight songs later, Beulah and Her Glory-ettes took the stage. Millie's attention had long since waned. *Come on, Beulah. Sing a little faster.* At least, Lou's group was next in line.

The applause was mediocre, but intensified when the Warble-Heirs climbed the steps leading to the stage. Millie's heartbeat went into a quickstep. That was her man up there, and he was looking her way. She fought the urge to stand and wave.

Marv blew into the microphone. "Testing . . . one . . . two . . . buckle my shoe."

The onlookers chuckled at Marv's attempt to be funny.

"Good evening, we're the Warble-Heirs. On my far right is our first tenor and my brother, Dooley Overton. On my left is our baritone, Lonnie Chandler, and on the end is Lou Blythe, our bass. My name is Marvelous Marv Overton, and I'm the lead singer."

Marv stepped back and poked Lou in the ribs. "I'd also like to introduce Lou's very special lady friend, Millie Drake. He's done nothing but talk about her for months, and we're so happy he finally asked her to come." A cheesy grin sliced across his face "Have any words for your sweetie, Romeo?" He held the microphone out to Lou.

The echo of cracking knuckles filled the auditorium.

Offstage, the Benton Brothers started to chant. "Lou-Lou-Lou . . ." and soon male voices throughout the room joined in solidarity.

Lou grabbed the mic out of Marv's hand. "Must you share everything, buddy?" He looked down at Millie. "I hope she'll still want to go out with me after this."

Blood pounded in Millie's face as she nodded her reply. She was embarrassed to the core, and yet, reveled in his attention.

Dooley's pitch pipe was barely audible. The quartet began their medley with *Wonderful Grace of Jesus*. The four voices blended in perfect harmony. Millie smiled at Hope sitting next to her. "They're fantastic."

After the Warble-Heirs finished their set, Millie eagerly watched Lou make his way to her at the display table. Curious eyes stared as he sat and took her hand.

Millie forced her attention to the Jovial Jubilees now on stage. She laughed at the curly-headed spokesman's comical introduction of the others. Lively music filled the auditorium, and the audience stood and clapped.

Lou handed her a small white dishtowel. "You're going to need this."

She stared at the towel and then at Lou. "Wha—?"

Millie's question was quickly answered as the crowd joined in the chorus of *I Was Under the Spout When the Glory Came Out.* White hankies flapped and swirled over a sea of equally white heads. Lou's hand grabbed her wrist and encouraged her to wave the towel.

When the frenzy died down and people returned to their seats, the shorter man took front stage. "Are y'all havin' fun?" He grinned, presenting a wide gap between his two front teeth. His brief testimony ended with a desire to walk the streets of gold. He opened an enormous suitcase and held up a small yellow packet. "These golden cakes are a reminder of heaven's pavement." Hands shot up all around as he tossed dozens of Twinkle Cakes into the cheering crowd.

Millie shrieked as Lou lunged in front of her to grab a Twinkle Cake on the fly. She giggled as he bowed low and presented it to her. The man was chivalrous to a fault.

The Rhettenmeyer Family began their first song. Millie remembered that Hope said this was the best time for a break. Better scurry to avoid the rush.

Right as she started to reach for her purse, Lou's arm went around her shoulders.

Who needed a break?

He swayed her in time with the music and whispered in her ear. "I hope you're having a good time."

Millie smiled and laid her head on his shoulder. His arm tightened around her, and she settled back to enjoy the remainder of the concert.

Millie glanced at the clock on the dash. Eleven fifty-three and they were still about a half hour from home. What kind of ruse could she possibly come up with to extend their evening? Her brain flat-lined.

"I hope Marv didn't embarrass you too much. I didn't expect him to broadcast my feelings for you."

"It's fine. Don't worry about it. I'm glad you told me first." She shivered and rolled the van window up. "I've had such a wonderful day, Lou. Too bad it has to end."

"Having you in the audience was special for me. I wish you could be there for every concert."

"Me too." Millie lifted her eyes to the midnight sky out the window. She watched the countless stars twinkle. A fictional world began to overtake her.

She could see it now, the trajectory of their lives making a big U-turn as they traveled the world with the other husband and wife team, Bill and Gloria Gaither. Dining and joking with all the well-known gospel singers and groups would be commonplace. Maybe they'd even get a private audience with England's queen.

Carol would help her learn to curtsy properly. They'd have to Google royal curtsy etiquette 101.

Outside Buckingham Palace, the lights dim while lasers and fog machines enhance the ambiance. Rigid guards with tall bearskin hats open the doors to the balcony. Cheers rise from the throngs of onlookers as Queen Elizabeth, the living symbol of unity between crown and people, straightens her heavy, oversized tiara and speaks into the jewel-encrusted mic. "My royal subjects, I give you, Lonnie, Dooley, Marvelous Marv, and of course, Lou, the Wonder Bass. Put your hands together for the world renowned, Warble-Heirs."

"Millie." Lou's voice broke into her regal daydream.

She turned her head and blinked moisture from her eyes. Fantasy time was over, and reality, in the shape of Mother, was waiting at home.

Lou made a right-hand turn into the church parking lot and pulled next to Millie's car. "Here we are, safe and sound."

Moonlight streamed through the van's windshield as she unbuckled her seatbelt. She had to leave, but her arms ached to hold him close. "Thanks again for a great time. It'll be a day I'll always remember."

"I'm not likely to forget it, either." Lou tenderly caressed her cheek.

Her skin tingled where he touched her.

"I want to kiss you, but this console is in the way."

"Hold that thought while I go to my office for a minute. Wait for me?" She pulled the door handle, but it didn't budge.

"Let me help you with that sticking door." Lou jumped from the van. In a split second, he opened her door and offered his hand.

She stood on tiptoe and kissed his cheek. "I'll be right back."

He walked her to the building, cracking his knuckles all the way. "I'll wait here, sweetie." He shifted from foot to foot.

Millie stepped into her office and rested her back against the wall. If her heart rate didn't drop soon, she'd have to call 9-1-1. Someone pounding on her chest and yelling "clear" was not the romantic ending she envisioned for this beautiful day.

She peeked out the window and saw Lou pacing only inches away. He stopped, checked his breath, administered breath spray, and resumed pacing. Was he preparing for an award-winning goodnight kiss?

Her heartbeat hit another crescendo as she wobbled to the chair and laid her head on the desk. She'd better get ready too, in case he didn't get cold feet. Within the confines of the desk drawer and beneath the purple post-em notes, lay the answer to a maiden's prayer—Sassy Lassie Breath Zappers. She popped a handful and reached for her tube of Lippity-Dew.

When she stepped outside, Lou was there to pull her close to him. Then, shutting his eyes he pressed her hand to his lips.

Millie swallowed. Was that it? She wasted half a bag of Sassy Lassies for one pathetic hand smooch? Just when she'd nearly accepted romantic defeat, Lou's lips paraded up her arm and conquered her neck. She desperately tried to curb the electrical current rushing through her. A 9-1-1 call might still be in her future. But what a way to go!

Lou cupped her head. His lips were warm and sweet on hers, and the kiss was as gentle as a summer breeze. Was this really happening? Don't fail me now, Sassy Lassies.

He ever so gently released her. "It's getting late. Your mother will be worried. Sit with me in the balcony tomorrow?"

Millie blushed, smiled, and nodded to the wonderful man who brought love and respect into their relationship.

"Good-night, Millie. I'll follow you home."

You can eat your heart out, Tawny Lamour. She grinned. Louis Elliot Blythe was now off the market.

CHAPTER EIGHTEEN

DEAR DIARY,

LAST WEEKEND WAS SO busy I didn't have time to share with you. Lou took me to a gospel convention in Armadillo Gorge. I may be prejudiced, but The Warble-heirs were hands down the best group there. Marv Overton introduced me and told everyone that Lou talks about me all the time. I was embarrassed and thrilled at the same time.

Marv's wife, Hope, is very sweet. She accepted me as one of them right away. But the best part of the day was the drive home. Lou's display of emotion weakened my knees. I felt like a heroine in a romance novel. When he wrapped me in his sinewy arms, I returned his kiss with a desire that belied my outward calm. Lou is back in my life and I will never let him go again.

Millie kissed a bright red heart sticker. As she placed it at the end of her latest diary entry, her bedroom door flung open with a bang. She jumped and quickly grabbed her private journal and shoved it under the pillow sham. "Mother. I'm getting ready for work. Do you need help with something?"

"I'm overwrought to the bone, Millicent." Penny barged into the room and shook her list in the air. "Do you realize Thanksgiving's coming and not a single soul will be here to help me? I'm not a well woman."

"We know you're not well. Why not have the tests done so the doctors will know what medications to prescribe to make you feel better?"

"Mark my word, Millicent, I do not intend to let the medical hacks put me through all that nonsense again. They couldn't find anything the last time. They probably think it's all in my head." She propped herself against the door and huffed. "The nurse told me they'd use all sorts of tubes, probes, and whatnot for those tests. And if you think I'm going to allow anyone to probe my core, you have another think coming."

How could she get Mother out of the room before she saw the diary? Millie slipped her shoes on, took the angry woman's elbow, and led her to the stairs. "I have to go to work. Why don't we go to the kitchen and talk so I can eat breakfast?"

"All you're doing is ignoring my Thanksgiving problems." Her mother stopped mid-stairs. "And does it matter one iota to you? Of course it doesn't."

"Why worry about Thanksgiving now? It's still three weeks away." Millie shook her head and urged her mother to continue down the steps. "It isn't a big deal."

"Au contraire, Millicent Marie. You all expect me to plan, order food, and do the shopping." She crossed her arms. "I shouldn't have to prepare a major feast for nine people and clean the whole house by myself as well."

"You're right. That's why Dad and I have helped you every single year. I know, let's ask Carol to do something this time. She'd be happy to. Since you don't want her here, maybe she can do some of the cooking at her house."

"Carol? Cooking? We're not having spaghetti for Thanksgiving dinner."

"I'm not talking anything big like the turkey, but she can whip up something simple, or buy a package of dinner rolls."

Penny stopped on the bottom step, brandishing her pen. "And that mother of hers wasn't much help before her accident, but now, she's totally useless with that big walker. And you waste too much time with that Lou person and your on-again-off-again romance. How will you bake your mincemeat pies or whip the potatoes?"

"I've done it the same way every year, Mother. I'll make the mincemeat pies and set the table the day before. That gives me plenty of time to help you in the kitchen. Dad and I will make time to be here for whatever you need."

Penny waved her off. "Which brings us to how much turkey should I buy? We've always had just five of us, and I got a twelve-pounder. Now, Carol and Andy have nosed their way in, and Pastor Frank will want to be with Carol."

"And why shouldn't he? They're engaged and so much in love." Millie followed her into the kitchen. "He's going to be a part of our family and has every right to be here."

Penny curled her lip. "You stood by and watched Carol rip him from your arms. Didn't I tell you she would? Of course I did. Now we're stuck with that missing link of yours who expects to join us too. If he's still sniffing around by then."

When was this lunacy going to end? Millie clenched her teeth. The day had started out so well. "Slow down, Mother." She put an arm around the older woman's shoulder and guided her into a chair. "You don't have to worry about Lou. He and Gabby are going to his brother's house in New Mexico."

"Well, thank goodness for that." She pointed her finger at Millie. "You do realize it's not too late to steal Pastor Frank back. Carol's been married before and every decent man desires an unblemished maiden."

Millie put her hands to her ears. "Stop it, Mother. Those romance novels have warped your mind." She turned away. "I'm with the man I love."

"Oh, Millicent, please come to your senses." She pressed her fingers to her temples. "He looks like a caveman."

With her neck and shoulders growing tighter, Millie frowned as much as she dared. "Let's not start that again."

Penny smoothed a wrinkle from the rosy damask tablecloth. "My dining room table only seats six, and we'll have eight people."

"We'll have plenty of room at the table if we scrunch together." Millie smiled behind her mother's back.

"Millicent Marie! Is it your lifelong goal to upset me? I'll not have us sitting elbow-to-elbow. Now where was I?" Penny ran her finger down the list. "Oh, yes. We'll have to set up the card table over in the corner for Andy."

"If I sit with him that will leave six at the table. Problem solved."

"Do not be flippant with me. You're my daughter, and you shall be seated on my right as always." Penny plopped on a dining room chair. "We'll put Sylvia and her big clunky walker with Andy. That will be perfect. She'll be much more comfortable there anyway."

"You've thought of everything. How considerate." Millie wondered if her mother noticed the sarcasm in her reply.

"Let's see, one of them can use that old melamine Benny Bunny plate. Oh, dear. That still leaves us one plate short. Totally unacceptable." She threw her list to the floor. "What am I going to do?"

"Things will work out. Who cares if we have an orphan plate?"

"May I remind you, I set a proper table?" She sniffed. "And this might be my last Thanksgiving to shine. I might be too weak to do any of this next year."

Millie let her rolling eyes speak for her.

Penny picked up her to-do list and headed for the kitchen. "I know. I have an extra meat platter in the same china pattern. Andy could use that." She clucked her tongue with disapproval. "The boy eats like a Clydesdale, anyway."

Millie sighed until her lungs felt depleted. Months of counseling for her mother had been a total waste of time and money. "I have to go to work."

"Of course you do." Penny crossed her arms. "Thanks for nothing."

CHAPTER NINETEEN

Thanksgiving Day

IN THE PRIVACY OF HER ROOM, Millie turned on the light and opened her secret diary. Maybe she could write out her thoughts of the day before Mother called her again.

> Dear Diary,
> Today was the worst Thanksgiving our family has ever experienced. I can't stop crying. If only Lou were here to hold me in his arms and say everything will be okay, but he and his mother are at his brother's house in New Mexico. He won't be back until Sunday night. Carol and I always share our problems, but it isn't the same as talking to Lou. I'd call him, but he only sees his family once a year and I don't want him to see me as a clinging vine.
> Sweet Aunt Sylvia collapsed at our dinner table. An ambulance came and rushed her to the hospital. I wanted to go support Carol, but Mother had been sick all day and needed me to stay with her. Actually, it was more like demanded. I'm waiting for Dad to call with an update.
> Meanwhile, Mother is being her usual obnoxious self. According to her, poor Aunt Syl is looking for attention. She said, "I'm a sick woman too, but does anyone care about me?

No, it's all about Sylvia."

The woman is devoid of compassion for anyone else; however, when it comes to her own health, she expects all of us to ooze with concern and sympathy. We're here to serve her every need while she lies around in bed and reads her sleazy books.

I really am sorry that Mother isn't feeling well, but it's difficult to take care of a prickly pear. Many weeks of sleepless nights added to mental and physical exhaustion is overwhelming.

Enough soul baring for one night. Millie shivered, closed her diary, and bowed her head. "Lord, please help me to love Mother, as I should. Open her mind and heart to You. Bring someone into our lives who can break through her chains of mental illness. Dad looks haggard lately. I can't imagine what he's going through. I'm concerned about his well-being. In Your name, I pray. Amen."

A shrill voice broke her concentration. "Millicent, I need you."

"Coming, Mother." She walked into the bedroom. "What do you need?"

"My feet feel like ice cubes. Would you put a pair of your father's socks on me and bring the electric blanket?"

Millie retrieved the blanket, pulled a pair of athletic socks from her dad's drawer, and sat on the end of the bed. "I hope this is warm enough. Want me to brew a cup of tea for you?"

"That would be nice. Oh, and maybe a cold turkey sandwich with tomato, lettuce, and a scant touch of mayo."

Millie nodded and turned to leave. A cold turkey club

did sound good. She'd have to make one for herself.

"And Millicent, would you mind bringing my December issue of *Soap Operas Today*?"

"Anything else?"

"That's all for now."

"I'll be back in a jiffy." Millie hurried down the stairs before Mother could think of anything else for her to do. Once the teakettle was heating on the stove, she dropped teabags in two cups and began making sandwiches.

When her hip pocket vibrated, Millie set the mayo-smeared knife down and pulled out her cell phone. "Hi, Dad. How's Aunt Syl?"

"The doctor said she suffered a moderate stroke. She's pretty weak, yet. They're hoping to move her out of ICU tomorrow."

"How are Uncle Max and Carol holding up?"

"As well as can be expected." Her dad cleared his throat. "Andy fell asleep on the couch and I'm heading down to the vending machines to pick up snacks. You should see the coffee bar. I've tried three different flavors so far."

"Go easy on the caffeine or you won't sleep tonight. Keep me updated on Aunt Syl's progress, Dad."

"So, how's your mother?"

Millie rubbed her temple. "She's had me running up and down the stairs a few times. I'm making sandwiches and tea for her now. Other than being cold, she seems to be okay."

"What's taking so long, Millicent?"

He laughed. "I hear that angelic voice now."

"In a minute, Mother." She softened her voice and talked into the phone. "I need to go. Your angel is still harping. Talk to you later." She prepared her mother's tea, positioned everything on a serving tray, and headed for the stairway.

"I'm still waiting on my magazine."

Millie's shoulders slumped as she came to a dead stop halfway up. Careful not to spill the tea, she maneuvered back down the steps to find the precious reading material. If only they lived in a one-story home.

"Are you coming?"

"I'm on my way." Millie grumbled and trudged up the stairs. Five minutes, just five lousy minutes of silence was all she needed. With an anemic smile pasted on her face, she hurried into the room and sat the tray on the nightstand.

"What is this? I can't eat two sandwiches. What were you thinking?"

Her mother's whiny voice grated on Millie's one remaining nerve. "I was thinking I'm hungry too." She picked up her plate and walked to the door. "I'll be in my room."

"Wait." Penny nibbled on her sandwich and set it down. "I don't think I want this after all."

Millie was tempted to ram it down her throat. "I'll take your plate down a little later. You might get your appetite back in a few minutes."

"One more thing, Millicent. I want you to call your father on the cell phone." She stuck out her lower lip. "My upset tummy needs a Kotton Kandy Karamel shake from the Kravin' Kream."

"I'll be sure to let him know." Millie closed the door of her bedroom, blocking the demanding clamor of her mother.

Back in her room, Millie took a large bite of her turkey sandwich. Mayonnaise mixed with the juice of the tomato and dribbled down her chin. She didn't care.

Her phone vibrated, and Lou's picture popped up on the screen. "Hi, Lou."

"Happy thanksgiving, honey. I miss you."

"I miss you too and wish you were here." She wiped the drippings from her chin. "How is the visit with your family going?"

"We're having the best time. I've told everyone all about us, and they can't wait to meet you."

"I look forward to meeting them too." Millie took a drink of hot tea. Speaking with Lou brought calmness to her frazzled nerves. Her shoulders relaxed. She wanted so much to be in New Mexico with him.

There was a pause before Lou spoke up. "How did your family gathering turn out?"

Her chest tightened at the thought. "Truthfully? Filled with drama as usual. The worst part is Aunt Sylvia had a stroke at the beginning of the meal. She was rushed to the hospital."

"Oh, bless her heart. How is she, now?"

"Dad said she's resting comfortably. Mother is another story. I drew the short straw and had to stay here with her since she's sickly. After everything she's done, I resent having to care for her."

Millie heard Gabby in the background asking what was going on. Lou related her story, then spoke into the phone "Sweetie, my mom wants to tell you something."

"Hi, Millie darling. I'm sorry you have such an awful time with your mother. Lou tells me today has been especially difficult."

"I get frustrated because Mother refuses to have those tests done. Then she complains because her pain is getting worse. Bottom line, she's a terrible patient, Gabby."

"Some people are more difficult than others, honey."

"The worst of it is we're used to her complaining and drama. Since she won't have the tests done, we don't know if it's real pain or if she's faking it. Meanwhile, I'm constantly at her beck and call."

"I ran across a verse while we were on the plane and thought of you and this situation. It's Matthew 25:40. "I tell you the truth, whatever you did for one of the least of these brothers of mine, you did for me." Now here's the secret. Everything you're doing for your mother, think of it as doing it for the Lord."

"Thank you, Gabby." Millie took a deep breath as peace settled over her. "That shines a different light on it altogether. I'm sure it will help."

"If you ever need to talk, pick up the phone. Love you, honey. Lou wants to talk again. We'll be home on Sunday."

"I love you, Sweet Cheeks. Wish I could be there to hold you. See you soon."

She smiled. "Thanks for calling, sweetheart. Talking to you and your mom gives me more comfort and confidence than you'll ever know. I love you too."

Millie hung up and imagined his kind, warm eyes. She ached to be in his arms. After years of Mother treating her like something scraped off the bottom of her shoe, God rewarded her, Millicent Marie Drake, with the love of a devoted man.

CHAPTER TWENTY

Early December

MILLIE SCURRIED FROM THE KITCHEN TO answer the front door. "Gabby." Millie hugged the short, vibrant woman. "Come in. What brings you to our humble home?"

"I heard your mother still hasn't gotten any better." Two deep dimples formed with Gabby's grin. "Thought it was time to come around to introduce myself and visit with her for a few minutes."

"That's so sweet of you." Millie wished she felt as positive as she sounded. "Mother's in the living room. Better wait here at the door and give me a minute to prepare her." She turned and offered a silent prayer. *Please Lord, Mother doesn't like Lou. Help her to be gracious just this once.* "Mother, Gabby Blythe is here to meet you."

"Who?" Penny frowned, lowered her romance novel, and propped herself on an elbow. "Who in the world is Gabby Brite, and what is she selling?"

"She's Lou's mom."

"Why would I want to meet his mother, pray tell? I thought she lived in Mexico or something."

"One of her sons lives in New Mexico. They were there for Thanksgiving."

"Oh, Millicent. You mean to tell me the woman has more than one spawn? Heaven help us." Penny pulled the pink and purple afghan to her chin. "Tell her I'm terribly ill and don't wish to meet anyone."

Millie returned to the foyer and placed a hand on Gabby's shoulder. "You probably heard that. I'm so sorry. This isn't a good time for a visit. Could you come back when Mother's in a better mood?" As if that would ever happen.

A crotchety voice came from the living room. "Is she still here, Millicent?"

"Yes, I'm still here." Gabby gave Millie a hug and whispered, "Don't worry." She squared her shoulders and ventured into the viper's den.

Millie crossed her eyes as her angst level reached immeasurable proportions. How would this play out?

Gabby took the initiative to speak first. "Nice to meet you, Penny. Your home is immaculate." She glanced around. "You've coordinated all the hues and textures perfectly."

"I've worked several years on mixing and matching to make each room flow."

"Your hard work certainly speaks for itself. You must have the patience of Job."

With a satisfied smile, Penny settled back into her velvety pillow. "You have a discerning eye, Gabby."

"Thank you." Gabby sat on an adjacent overstuffed chair. "Have you always lived in Apache Pointe?"

"I was born and raised in Phoenix and moved here after Stuart and I got married. He wanted to be near his family."

"I see you're a reader too. What book is that?" She glanced at the cover of Penny's paperback. "Oh, you like stories from the Regency Period. So do I. My favorite is *Pride and Prejudice*. Have you read it?"

"No, but I loved the movie."

"Would you believe I played Elizabeth Bennet in our college stage production?" With a theatrical air, Gabby laid her hand on her throat and gazed into the air. "In marrying your nephew, I should not consider myself as quitting that sphere. He is a gentleman; I am a gentleman's daughter; so far we are equal."

"Elizabeth was some gal." Penny snickered. "That's what I like, a strong woman who isn't afraid to speak her mind."

The sudden camaraderie between the two women shocked Millie. Had Gabby actually won Mother over? She pried her chin from the floor and peeked at her watch. In less than ten minutes? Who would've guessed it could happen that fast?

"Don't you simply adore the relationship between Elizabeth and Mr. Darcy? It's been called the quintessential romance novel." Gabby inched her chair a bit closer. "Would you like to borrow my copy?"

Penny's eyes bulged and a half-smile tugged at her lips. "Of course I would!" She turned to Millie. "My friend and I would like some chamomile tea."

With her head spinning and heart soaring, Millie nodded and retreated to the kitchen to put the kettle on. What had happened? Did Mother really call Gabby her friend? She grinned and lifted the antique teapot along with matching cups and saucers from the china cabinet. To her knowledge, Mother never had a friend before. God worked a miracle through Gabby. Millie couldn't wait to tell her dad and Lou what she'd witnessed. Her next diary entry would get a gold star, maybe two.

Christmas morning

Millie sat at the desk in her bedroom while she spoke to her cousin on the phone. "I can't believe it, Carol. Mother's changing right before my eyes."

"All of this because of Gabby Blythe? What kind of magic does that woman possess?"

"Gabby's double doctorates might have sweetened the pot a bit. At any rate, I'm sure it impressed her. Whatever her gift is, Dad and I are enjoying the unexpected fallout." Millie doodled a picture of Gabby complete with a halo. "Gabby's been doing her best to knock down that brick wall with positive input. It's working."

"That's amazing, Mills. Now you have to marry Lou to keep the Penny Whisperer in the family." Carol's laugh ended with a soft snort.

"Good one, Cuz. The Penny Whisperer. I'll have to remember to tell Dad." Millie made a quick note on her doodle paper. "She makes it look easy too. If I compliment Mother, she thinks I want something, but when Gabby praises her, she eats it up."

"Last week Uncle Stu told me your mom agreed to have Christmas dinner catered. Did I hear him correctly?"

"That's another miracle. Gabby suggested it, and Mother acted as if no one had ever mentioned it before. Dad went to pick up the food a half hour ago. He asked Mother to go along because she wanted to get out of the house."

"I'm in shock and can't wait to see my new and improved aunt."

"Since Lou and Gabby are coming, you'd better get here at twelve, on the dot, or the old Penny might come back to haunt us all. The table's set and ready for action."

"I guess I'd better kick start my son so we can get there promptly at noon." Carol paused. "See ya."

Millie reached for her real diary and opened it to the next blank page.

Dear Diary,

  I'm still in shock and awe that Mother and Gabby have a growing friendship. Where has this blessed angel been all my life? And to think, God used *Pride and Prejudice,* of all things, as the catalyst for this transformation.

Mother hasn't been perfect, but seeing her with a genuine smile during this Christmas season has been the best gift I could have ever received. She's even starting to accept Lou. A little. Dare I hope this change is permanent?

This is the first time in forty-five years Mother didn't feel like preparing a holiday meal. We're having it catered.

What other surprises does the New Year have in store?

The sound of guitar music caught her attention. She placed the diary in the desk drawer and listened. Where was it coming from? A deep bass voice lured her to the window.

"Wise men say . . . only fools rush in . . ."

"Lou?" Millie ran downstairs and opened the front door, relieved her mother wasn't there to ruin his performance. She wept as he sang the next verse.

"Take my hand . . . take my whole life too . . ."

Her knees threatened to give way, and she leaned against the doorframe for support.

A car pulled into the driveway next to Lou's van. Her stomach plummeted. Mother and Dad. Could they have picked a worse time? The passenger door opened, and an indomitable figure struggled to get out. Was Dad man enough to hold back the gale forces of Mother's wrath? Would Lou bolt?

Not missing a note, Lou's head veered slightly to the Drakes' car, his heavy brow furrowed.

Gabby jumped from the driver's side of the van, hurried to Penny's side, and pulled her into a hug.

Lou walked closer to Millie, his robust voice more determined as he repeated the chorus.

Her breathing quickened and chest pounded. She was pretty sure a cardio workout could never be this intense.

Lou finished his song and placed the guitar on the ground. He popped his knuckles, took her hand, and dropped to one knee. "Miss Millie Drake, I've been hopelessly in love with you for years. Will you do me the honor of becoming my wife?" He held up a velvet-covered box with a tiny red bow.

Penny screeched, hobbled across the lawn to the couple, and then bent over to kiss the top of Lou's head. "This is so romantic. Of course she will."

CHAPTER TWENTY-ONE

January

"MOTHER, PLEASE." MILLIE RUBBED HER POUNDING temples. "You're blowing this out of proportion. I don't need twelve bridesmaids or a seven-course dinner at the country club." She reached for the pink cozy-covered teapot, which matched everything else in the house, and turned to her future mother-in-law. "More tea, Gabby?"

"Thank you, dear." Gabby's trademark dimples appeared with her gentle smile. "It's generous to want your daughter to have an elaborate ceremony, but it takes more time to prepare. They're getting married in April. We only have three months, and the kids do have their hearts set on a small wedding anyway, Penny. Let's try to keep their wishes in mind."

"But ever since Millicent was born, I envisioned her wedding with all the glamour and glitz of Hollywood that my family could never afford." Penny took a deep breath and her hand swept the air as if to bring life into the fantasy. "She would be clad in billowing Irish lace and glide to the altar on the arm of her father, Cary Grant."

"Cary Grant?" Gabby chuckled. "Whatever happened to poor ol' Stuart?"

Penny ignored the question. "When I was a young girl, I always dreamed of having a big, expensive wedding."

"But I thought you and Dad eloped. What happened?"

"It was during the war, and Stuart was in the Army in Saigon." Mother smoothed the side of her burgundy-colored hair. "When Father found I'd been secretly writing to a soldier overseas, he went into a drunken rage. I barely escaped with my life. He called Stuart a pansy because back home he was a lowly florist. Father forbade us to marry."

Millie's eyes narrowed as she set her teacup down. Aha! Her mother's caustic genetic code finally unraveled. Hopefully future generations wouldn't be carriers of her warped DNA. "So, you went behind your father's back and married Dad anyway?"

"We went to the Justice of the Peace and had a one-night honeymoon in Iguana Bend. Our whole wedding was a huge disappointment. No pictures, no wedding cake, no family or friends. I carried one lone carnation that Stuart plucked from a funeral bouquet on his way out of the flower shop." She sniffed. "This, dear Millicent, is why I vowed you would have a gorgeous, drop dead ceremony."

"I'm sorry, Mother. I wish you could've had your fairytale wedding."

Gabby patted Penny's hand. "That's sad. Barton was in the air force during the war, so we were married on base in Texas before he went to the Philippines. Only our parents were able to attend."

"I'm sorry you both had quick weddings, but I still don't want all the pomp and circumstance with a dozen attendants."

Penny crossed her arms. "But I must insist you have more than one bridesmaid."

"Okay, so let's put our heads together and come up with a workable compromise." Gabby sipped her tea. "What friends or relatives would you like to have as additional bridesmaids, Millie?"

"I can't think of anyone to ask other than Carol."

"Here's an idea. Lou's brother, Spence, was going to be his only attendant, but he has two other brothers and three sisters-in-law that could step in."

Millie straightened in her seat. "That's a good solution, Gabby. Do you think they would do it?"

"I'm sure of it. I have a picture of the boys." She reached for her purse, pulled out a snapshot, and handed it to Millie. "Lou was about fifteen here."

"Oh, he's so cute. The Blythe boys sure resemble each other." Millie reluctantly handed the photo to her mother.

"They're all tall, dark, and handsome like their dad." Gabby pointed to her sons' images. "There's Bart, Jr., Spence, Nick, and of course, your Lou."

Millie glanced at her mother half-expecting a grimace to surface. With no scowl forthcoming, Millie released her pent-up breath and wrote the names of Lou's siblings on her list. "We're still shy one groomsman." She snapped her fingers. "Maybe Andy could be the fourth. It isn't a dozen attendants, Mother, but it's more than one. Would that work?"

"I suppose." Penny's tone was flat as she picked imaginary lint from her fuchsia robe.

"At least I won't have more people at the altar than in the pews." The words no sooner passed Millie's lips, then the familiar doomsday mask emerged on her mother's face. Millie clenched her teeth and waited for lightning bolts to usher in the first emotional monsoon of the new year. Now might be a good time for more tea. She hurried to the stove and returned with the teapot.

"Good, that was an easy fix." Gabby closed her notebook and tapped it with her pen. "We're moving along like a well-oiled machine, ladies."

Penny's pencil snapped in half. "Oh, look what I did. I'm such a klutz." A dark warning cloud settled deeper on her features, and her mouth contorted into a defiant stare. The atmosphere crackled.

"More tea?" Millie's hand shook and steaming liquid

sloshed from the spout. "Anyone?"

"Maybe half a cup, thank you." Gabby stood and pointed down the hall. "I need to visit the powder room. Excuse me."

Cold silence filled the kitchen until the bathroom door clicked shut.

Millie's composure faltered under Mother's lethal glare. Would she ever get the hang of this stand-up-to-Mother routine?

"I don't understand you, Millicent. Are you going to sit there and allow an outsider to dictate your wedding plans?"

"We compromised, Mother." Millie sat, poured Gabby's tea, and then filled her own cup. "Besides, she's the mother-of-the-groom, hardly an outsider."

Penny smacked the table. "She expects us to add all her sons and their wives to the bridal party." Her voice lowered. "Did you see the picture of those boys? It's going to look like we're hosting a knuckle dragger's convention. We might as well pitch a tent and sell tickets."

"Don't talk like that. They're Lou's brothers and have every right to be in our wedding." She pushed her chair away from the table and waited for a hostile reply.

"We'll be a laughing stock. I won't have it." Penny's face twisted. She moaned and held her stomach.

"Well . . ." A soft voice came from behind them. "It was only a suggestion. Maybe you can come up with a better solution."

Another hush settled around the table. How much had Gabby heard? Millie swallowed and watched her mother shrivel in her seat. She had to be upset about sharing control of the situation even if she did like Gabby.

"I'm sorry, this is my fault." The calmness in Millie's voice belied her humiliation. "Lou and I agreed on a simple wedding. I should've thought to include more of Lou's family in the first place. Your idea is perfect."

Penny straightened the ruffles on the front of her silky robe and mumbled, "Fine."

"Mother, think of it this way. Gabby's trying to make this a bigger wedding to please you." Millie held her breath for a terse reply, determined to stand her ground.

Penny's face blushed. "I guess you're right." She dabbed her eyes behind heavy, red-rimmed glasses. "Can we still have my candles and twinkle lights?"

"Does that work for you, dear?" Gabby winked at Millie.

Millie nodded and hid a victory grin in her teacup. "Candle and twinkle lights, it is." Mother had passed a test in the fine art of give and take.

"Excellent." Gabby adjusted her short-sleeved jacket and smiled. "I'll contact the wedding planner, and we're all set."

Even the wedding gown. Millie mentally clicked her heels, thrilled that she and Carol had managed to purchase the perfect gown without Mother's nagging participation . . . or knowledge.

"Now," Gabby turned in her chair. "Penny, you're looking a little jaundiced, and I'm worried that pain in your stomach might be pancreatitis. You don't want to mess around with it. Have you gone to see the doctor like you promised?"

Penny waved her off. "I will. I'll call for an appointment next week."

"That's not good enough." Gabby stared her down. "Either you call right now, or I'll do it for you."

How does Gabby get away with challenging Mother without being subject to her nuclear fallout? Millie held her breath and squirmed in her chair, prepared to skedaddle at a moment's notice.

"I want you to get better, Penny. I need to move out of

Lou's place, and you promised to help me find a suitable condominium." Gabby's eyes twinkled. "Our newlyweds don't need a mother breathing down their necks."

"Fine. Give me the phone."

Millie's heart soared. Her future mother-in-law was beyond perfect.

"We barely have enough room in this little kitchen." Millie nudged the dog with her foot as she pulled the dinette chairs out of the way. She turned to Lou. "Would you call Farfel and move the table to give your mom a little more space?"

Gabby helped him scoot it away from the window. "That should do it." After taking her seat, she retrieved her laptop from the black bag and placed it on the table. "Have you considered finding a bigger place for your new bride?" She laid a yellow legal pad next to her computer.

Millie nudged him. "We've been talking about it."

"Newlyweds don't need much space." Lou's eyes twinkled. "It's nice and cozy, besides, we have the basics."

With a laugh, Gabby shook her head. "You young people. Combining your lives will often try your patience. Trust me, you won't want to be breathing down each other's necks." She tapped her pencil on the computer. "While we're looking at condo listings for me, let's take a gander at a larger place for you."

Millie clapped her hands. "Could we, Lou?"

"Won't hurt to look, Sweet Cheeks." He kissed her forehead. "Let's get these laptops a-hummin'."

Farfel nosed his food bowl across the kitchen floor to his daddy. Lou ignored him until the basset whined pathetically. He finally got up from the table and filled the bowl with dry kibble. "This should keep you busy, Farf." He sat down and let the air ease from his lungs. "Okay, ladies, let's get down to business and see what we can find."

The doorbell rang.

"I'll keep looking while you answer the door." Millie grabbed his computer and Googled: Apache Pointe Homes and Condominiums.

His long legs sauntered through the living room and opened the front door.

"Lou!" A giggling blonde in a blue shirt and khaki-colored slacks jumped into his arms and kissed him on the mouth. "I've missed ya so much."

Icy needles stung Millie's skin. She positioned her chair for a better view of the girl hugging Lou. What was going on? She searched Gabby's eyes for a clue.

With a determined set of her chin, the silver-haired woman patted her hand and whispered. "Take a deep breath. It's gonna be okay."

Old fears and uncertainties reared their ugly heads, but at least Gabby was there to lend her moral support. Millie doggedly resolved not to whine and whimper like Farfel in front of her future mother-in-law.

"Gemma . . . so nice to see you again." He gently released her arms from around his neck. "What are you doing here in Apache Pointe?"

Who was this bubbly creature? Millie's shoulders grew rigid as she strained to hear the answer. It had better be good.

"I had some time off and I wanted to see ya, don't ya know."

The thick accent jumped all over Millie's last nerve. Worse yet, Miss Bubbles was all curves, shapely legs and big white teeth. Every blonde hair was in place. Even her rosy cheeks added to her allure.

Gabby cleared her throat. "Lou, invite your friend in so we can meet her."

"Where are my manners?" With his hand on the young woman's elbow, Lou led her toward the kitchen. "Come on in and meet my mother and fiancée."

Gemma hesitated and lowered her voice. "Your fiancée? Oh, Lou, ya didn't tell me ya got back together. I'm sorry, I shouldn't be here."

"Don't worry. They'll be happy to meet you." He looked heavenward, and took a deep breath. "Mom, this is Gemma Carr, the cruise director on the Caribbean Breeze. Gemma, this is my mother, Gabby Blythe."

While they shook hands, Lou stood behind Millie, his hands nervously massaging her shoulders. "And this lovely lady is my bride-to-be, Millie Drake."

The man was trying to cover up the seriousness of the situation. With lips twitching, Millie's eyes strayed to Gabby. Apparently, his back peddling didn't work with her either.

"I've heard a lot about you, Millie." Gemma giggled and presented her hand. "It's nice to put a face to the name."

Stay calm, Millicent Marie. She hoped disdain didn't leach into her voice. As if in slow motion, she reached for the extended hand. "Nice to meet you, Miss Carr." Interesting. Lou hadn't told her a thing about Miss Bubbles. She offered a light smile in spite of her uneasy stomach.

"My friends call me Gem." She glanced out the window. "So this is Apache Pointe."

"Must be a lot different from the lower mandible of Moose Jaw, Minnesota." Lou choked on a laugh. "Have you been home lately?"

Millie arched her eyebrow. He knew where she lived?

"Actually, I came here on my way there." Another giggle erupted.

"Wait a minute, Gem. You left Florida and came to Arizona on your way to Minnesota?" Lou chuckled and his eyes begged for Millie to understand.

She didn't. Millie was no navigator, but she knew Miss Bubbles was far off course. In more ways than one. They had to be more than nodding acquaintances for the woman to travel thousands of miles out of her way simply to see Lou.

Gabby stood. "Did you eat that airplane food?"

"They only served a snack." Gemma nodded. "I had cheese, crackers, a small box of raisins, and a ginger ale."

"That's hardly enough for a human to live on." A faint smile came to Gabby's lips. "How about a ham sandwich?"

What? Millie looked at Gabby as their bond of camaraderie seemed to crumble. The last thing they needed to do was feed this stray cat. They'd never get rid of her.

"Have a seat, Gemma." Lou grinned lopsidedly and held the chair for her. "I'll get you something to drink."

"Okay, then." She sat in the offered chair. "Would ya happen to have bottled water? By the way, Betsy Barnum sends her love. She and Nadine . . ."

Millie shifted positions. How many women were chasing him on that ship? She eyeballed Gemma nibbling on her sandwich. As visions of force-feeding Miss Bubbles began to dance in her head, a still small voice pricked her conscience. Millie closed her eyes. *I'm sorry, Lord. That wasn't a kind thought. Curb my jealously. Help me deal with this problem.*

A half-hour and at least a dozen stories later, Gemma finally took the last bite of her food and peeked at her watch. "I'd better get going. Okay then, I guess this is good-bye, Lou. Thanks for the food and hospitality. Good luck with the search for your homes." She looked at Millie. "It's been nice meetin' ya, and I hope ya have a wonderful life together."

Lou walked her to the door. "I'll be praying you find your Mr. Right. Good-bye, Gem. Nice seeing you again."

After giving him a quick hug, Gemma wiped her eyes, then turned and left.

He closed the door but continued to watch from the window.

"Lou." Gabby stood with her arms crossed. "I think she's old enough to walk to her car without your supervision."

He shuffled into the kitchen and took Millie's limp hand. "I didn't know she was coming for a visit. I'm sorry."

"That isn't the point. I opened up and told you everything about Kent. Then I asked if you had anything to share. You didn't even hint of her existence."

"In my defense, you were feeling so low and helpless; I didn't want to hurt you any further." He stepped back, an anxious frown fixed on his face. "I was sparing you additional pain. How was I to know she'd show up on my doorstep unannounced?"

"Let me get this straight. If you had known she was coming, you would have told me?" Her tone hardened. "Or would you have met her elsewhere to spare me more pain?"

He sank in a chair and planted his elbows solidly on the table. "I said I'm sorry." The pain in Lou's dark blue eyes deepened as his mouth tightened into a flat line. "Since we're laying all of our cards on the table, Gemma would've been a bigger temptation if she had known the Lord."

Gabby groaned. "Okay, kids. Play fair."

His hand rose, cutting her off. "I have two words for you, Millie. Kent Sheridan." He sat up straight obviously pleased with his comeback.

"Like I said before, I told you everything." Millie cast a

piercing glare his way. "Since you walked out on me and kept your relationship with Gemma a secret, maybe we're not ready to get married. You can't do things like that and expect me to trust you."

"She's right, Son." Gabby looked from one to the other. "That's a recipe for disaster. But it goes beyond that. Millie, you know I love you like a daughter, but you were wrong too. When Lou left, you should've gone after him and straightened things out right away. Maybe it's a good idea to put your marriage on hold until you've worked through these trust issues."

Millie clamped her mouth shut and waited for his reaction. She'd let him speak first.

He scowled out the window and cracked his knuckles, one-by-one.

"Perhaps your mother is right." Millie laid her engagement ring on the table and left.

CHAPTER TWENTY-TWO

Post Valentine's Day

THE INVITING SMELL OF FRESHLY GROUND coffee beans welcomed Millie into Java Joe's Coffee House. She stood at the counter and ordered a hot ham and cheese sandwich and her favorite Mint Chocchiato from the menu. She paid for her items and scanned the room for her cousin.

Carol sat at a corner table sipping her coffee and waved when she spotted Millie. "Over here, Mills."

She balanced her tray and zigzagged through the maze of tables while customers talked above the noise of the coffee grinder.

"Have you been waiting long?" Millie placed the tray on the table and removed her lunch. "I got away as soon as I could. Not to mention any names, but somebody's husband is a real taskmaster."

"Frank's kept you busy this morning, huh? And he knew we were having lunch together. I'll have to speak to him about that."

Millie laughed. "He also knew I wasn't coming back to the office this afternoon. I got all my work done, so we're both happy." She sniffed the air. "Smells like they just took cinnamon muffins out of the oven."

"I love their cinnamon muffins. We'll have to share one before we go." Carol picked up her sandwich. "Did your mom's tests go well?" She took a bite.

"The diagnosis was worse than we expected. She's

such a hypochondriac, we didn't take her complaints seriously." She unwrapped her sandwich. "Now we find out it's stomach cancer. They've decided to operate first because the doctor said sometimes the cancer has spread more than the tests indicate." She bit into her sandwich.

"Oh, no! Poor Aunt Penny. I'm sorry to hear that." Carol looked down at her hands. "Will they give her any other treatments?"

"Doctor Swanson will know more of what to do after surgery. He said they'd give her chemo and maybe radiation later." Millie held her warm cup and sipped the Chocchiato.

Carol grabbed Millie's hand. "Is there anything we can do for you or Uncle Stu?"

"Thanks. I'll let you know if something comes to mind. Please pray for us. That's what we need the most." She nibbled on her ham sandwich.

"Frank and I pray for all of you every day and so does Andy." Carol took the last bite of her lunch and wiped her mouth.

"I appreciate that. Andy sure is growing up to be a fine Christian man. His dad would be proud." She leaned forward and grinned.

Carol lightly stirred her cafe au lait. "Is that your cell ringing?"

"I'm finally remembering to bring it with me." She pulled the phone from her purse. "It's Dad, I have to take this."

"Sure, go ahead."

Millie covered her free ear to hear him better. "Hi, Dad. What's up?"

"We're at doctor's office. He wants to operate first thing tomorrow. She fought his orders to go right to the hospital, so he called an ambulance to transport her." He released a heavy sigh. "When they got here and tried to put her on the stretcher, she screamed your name, and kicked at them. Oh, Millie, they had to sedate her."

Her heart raced as she listened to her dad's report. "Okay, I'll be there in a few minutes."

Carol sat her cup down. "What's going on?"

"Mother got loud and combative at the doctor's office. They had to put her out and an ambulance took her the emergency room. She was yelling for me." She looked up. "I need to call Gabby."

"Why not Lou?"

"We're taking an engagement hiatus. Anyway, he's in a computer repair class in Denver."

"Too bad about your engagement. I'm sure you'll work things out. Do you want me to come to the hospital with you?"

Millie nodded and speed dialed Gabby's number. "Dad and I could use the extra support. He said Frank's on his way now."

"I'm sorry Lou can't be here." Carol pouted and gave Millie a hug. "I'll meet you there. Be careful driving."

Millie left a message for Gabby, then headed for the hospital, praying at each red light. Her thoughts and sympathy went to the unsuspecting medical staff. Penelope Joy Drake wrote the book on gloom, despair, agony, and defeat.

Carol was waiting for her inside the Emergency Room entrance. Millie rushed to the receptionist's window. "I'm here for Penelope Drake,"

"Are you a relative?"

"I'm her daughter."

She turned to her computer. The rapid clack of acrylic nails on the keyboard sent Millie's nerves over the edge.

The copper-haired lady sipped a bottle of water. "Have a seat in the waiting room. I'll let you know when you can go back."

Forty-five minutes later, a man with a clipboard called Millie's name. Following the orderly to her mother's cubicle, Millie tried to prepare herself for whatever shock might be in store. She slowly placed a hand on the cold metal bedrail while monitors constantly beeped. They had strapped Mother to the bed with IV tubes. Her make-up was gone and a pasty complexion remained. Millie couldn't remember the last time she saw that face so clean.

Her dad stood next to the bed, his face drawn and spent. She gave him a hug.

"I'm glad you're here, Princess. This has been a long day; at least your Mother has been sedated." Stu pointed to the nurses' station. "All the rooms are filled so they've been trying to find a bed for her somewhere."

A nurse pulled back the curtain, and two men in white coats came to take her away.

"We found one available bed on the fifth floor. The only problem is it's in the Psych Ward." She looked at Stuart. "Is that a problem?"

"Not at all. We're grateful you found a place for her."

"Give us a few minutes and we'll have her settled. You can visit her then."

Millie put her arm around her dad's shoulder. "Did you eat lunch?" Before he could respond, she added, "Let's get Frank and Carol and go to the cafeteria for a quick bite."

While the four of them were eating, Millie's phone rang. "It's Gabby. I'll take it over there to spare you." She pointed to an empty table.

She returned as her father was finishing his sandwich. He tossed the wrapper on the tray and Frank took it to the trashcan.

"Gabby will be here later." She patted her dad's arm. "You look exhausted. Why don't you go home after you see

Mother?"

"Would you mind? I am pretty beat, and her surgery is early in the morning."

"I'll stay with her and give you a call if anything changes."

They left the cafeteria and took an elevator to the fifth floor. Moans and cries carried throughout the hall as they walked to the last room on the left.

Millie took her dad's arm as they quietly entered. Another patient loudly snored in a bed next to the wire-meshed window looking out over the parking lot.

As expected, beeping monitors kept track of Mother's vitals. An IV pole beside the bed held a clear bag of fluid. She didn't anticipate seeing her mother's arm strapped to a board and attached to the bed's railing. Her heart ached and tears filled her eyes as she touched the cold hand.

Millie looked at the others. "She's still out."

"That's a good thing. Hopefully she'll sleep all night." Stuart bent down and tenderly kissed her cheek.

Penny's clouded eyes popped open. "What do you think you're doing, Stuart?" She smacked him with her free arm. "This is neither the time nor the place." Her cough changed to a gargling sputter before she dozed off again.

Frank and Carol left the room laughing. A short time later, Millie and Stuart joined them in the hall where the weak voices of other patients begged for attention. Millie gulped and tried to calm her fears. Why had she offered to stay with Mother overnight?

Taking Millie to the side, Carol whispered in her ear. "You don't need to be here by yourself, Cuz. I'll stay with you."

"Are you sure?" Millie rubbed her arms. "Thanks. It is scary up here, isn't it?"

"Let's pray before we go."

They formed a circle and Frank took their hands. "Dear Lord of Mercy and Father of Comfort, You are the only One we turn to in our moments of need. We come before You on behalf of Penny Drake. Please turn her weakness into strength, suffering into compassion, sorrow into joy, and pain into comfort. We trust You to watch over Millie and Carol as they stay here tonight, and please prepare Penny and the medical team for surgery tomorrow. In Your blessed and holy name, Amen."

After the men left, Millie and Carol returned to room 554 and pulled the two chairs close together.

Carol pulled a candy bar from her purse. "Want half?"

"Have I ever turned down chocolate? Yeah, I want some."

The patient by the window began to scream. "Kill those bugs! They're crawling up my blanket."

Penny startled awake. Her eyes bulged as she attempted to sit. "Why doesn't someone help her?" Her voice was raspy as she yelled, "Somebody get the RAID."

Another scream. "Snakes! Now, there's snakes! Kill 'em, get 'em outta here." She shook the bedding and released another howl.

A nurse hurried into the room. "Sorry, ladies. She has a severe case of the DTs. It should pass soon."

Penny clutched her blanket under her chin. "I want to go home, Millicent."

"I'm sorry, Mother, but you're not well enough to go home." Millie rested a hand on the quivering woman's shoulder. "Lie down. Everything will be okay in the morning. I'll stay here with you." She leaned over the railing and rubbed the wrinkled forehead until her mother relaxed.

In spite of the moans and whimpers from the next bed, Penny was asleep within minutes. Millie quietly shared her breakup with Carol.

Carol gave her a hug. "I totally understand your trust issues. He should've told you about the cruise director after you admitted dating Kent."

"Between you and me, I miss Lou. Should I forget what happened and ask him back?"

"This needs to be resolved, Mills. You both need to apologize for any wrongs and do that continually through your marriage. I know you've heard this before, but never go to bed angry."

"Thanks, Cuz. You always give me the best advice." Millie yawned. "I'm getting tired. Wanna go for a walk while Mother's sleeping?"

"Let's go."

Around eight o'clock the next morning, Frank walked into Penny's room.

Stuart greeted him with a handshake. "Hi, Pastor Frank. Thanks for coming."

"Sure, I wanted to be here with my family." He put his arm around Stuart's shoulder and led him beside the hospital bed. "Penny? Can you hear me? We're going to pray for you."

By the time his prayer was finished, two men in green scrubs came to take her to surgery.

Millie kissed her cheek. "See you later, Mother."

Stuart took his wife's hand. "Know we love you. Millie and I will be here when you wake up." He leaned over and kissed her forehead then they wheeled her from the room. Stuart turned to the others. "It's going to be a while. Anyone for breakfast?"

"Sounds good to me, Dad. I'm starving." Millie took his arm and the foursome headed for the elevator.

Frank pushed the first floor button. As the doors closed, Millie became aware of the weary expression settling on her dad's features. The creases between his brows were unusually deep. Millie was puzzled at his concern. Even though Mother had emotionally beaten him down for over four decades, he was still committed to her.

Millie's heart nearly stopped. Could she be that committed to Lou? She cancelled their engagement over something much less distressing. For years, he'd lived alone, so how could she expect him to grasp the significance of respecting her feelings by not keeping secrets?

During their breakfast, Frank and Stuart listened with great interest as Millie and Carol shared stories of spending the night on the Psych Floor.

Frank looked at his phone and stood. "Duty calls. I have to go." He looked at Carol. "You want me to drop you off at home or do you want to stay longer?"

"Aunt Penny's going to be in surgery for quite a while. If it's all right with Millie, I'll go home and freshen up."

"Why don't you take nap too? I'm going to do the same thing when Mother gets out of recovery." Millie hugged her. "Thanks for staying with me last night."

Millie gathered her belongings. When she and her dad got to the waiting area, the receptionist led them to the conference room.

"The surgeon will be with you shortly." She closed the door behind her.

They exchanged glances and took their seats around the polished oak table. Millie licked her lips. "It's been less than an hour. Doesn't look good does it?"

Stuart held her hand as they prayed for strength to receive the news.

A tap on the door interrupted them. It opened. "Mr. Drake?"

Stuart nodded. Worry lines etched between his brows as he stood. "We didn't expect you be done so soon."

"I'm Doctor Hunt." The doctor shook his hand. "Mrs. Drake is in recovery." He took a deep breath. "The surgery took about forty-five minutes. I'm sorry to tell you we discovered cancer has invaded the entire digestive system. It was too extensive for us to remove. Again, I'm sorry. We'll do our best to keep her comfortable."

Mother couldn't be that sick. Maybe they made a mistake. Millie's hand went to her throat as a sudden coldness came over her.

"Do you have any questions?"

"I have a couple." Stuart rubbed his chin. "Will she be able to come home?"

Doctor Hunt nodded. "We're going to keep her here for a couple of days and work up a plan for chemo treatments along with pain management and diet."

Millie fought back tears and gripped her dad's arm. She opened and closed her mouth a couple of times before the words came. "How l-long?"

"My best guess at this time is about three months; however, chemo might prolong it." He offered a concerned smile. "You can pick up beeper at the receptionist's window. They'll let you know when Mrs. Drake is out of recovery. Any other questions?"

This was real. She wrestled with the urge to run away.

"Thank you, doctor." Stuart shook his hand. "I can tell that wasn't an easy message for you to deliver. We appreciate your kindness."

"Your faith in God will keep you grounded. That will help a lot in the next few months." He glanced at his clipboard and scribbled on the paper. "I'm sorry you have to go through this. If there's anything we can do, please let us know. An oncologist will be in touch."

Millie and Stuart hugged in the quietness of the conference room.

His shoulders lifted as he took a deep breath, held it, and released a strangled sigh. "What'll we do now, Princess?"

"This is such a shock. I guess we take it one step at a time." Tears continued to form in Millie's eyes. She gave him an extra squeeze, then turned. "Would you call the church while I contact Gabby? Let's meet in the cafeteria for coffee about an hour from now."

Stuart nodded and reached for his phone.

Wanting fresh air, Millie went outside and dug in her purse for the cell. As she pulled it out, the phone rang. Gabby's number popped up on the screen.

"Hi, Gabby. I was about to call you." She broke down while relaying the news of her mother's diagnosis.

"I'm sorry. I'll be with you as soon as I can. Trust the Lord in this. Love you."

Millie finished her messages, then grabbed a cup of coffee in the cafeteria, and met her dad. "Any news from the beeper?"

"Not yet. It should be another couple of hours before they move her." He smiled. "Why don't you go home, freshen up, and get some rest?"

"That sounds wonderful. Gabby, Carol, and Frank should be here soon. They can keep you company. Will you be okay until then?" After he nodded, she kissed his cheek. "I'm going now before anything else happens. See you this evening to give you a break."

Late the next morning, Millie once again returned to the hospital. She repositioned herself in the chair and picked up another worn magazine. Great. *Field and Stream*, circa 1961. She flipped through the pages with little interest.

The evening before wouldn't have been as nerve racking with Lou by her side. She should have swallowed her pride and called him before now.

She glanced at her mother's roommate, Fran. She was

also in her sixties and had a kidney transplant the week before. Both women were dozing, so Millie walked to a nearby waiting room for a magazine exchange. While she was there, she called Lou. It went to voicemail. "This is Millie. I need to talk to you. Call me when you can."

When she got back to her mother's room, she jerked to a stop, unable to believe her eyes. She shook her head, sure it must be an illusion, but the image remained. A naked old man with a Shar-Pei body was climbing in Mother's bed. Mother's eyes popped open. She jumped with a start and screamed. Her monitor beeped frantically, setting Millie's nerves to screaming. Her lack of sleep made her feel like she was moving at a snail's pace as she headed across the room.

Fran woke up. "What's going on?"

"Call the nurse." Millie rushed to the bed and jerked on his arm. "What are you doing?"

He pointed to a pile of cloth at the foot of the bed. "Wet. Wet."

Millie shuddered. "Eewww! And I touched him."

"Do something, Millicent Marie. Don't let him have his way with me!" Mother continued to screech and slap the old guy's hands.

Meanwhile, Fran sat up in bed and laughed so hard that she doubled over. She pulled herself together long enough to push the call button and scream at the top of her lungs, "GET THIS OLD GOAT OUT OF HERE!"

Afraid of touching him again, Millie, grabbed latex gloves from the sink and attempted to put them on for naked jaybird removal.

"He's not going away, Millicent." Penny's squawking was ear-splitting. "Quick, give me something to clobber him with."

Within minutes, two nurses rushed into the room. One bagged the dripping cloth and bedding while the other led the waddling man away.

Stuart entered the room and scratched his head. "What was that guy doing in here dressed in his birthday suit?"

Laughing and moaning at the same time, Fran rubbed her abdomen. "This is the most fun I've ever had in the hospital, Penny."

She pouted. "I've never been so insulted in my life. I feel like a soiled dove on *Frontier Passion*."

"Soiled dove?" Fran cackled. "Stop making me laugh! I think I popped a stitch."

"I'll give you the abbreviated version later, Dad."

One nurse returned, drying her hands. "Poor guy wet himself and was looking for a dry place to land." She giggled. "I'm sorry you had to witness that, ladies."

Millie playfully rubbed her eyes. "Some things you can't unsee." She smiled. "Living with Penelope Joy Drake is never boring."

Millie came from the workroom and placed a new floral arrangement in the shop's refrigerated showcase. "Dad called, Carol. He said he's on his way to the shop from visiting Mother at the hospital."

"He's been going every day, no wonder he's so worn out." Carol wiped the counter clean. "Thanks for filling in for him this morning, Mills."

"Happy to do it. I knew you and Uncle Max needed help." Millie joined her cousin at the counter. "I wish Dad would take a day off to rest. I don't want to lose him too."

"Aunt Penny's prognosis must've hit him harder than we realized."

"Who would have guessed she only has three months

to live? Her mood swings go from pity Penny to book-throwing anger." Millie mimicked her mother's shrill voice. "Why did God give me cancer, Stuart? It must be a mistake. It isn't fair, Millicent Marie. You know I've been a religious person all my life and don't deserve any of this."

"She's working through the stages of grief, Mills."

"I'm trying to keep that in mind, but her pompous attitude makes me angry. Then I feel guilty. It's a vicious circle." Millie released a frustrated sigh and pushed her hair away from her face. "I regret my only memories of Mother will be of her temper tantrums and a life filled with drama."

"Your mother had some good points." Carol grinned. "For instance, I'm jealous she taught you how to be a great cook and fix something other than spaghetti. Because of her you know how to set a nice table, even with that cute Benny Bunny plate."

"Thanks for the awesome memories." Millie laughed through tears. "Because of Mother, I also know how to make a bed with hospital corners. Oh, and I've learned to be punctual."

"See, you came up with a few good thoughts." Carol cocked her head. "All you have to do is focus on the positive."

The bell over the shop's front door jingled.

"Yoo-hoo!"

Millie and Carol turned to greet the customer.

"Sue North!" Carol ran from behind the counter and hugged the woman. "What are you doing here, and why didn't you tell me you were coming?"

"I'm sorry, but it was a last-minute decision, and I barely had enough time to pack. It's only a two-day visit, but I still wanted to drop by and see my very best friend."

"I'm so happy you're here. Come meet my cousin." She grabbed Sue's arm and pulled her to the display counter.

"Mills, this is Sue North, my friend from Vermont. Her daughter is Ethan's fiancé. Sue, this is Millie Drake."

"Nice to meet you, Millie. Carol has shared about you two growing up together. I loved when you glued the last pages of your mother's novel together. How about the three of us go out and get into trouble some time?"

"Sounds like a lot of fun. Let's do it." Millie laughed. She liked Sue North. Maybe the woman's outgoing personality would rub off on her. "Hey! We have semi-fresh coffee in the break room."

"I could use a cup of coffee about now. Oh, and Mills, bring our secret stash of cookies too." Carol turned to her friend. "You want any, Sue?"

"I sure hope they're Grizzly Bars. Rikki wants me to make them for the bridal shower."

Carol giggled. "Hers or yours?"

"A bridal shower for me? Not on your life. I'm not seeking another opportunity to marry now or in the future, thank you very much."

The shop phone rang.

"Can you get that, Carol?" Millie turned abruptly and headed for the break room. "I'll be right back with the coffeepot and Grizzly Bars."

"That would be great. I'll clean off the counter. Thanks, Mills." Carol reached for the phone.

Millie grabbed three Styrofoam cups, the coffee pot, and a plate of the chocolate bars. After placing them on a tray, she returned to the showroom as Sue was talking.

"My plan is to visit the reservation where Rikki and Ethan plan to work. I want to see what needs the children's home has. I know it's spur-of-the-moment, Carol, but can you go with me today?"

"Sorry, wish I could, but Frank and I are expected to attend a regional ministerial dinner in Phoenix this evening."

"Bummer. I was hoping you could help make a list of things that I can bring the next time through." Her purse vibrated. "I need to return this text from Rikki. Excuse me." She headed for the front window.

"Wish I could go with her." Carol turned to Millie. "I heard the backdoor. Your dad must've returned from the hospital."

"Dad was supposed to talk to the doctor. Maybe he has an update."

Stuart came in from the workroom carrying a foam cup. He gave Millie a hug. "Hi, ladies. I assume the coffee pot's in here." He filled his cup. "How's business going?"

"Two local funerals, so we've had a lot of phone orders. Uncle Max is making deliveries." She tugged on his sleeve and pointed to the woman walking toward them. "We have a surprise visitor, Dad. This is Carol's best friend, Sue North, from Vermont."

Carol took over the introduction. "Sooze, this is my favorite uncle, Stuart Drake."

"Hi. Any uncle of Carol's is an uncle of mine."

"Nice to meet you, Miss Suzie-Q. What brings you to beautiful downtown Apache Pointe?" He offered his hand.

Sue returned the gesture. "My daughter is Ethan's fiancée, and I'm here to visit the Native American Missions children's home where they're going to work." She put her arm around Carol's waist. "Since I'm out here, I had to stop in to see my old friend and ask her to go with me."

"Oh, you're Rikki's mom. Ethan brought her by the flower shop a few times last summer. She's a sweet girl."

"Thank you. Ethan's probably mentioned they're going to move here in August after he and Rikki graduate and get married. I want to find methods to help the Maverick Ranch for Children by way of donations and to set up a charitable foundation in the near future."

Carol refilled her coffee cup. "Sue has a deep passion

for charity and her daughter's welfare."

"That's wonderful." Millie nudged him. "We were talking about you volunteering there, Dad."

Stu's eyes widened as he straightened his shoulders. "I've always had an interest in that mission because my mother's grandfather had Apache ancestors. I'd really like to help out at the ranch."

"My plans are to go this afternoon, but I'm a little nervous about driving that far without company." She smiled at Stuart and took a Grizzly Bar from the plate. "Would you and Millie consider going with me?"

He looked at Millie and grinned. "How about it, Princess? I'm game, are you?"

"Sorry. Daddy." She shook her head and handed him one of the chocolate treats. "I'd better stay here and help them catch up on all these funeral orders or we'll be swamped tomorrow. Maybe next time?"

"Looks like it's just you and me, Suzie-Q. I enjoy going out there. Mind if I tag along?"

"Not at all. I'd be glad to have your company." She linked her arm in his. "May I call you Uncle Stuart?"

"I would be honored."

"I'm glad you're going." Millie kissed her dad's cheek. "You've been at the hospital with Mother all week, so you deserve to get away and do something different to relax. Have a good time."

"Now would be the perfect opportunity for you to call and patch things up with Lou." He gave her a wink. "Gabby told me he's downright miserable without you and your moping around makes it obvious the feeling's mutual."

That was all the encouragement Millie needed. She pulled her cell phone from her pocket and noticed two missed calls. "I'm on my way to call him now." Why was she always leaving her phone behind?

He gave her a thumbs-up and left the store with Sue.

"Carol, can you man the front desk while I call Lou?" She dialed his number and headed out the front door. His phone rang.

"Hello?"

"Lou? I'm sorry I didn't trust you. Can we—" A familiar rumble broke her train of thought. She turned to see a red van pull to the curb. There was a moment, a heartbeat of time before the realization sunk in. "Lou!"

He climbed from the van, stepped to the sidewalk, and opened his arms. "I love you, Sweet Cheeks." He flashed his ready grin.

Millie ran into his embrace and held him tight. She felt his uneven breathing on her neck, then she leaned up and kissed him, savoring every moment.

"I'm sorry, Lou. Do you forgive me?"

"It was my fault for not telling you about Gemma. I can understand why you were so upset with me." He dropped to one knee. "Millie Drake, will you marry me?"

"Yes!"

Applause and cheers broke loose behind them. Carol, along with Uncle Max and design crew, stood at the flower shop door.

Carol's voice raised above the others. "It's about time."

CHAPTER TWENTY-THREE

Late February

DEAR DIARY,

JUST OVER A MONTH until I'm Mrs. Louis Elliot Blythe. Gabby is determined to find a condo before the wedding, but so far she hasn't found one that meets her needs in the immediate area.

Dad and I made plans for Gabby to come over for lunch today. She wants to help us sort out our feelings for Mother and deal with her inevitable prognosis.

I haven't seen much of Lou this week. Blythe Computer and Technical Support has had another growth spurt. Lou and his business partner are training two new techs. I'm thankful that business is good, but I miss my man.

Carol's friend, Sue, was here a week ago. I liked her very much, and I'm glad she'll be coming to Apache Pointe to visit her daughter and Ethan. She re-ignited Dad's passion for Native American missions. It's good to see him smile and be excited about getting involved in helping others.

Mother's chemo treatments have caused her hair to fall out. It's humbled her somewhat. However, she's so self-absorbed, Dad and I are afraid she'll go into an emotional tailspin.

Millie hurried to answer the front door. "Hi, Gabby, we've been waiting for you." She leaned over to kiss the older woman's cheek. Her God-given wisdom coupled with a degree in psychology was definitely heaven sent.

"I brought the Bucket O' Cluck we agreed on yesterday. It's hot, crispy, and ready to devour while we have our talk."

"Thank you, sweet lady. Come on in. Dad and I appreciate your willingness to help us sort out a lot of difficulties with Mother." She took the deep-fried offering and led her future mother-in-law to the kitchen. "Chicken is one of Dad's favorites. Go ahead and have a seat while I get him."

Gabby pulled out a small notebook and pen, laid them by her plate, then put her purse on a chair. "Shall I set the table?"

Millie nodded and hurried out of the room. Gabby's gentle and unassuming spirit was much different from Mother's harsh, self-serving control. A thought tickled her mind. Dad needed and deserved a sweet woman like her. It would be interesting if he and Gabby got together after Mother passed. After a respectable time, of course.

She went to the garage. "Get washed up, Dad. Gabby's here for our talk and brought our chicken dinner too."

He looked up from under the hood of the car. "Woo-hoo! I'm on it, Princess."

Back in the kitchen, Millie pulled the fixings for a tossed salad and two kinds of dressings from the refrigerator while Gabby filled the last glass with lemonade and put the chicken on a platter.

With their tasks completed, they sat side-by-side at

the round table.

"Nice to see you, Gabby." Stuart walked over and stood behind them. "We haven't had much time to cook around here, so thanks for lunch. It sure smells delicious." He rubbed his hands together, and then placed one on his daughter's shoulder and one on Gabby's. "Ladies, let's return thanks before we dig in." He bowed his head.

"O Gracious Heavenly Father, we give You thanks for Your abundant love and generosity. Please bless the food Gabby brought and give her added insight during today's counseling session. Thank You for our family and friends and especially be with Penny as she undergoes more cancer treatments. Keep our hearts open to Your will. We ask this through Christ, Your Son. Amen." He gave Millie's shoulder an extra squeeze and went to his chair.

"Thanks for your faith-filled prayer, Stuart." Gabby reached for the salad. "I don't know about you, but I'm starved."

"Me too." Stuart took a couple of chicken thighs from the platter and dropped them on his plate. He wiped his fingers, passed the serving dish to Gabby, and reached for the salad.

She speared a piece of chicken with her fork and placed them both on her plate. A concerned look settled on her features. "A couple of weeks ago you and Millie asked me to help you sort through your feelings about Penny. I know you've struggled many years with her dysfunction. Let's use this opportunity to make sure everyone's heart is prepared for this life transition. Stuart, do you have any questions or comments to get things started?" She poised her pen over the small notebook.

He swallowed and laid his fork down. "I'll start at the beginning. I was young and naïve walking into a marriage with Penny." With fingers steepled under his chin, Stuart's voice softened. "I admit thoughts of leaving her often crossed my mind, but when Millie was born a year later, the main concern was for my daughter." He patted Millie's hand. "That's when I chose to stay and honor our wedding vows. You know, for better, for worse and so forth?"

"You stayed for me, Daddy?" Millie wiped her tears, stood, and kissed the cheek of the hero who put her needs ahead of his own. She scooted her chair closer to him and sat down.

Gabby had been silent through their exchange. She shifted in her seat and jotted in her notebook before turning to Millie. "What are your thoughts about you and your mom, honey?"

After a moment, Millie looked at her, not quite sure of what to say. Had she somehow brought this disaster on herself? She rubbed the back of her neck. "The only word I can use to describe our relationship is strained. She's never showed me any tenderness or tried to connect on an emotional level."

"And how did that make you feel?"

Millie gazed into Gabby's face and found a willingness to listen. "It made me wonder how anyone could love me if my own mother didn't."

An obvious tone of anger crept into Stuart's moan as color flamed into his face.

Gabby reached over and patted her hand. "Millie, honey, your mom's failure to show love is a failure in her, not you. You're a very loveable young lady."

"Do you think it's too late to make things better between us? I've always wanted a close bond with her, but could never break through her wall of indifference. She constantly pushed me away."

"Considering our time constraint, things will probably never be perfect, but it's definitely not too late to make things better." The silver-haired woman flipped back a few pages in her notebook and studied them. "I talked with your mom the other day. Apparently while growing up, she didn't receive the emotional attachment needed, so she had little in reserve to pass on to you."

A flicker of weariness grabbed Millie's heart. "I kind of assumed it was something like that since she rarely interacted with me when I was little."

"What do you remember?" Her voice was gentle and earnest.

Millie focused on her hands, which tightened around her napkin. A moment later she peeked up. "Mother was usually reading or watching TV while I quietly played by myself."

Stuart wiped his mouth. He leaned forward and looked straight into Gabby's eyes. "One day I came home in the afternoon, and they were sitting together watching soap operas."

"That was after I learned to sit still and not interrupt her until the commercial." Millie nodded. "Watching her stories is the only bond that comes to mind from my younger years." She glanced up. "Later Mother taught me how to set a pretty table and cook so I could help her every Sunday and on holidays."

Gabby's eyes were intent on understanding Millie's mood. "Did helping her in the kitchen draw you closer?"

"It should have, but she was too critical." Millie grinned. "But thanks to her, I can whip potatoes to perfection and make a mean mince pie."

"That she can!" Stuart's eyes brightened as he chuckled and pulled her into a quick hug.

"I look forward to sampling both." Gabby released a gentle laugh. "Now, let me ask you this, Stuart. How did you feel when you saw your daughter watching the soaps?"

The rigid set of his jaw indicated disgust as he put his glass down a little harder than necessary. "The soaps were on during work hours so I didn't know about it at first. It made me downright angry, but I still kept my mouth shut. Penny got so furious when anyone challenged her, and she would've made my little girl suffer the consequences when I left."

"That was your way of protecting Millie. Remember, nothing can change what happened a long time ago. Guilt can beat you down if you allow yourself to dwell on it."

Without blinking, Stuart nodded and sustained his pensive gaze.

"Your lives seemed to run smoother if you didn't cross swords with her, right, Stuart?" Gabby wiped her fingers, scribbled a note, then slanted a glance at him.

"Exactly."

Millie laid her red-rimmed glasses on the table and hid her face in a tissue. "Both of us learned that lesson quickly." She leaned into her dad's shoulder.

"Now, let's see if we can find ways to heal your mother's broken spirit as well as your own." Gabby's gentle expression revealed sympathy. "That's where forgiveness comes in."

"Do I simply forgive and continue to allow Mother to walk all over me?" Millie shook her head. "It's hard to forget all the years of pain, misery, and humiliation."

"You have to give it to God. Let Him be the judge." Gabby pushed her empty plate away. "Do you think He still loves Penny in spite of the wounds she's inflicted?"

Stuart cleared his throat. "We know He loves all of us even though we don't deserve it."

"What about you and Millie? Do both of you love her?" Gabby took a bite of chicken while waiting for their replies.

His shoulders went up in a half-hearted shrug as he focused on the nearby window. "I struggle with it, but constantly ask God to help me. My love for her is hidden under a lot of hurt and frustration." He licked his lips.

"Actually, my feelings alternate between empathy and love. I hurt for Penny because of her violent upbringing."

Dumbfounded at the revelation, Millie raised her hand. "Wait, Dad. This is the first time I've heard of Mother's violent childhood. I remember you told me it was rough, but violent?"

"Unfortunately, yes. Your grandparents had to get married. Penny's dad was an alcoholic and often told her she wasn't his. He mentally and physically abused his whole family." Stuart's countenance was grave as he put his arm around Millie. "Since Penny was the oldest child, her mother blamed her for being stuck in a turbulent marriage."

"Why didn't her mother run away from the monster?"

"Back in those days, your Grandmother Krause had nowhere else to go. She had no money or means of support."

"I've never heard Mother's side of the story before. No wonder she's so full of anger." Millie looked into the distance, amazed at the tender feelings growing within. She closed her eyes. *Lord, Your Word says I can't expect You to forgive me if I refuse to forgive Mother. Please help me to let go of my grudge and love her as You do.*

CHAPTER TWENTY-FOUR

March

MILLIE PEERED OUT THE FRONT WINDOW of the Knuckle Sandwich shop. "I hope your mom gets here soon, Lou. I have to get back to the church office." She straightened the collar of her dark blue blouse.

"Mom's always punctual." Lou shifted in his chair and checked his watch. "She was going to see your mother this morning. Maybe she got hung up with something."

"Gabby's been wonderful to Mother. I've noticed small changes in her this past month. The other day I actually saw her reading the Bible even though she's sick with chemo." She looked at Lou. "Do you realize what a big deal that is?"

"That's great, honey."

"I'm anticipating that the two of us will eventually grow closer." She brushed the hair from her eyes. "Or at least have an affable connection."

"I hope you reach a level of contentment in your relationship. No one deserves it more than you."

Gabby, dressed in pleated trousers and a white shirt, rushed to the table. "Sorry to be so late."

"I ordered your favorite chicken salad sandwich and sweet tea. I hope that's okay." Lou seated his mom and kissed her cheek.

"That's perfect, Son. Penny and I got into a deep conversation, and I didn't want to leave her questions unanswered. Keep praying, kids. The Lord's working in her heart."

"I've heard how God has been using you in Penny's life. I'm proud of you, Mom."

Millie looked into the woman's sparkling blue eyes. "He's given you the personality and ability to break down Mother's concrete walls that nobody else has been able to chip away."

"I'm glad the Lord's bringing it about. It must be His timing." Gabby cocked her silver head to one side. "That poor soul realizes the end is coming soon. She finally sees the need to make amends."

"I can't believe Mother said that. She's never apologized to anyone as far as I know." She unwrapped her straw and plunged it into her lemonade. Did Mother actually mean it, or was she trying to impress Gabby?

"I remember you mentioned that, but after watching Penny's reactions, I honestly believe she's sincere."

A voice came over the speaker. "Blythe, your order is ready."

Lou scooted from the table. In his best Arnold Schwarzenegger accent he said, "I'll be back." He hurried to the counter.

"Can you believe your wedding is only three weeks away? Are you ready to have me for a mother-in-law?"

"You bet I am. I can't wait to be Lou's wife and be a part of your family." Millie laughed. "From what Lou tells me, the Blythe ladies are wonderful. He also warned me about his goofy brothers, but I still look forward to joining the clan."

"Believe me, we've all been counting the days. Do you have all the ordering done and plans finalized? Flowers, cake, dresses and accessories?"

"Lou and I tasted cakes and decided on the raspberry truffle for one layer and a lemon swirl for another. We don't have to worry about the flowers because Dad, Uncle

Max, and Carol are on top of it. The church and fellowship hall were booked well in advance. I go in for my final dress fitting next week." Millie felt heat rising in her cheeks. "Lou said he'd take care of the honeymoon plans."

Lou set the food-laden tray down. "Did I hear my name and honeymoon mentioned in the same sentence?"

"That's what I wanted to talk to you about today." Gabby reached for her chicken salad plate. "I gave your brothers each a cruise for their honeymoon, and it's only fair for me to give you the same, Lou."

He leaned over and kissed her cheek. "Thanks, Momma. You're the best." He looked at Millie. "How does going on a cruise sound to you, honey?"

"What a generous gift, Gabby. I love it. You're spoiling me already. Thank you."

"All the travel agent needs to know is the destination." She grinned at Millie. "And young lady, I want you to call me Mom Blythe like my other daughters."

"Okay . . . Mom Blythe. A cruise sounds fun and romantic. I've never been on a boat." She glanced at Lou and put her hand on his shoulder. "I was jealous of you going on that six-week trip this past summer."

"Now we get to go on one together." Lou wiggled his eyebrows and kissed her hand. "And since we'll be married, I guarantee it'll be a hundred percent more pleasurable."

Mortified at what he had implied in front of Gabby, Millie nibbled on a French fry and glanced away. Some things weren't kosher for a mother's ears.

"Don't embarrass her, Louis Elliot." Gabby shook her finger. "You've been around your older brothers too much."

A glint sparkled in his blue eyes. "It's finally my turn to crow, Mom." He laced his fingers together and cracked his knuckles simultaneously.

"Not at the expense of your fiancée." Gabby sent a wink to Millie. "Another reason I wanted you to join me today was to ask if the connection with your mother has improved any?" She crunched into a potato chip.

"Since Dad told us about her childhood, I've found it easier to show her more love. She seems to be responding to it, but then again, it might be her meds. Either way, she's mellowing."

Gabby swallowed her chip. "I'm sure it's a little bit of both. Even a difficult person will often respond to unconditional love."

"Now that I've had a glimpse of this side of Mother, I'm mourning the relationship that could have been."

"Continue to work on healing your damaged lives, and the mother/daughter bond you long for can still come about. Remember, Millie, it might not be at the same level you desire, but there will certainly be a marked improvement. You'll have good memories of her for the rest of your life."

Lou pushed his empty plate aside, leaned forward, and placed his elbows on the table. "That's a good thing."

"Mother and Dad are getting along better too. He's been taking her out for short drives to see the sunset. She sleeps better when they get home."

"It's good he's willing to go the extra mile for her." Gabby picked up another potato chip. "By the way, what's the story between your mother and Sylvia? I've noticed some silent animosity there."

"I'm not sure what started their family feud, but it began over forty years ago. Mother is so jealous of anything Aunt Syl has or does. She sets verbal traps for my poor aunt. Those barbs are so filled with judgment, Aunt Syl responds the only way she knows how, by slamming kitchen cupboards and drawers."

"I see. Exciting family get-togethers, right?" Gabby

pulled a small notepad from her purse and jotted a few lines. "Thank you. This will help me know how to approach her. She needs a constructive way to release her hostility."

"Aunt Syl had a stroke on Thanksgiving, so she isn't well, either. She needs to let go of the hurt Mother's caused." Millie took a drink of lemonade. "It would be wonderful if both ladies could forgive."

"It's going to take a lot of thought and prayer." Gabby drummed her fingernails on the table. "If you could give me a little clue to something they have in common, I may be able to help your mother come up with a peace offering to get the ball rolling."

"That would be awesome, Mom Blythe." Millie tried to swallow her doubts. Mother taking the first step to apologize to her sister-in-law would be a first-class miracle. She'd rather smack her over the head with a baking pan. Baking pan? An idea came to mind. "You know what? Aunt Sylvia loves Mother's pecan rolls."

"Done!" Gabby gave her a thumbs-up and winked. "We make a good team."

Mother showing a hint of conciliatory spirit? Millie settled back in her chair. She'd have to see it to believe it.

CHAPTER TWENTY-FIVE

Later that week

MILLIE TOOK A SEAT NEXT TO Gabby in the living room. "Mother's having a good day today. She's in the kitchen wrapping the pecan rolls to take to Aunt Sylvia's. Thanks for going along with us."

"Wasn't Sylvia's stroke only four months ago? I hate to go too early. Are you sure she's up to having company?"

"I called her this morning to be sure. She's eager to meet my future mother-in-law. We set the time for around one this afternoon." Millie lowered her voice. "While we're alone, I want to tell you how much we appreciate your influence on Mother. It's hard to believe that after all these years she finally agreed to make peace with Aunt Syl. This never would've happened without your guidance, Mom Blythe."

A relaxed smile played at the corners of Gabby's mouth. "I'm simply using the tools the Lord gave me and following His lead. Remember to be patient because permanent change never takes place overnight." She stood and brushed the wrinkles from her melon-colored blouse. "Let's trust the Lord to have His way in today's visit."

Millie's level of anxiety continued to grow as she pulled her car into Max and Sylvia's driveway. She prayed Gabby would intervene between the two women, should any fangs or claws be displayed. They'd been at each other's throats for over forty years, and old habits were definitely hard to break.

Her molars ground together as she envisioned her mother and sweet Aunt Sylvia coming to blows over some insignificant insult. How would she explain the two cold bodies to the authorities? Good thing she'd called ahead. It gave Aunt Sylvia time to gulp down a tranquilizer and get out her breastplate and helmet.

The last one to get out of the car, Penny carried the pan of warm pecan rolls up the steps and to the front door.

Millie inwardly grimaced. Was this an actual peace offering or merely another attempt to impress Gabby? The stress of not knowing evaporated her energy. With her arm as limp as a stringless marionette, she rang the doorbell, stood back, and waited for Drake feathers to fly. Please, Lord, keep the conversation civil.

The aroma of freshly brewed coffee greeted them as the door slowly opened. Aunt Sylvia's thick robe hung loosely from her frail shoulders as she leaned on a walker. Her once beautiful eyes were now sunken and dull. The silver in her hair was more prominent.

Millie stepped inside. She held her aunt's arms to keep her balanced and cautiously kissed her forehead. "I'm glad to see you're up and around. What a pretty robe, blue is a good color for you."

Before Sylvia had a chance to reply, Penny displayed the covered baking pan. "Hello, Syl." Her voice trembled. "I thought we might enjoy these pecan rolls together. Millie helped so I wouldn't tire too much."

"Thank . . . you. Smells good." Sylvia's squinty eyes displayed a hint of skepticism. "Have with coffee. How are you?"

"It's been a rough week, but today's pretty good. My

nausea pills help."

Millie took the pan from her shaking mother. "Aunt Syl, I'd like you to meet Gabby Blythe." Joy filled Millie's heart as she added, "My future mother-in-law."

"Happy to meet Millie's favorite aunt." Gabby patted Sylvia's frail hand.

Sylvia's smile was a little off-center as she nodded. "You too." She pointed to the nearby dining room; her body swayed as she turned her walker in that direction, and took slow, deliberate steps.

Millie shook her head as her mother followed Sylvia through the living room like a three-toed sloth pursuing a slug.

"Aunt Syl, you sit here, while I get the cups and plates." Millie pulled out a chair, made sure her aunt was comfortable, then retreated to the kitchen. She was relieved that her mother wasn't blathering in her usual condescending tone.

Laughter flowed from the dining room causing Millie's shoulders to relax. She put the dishes, coffee pot, and plated pecan rolls on a tray. Maybe it was possible for the sisters-in-law to get along. She took a deep breath and joined the others.

Gabby glanced around the room. "You have such a nice condominium, Sylvia. It's so bright and cheery."

"Thanks." Her voice was thin and shaky.

"How long have you lived here?" Gabby poured a little more coffee in her cup.

Sylvia held up her hand. "Five years."

"They really like it here." Millie smiled at her aunt. "Their neighbors check in on her while Uncle Max is at work."

"How fortunate you are." Gabby selected a gooey roll from the plate. "I've been looking for a condo in this area."

Penny immediately jumped into the conversation.

"Gabby asked me to help her find a nice place."

"Good." With hands shaking, Sylvia managed to lift her half-filled coffee cup without spilling any. "Try here?"

"Yes, we have." Millie set her drink on the table. "Lou and I spoke to the manager. They have a couple of new units available on the north side of the complex."

Penny laid her hand on Gabby's. "Shall we check tomorrow morning if I'm up to it?" She tossed her sister-in-law a proud glance.

A red flag flapped a warning in Millie's mind. She recognized her mother's attempt at baiting Aunt Sylvia.

"Sounds like a good idea, Penny." As if reading Millie's mind, Gabby quickly changed the subject. "These pecan rolls are amazing. I hope you don't make them on a regular basis, or I'll have to work out with Richard Simmons."

Millie wiped her fingers on a napkin. "I'd hate to see you deal with such torture. Allow me to ease your suffering." She playfully reached for Gabby's plate.

"Excuse me?" Gabby's eyebrows rose as she moved her pastry out of Millie's reach. "I'm capable of using self-control when necessary. Even if my willpower fails, God has given us Spandex for a reason."

Relief settled over Millie as she watched the older ladies snort with laughter. However, her reprieve from stress was short-lived when she remembered her mother still had to offer Sylvia a heartfelt apology.

When the room drew quiet, Sylvia pointed to the diamond ring that sparkled on Millie's left hand. "P-Pretty."

Penny beamed and placed her half-eaten pecan roll on the blue and white dessert plate. "They're getting married in two weeks."

"Oh!" Sylvia searched Millie's eyes. Her lips puckered as she struggled to form the next word. "P-Pearls." She paused. "P-Promise."

"Thank you, Aunt Sylvia. I remember you offered your necklace and earring set for my wedding. Don't let me forget to take them." Millie smiled and sipped her coffee. Bless her heart, she remembered even after a stroke.

"Bedroom." Sylvia gestured to the hall. "Top d-drawer."

Penny's head hung low. She sniffed, lifted her red-rimmed glasses, and wiped a tear. "I wish I had memories of a big, fancy wedding like you, Syl."

And there it was. Mother's typical all-about-me moment. Millie rose from the table and headed for the bedroom. She needed time away from the mama drama before her silent scream became audible.

Millie opened her aunt's dresser drawer and pulled out a black velvet box. She lifted the pearl necklace to her throat and peered at the image in the mirror.

She formed a mental picture of Aunt Sylvia on her wedding day, dressed in white lace and wearing the same pearls. Uncle Max must have been so proud of his sweet, blushing bride. She smiled. He still was.

God had certainly blessed her with a loving aunt and uncle. Millie hoped her marriage to Lou would mirror Max and Sylvia's happiness and loyalty even through difficult times. She closed her eyes and breathed a prayer for the couple and their health needs.

She plucked a tissue from its box on the nightstand. With a quick swipe at her nose, she returned to the dining room, where a mind-blowing scene came into view.

"Yes, yes, yes! I'm so sorry we've had such a strained relationship over the years." Mother dabbed her eyes. "Bless your heart, Syl. You finally understand my pain. Stuart's going to love your idea." The two huddled together, weeping in each other's arms. "We're going to do better from now on, aren't we?"

Was it possible for Mother to change so dramatically?

Millie frowned and looked at the bedroom door. Had she wandered through some strange portal to a parallel universe? She searched Gabby's face for an answer.

The woman responded with a perky grin as her fingers formed the victory sign. "Your sweet Aunt Sylvia came up with the most brilliant idea."

Millie inwardly moaned. She took a deep breath, almost afraid to find out. "I can't wait to hear what you've come up with."

"She suggested your mother and dad might renew their vows with a fancy ceremony on their next anniversary."

Millie's mind did a freefall as the implication hit full force. The opposing sisters-in-law had apparently made peace, but how would her poor dad feel about going through an elaborate wedding rehash. Maybe he'd embrace the idea to make her happy. She smiled. Since learning about Mother's abusive childhood, Millie wanted her to have that final wish.

CHAPTER TWENTY-SIX

Rehearsal dinner

MILLIE FIDGETED BY HER FIANCÉ AT the church entrance. "It's nearly eleven-fifteen, Lou. Your brothers are aware the wedding rehearsal was set for eleven o'clock, right? You know how Mother hates tardiness."

"Maybe they got turned around and can't find the church. I'd better call them." Lou pulled out his phone and speed dialed his brother. "Spence? Where are ya, bro? You guys are fifteen minutes late."

Even though Mother had mellowed since meeting Gabby, a late start was enough to revive the old habits. Woe be to the one who caused the delay. Millie licked her dry lips. "Is that their van turning in, Lou?"

He stepped to the door. "Oh, yeah. I see Patty waving in the van."

Millie's hands shook as she pulled at the skirt of her light blue dress. She stepped aside as Lou opened the door for his family members. Would they accept her right away as Gabby did? She drew in a deep breath while Lou hugged each couple.

"I want all of you to meet my sweetheart, Millie Drake." Lou turned to Millie. "Honey, this bushy guy is Bart, the old man of the group."

Millie's concern of acceptance into the Blythe family dissipated when bearded Bart pulled her into a hairy bear hug. She let out a loud squeal when he lifted her off the floor and spun her around.

With a gentleness that belied his large frame, he set her down. "Hi, little lady. Good to finally meet you. And this beautiful blonde is my wife, Tara."

Her dimples flashed as she smiled and embraced Millie. "I apologize for my over-enthusiastic husband."

A few minutes later, Carol came down the hall pushing Penny in a wheelchair.

With her trademark accordion pleated brow in place, Penny tapped on her watch as they joined the group. "Do you realize we're almost half an hour late? I scheduled the dinner for precisely twelve-thirty. We don't want dehydrated chicken and withered baked potatoes, do we?" She readjusted her position and added, "Of course we don't."

Perfect! The Grand ol' Duchess had to take this opportunity to rematerialize. What a great first impression. Millie turned to her future in-laws, rolled her eyes, and silently mouthed, "I'm sorry."

The four couples fell into step behind drill sergeant Penny.

The thirty-minute wedding practice progressed better than Millie expected. Thankfully, Gabby's calming presence kept the fussy mother-of-the-bride focused.

Frank nudged Lou. "This is where I'll pronounce you husband and wife and say, you may kiss your bride."

Lou's bright blue eyes twinkled as his arms went about her waist. Without warning, he swept Millie into a swoon-worthy embrace leaving her in a near giddy state.

"That'll work, Lou." Frank cleared his throat. "I'm getting a signal from the caterer." He glanced back at the couple. "Looks like our rehearsal dinner is ready, so whenever our groom comes up for air, we'll offer thanks."

Lou's three older brothers grunted their approval in unison. "Wooh . . . wooh . . . wooh!"

After the cacophony settled, Frank delivered a brief

prayer, and then clapped his hands. "Dinner's ready. Bridal party, lead the way."

Millie hooked her arm through Lou's, and they followed the aroma of roasting chicken waiting for them in the church fellowship hall.

They were ushered to one of the six round tables draped in soft pink-colored cloths. Dark pink and white candles flickered in the middle of each one. A canopy of twinkle lights and tulle cast a soft glow around the room.

Lou held a chair for Millie and scooted her closer to the table. "One more day. I love you, Sweet Cheeks."

His sister-in-law in the purple dress sat beside her. "Hi, I'm Patty, Spence's wife. I've been eager to meet you." She pointed to Gabby. "Mom Blythe thinks you're the perfect match for her widdle Squishy."

Millie turned to Lou. "Did she just call you Squishy?" She giggled. "There has to be a story behind that."

His face turned cherry red. "And the teasing begins. The story will come another time, but you're not gonna hear it from me."

Millie looked at the pretty, blonde-haired lady. "By the way, I'm happy to meet you too, Patty. Maybe we can have coffee together so you can tell me the scoop behind the Squishy story." Millie made a mental note—Patty in purple with blonde hair. How would she ever keep his family straight?

One of Lou's three brothers sat next to Patty. They must be a couple. Now to put a name with purple Patty's partner.

Lou leaned forward. "Glad to see you got a haircut, Spence."

Finally, some names to work with! Millie turned to look at the man with a front tooth gap. Purple Patty and Spence with a space. Got it.

Spence nodded to his wife. "Patty insisted. She's been

calling me Fred Flintstone for the last month."

Millie nearly choked on her water. She glanced around the room. Mother wasn't within earshot, thank goodness.

"In my opinion," Patty leaned closer to Millie, "the mangy mullet style should've been outlawed a long time ago."

Millie looked up as the third brother came to the table. Bart with a beard and Spence with a space. The process of elimination told her this thick-necked guy was Nick, and the one closest to Lou's age. Nick's thick neck.

Nick pulled a chair for his wife. "Hey, Bart, remember the church directory portrait where our whole family had those cool mullets?"

"You mean the picture with the matching plaid outfits?" Bearded Bart chuckled into his napkin. "We thought we were really stylin' back then."

Nick nodded to Millie. "By the way, I'm Nick, the handsome one, and this is my wife, Kate. She's quiet and I'm not."

Millie mentally quizzed herself. Quiet Kate with thick-necked Nick. Spence with a space and Purple Patty. Bearded Bart and Tara with dimples. She'd have to work on the dimple alliteration.

Quiet Kate smiled and pointed to another table. "That's our son and daughter sitting with the young man over there."

"He's my cousin's son, Andy." Millie reached for her water glass and took a sip before continuing. "You and Nick have cute kids."

The kitchen door opened and servers entered the fellowship hall with piping hot chicken dinners. They positioned a plate in front of each guest.

Millie tried a bite of gravy-laden meat and checked her mother's reaction to the meal. The frown was gone. So far, so good.

Lou shoveled a huge bite of mashed potatoes into his mouth. He eyeballed her roll and pointed with his fork. "You gonna eat that, Sweet Cheeks?"

"Help yourself." She shook her head and pushed the bread plate his way. "I have to fit into my wedding dress tomorrow."

"Thanks." Lou picked up his knife. "Somebody pass the butter, please."

Millie cut off a bite-sized piece of roast chicken. Being part of a loving family had always been her dream. She swallowed and took a forkful of mashed potatoes. Why did clever topics of conversation escape her mind around these wonderful people? She sighed. That's one more thing she hadn't learned at Mother's knee.

Across the table, dimpled Tara put her glass down and dabbed her mouth with a napkin. "I think the rehearsal went rather well, don't you, Millie?"

"I'm very pleased. It means a lot to have the entire Blythe family come and celebrate with us." She smiled. "You make me feel loved."

Patty in purple covered her mouth and giggled. "I never would've guessed our little Squishy could kiss like that."

The sisters-in-law looked at each other, grinned, then broke into their female version of man grunts in three-part harmony. "Wooh . . . wooh . . . wooh!"

Quiet Kate smiled and fumbled with her napkin. "The three of us have practiced that since you set the wedding date."

"We even rehearsed over the phone." Tara's dimples popped. "Bart and I couldn't wait to be a part of your wedding. Thank you for asking us. Lou's such a sweetheart. He's talked about you for quite some time, so it feels like you're our little sister already."

"Thanks for accepting me so quickly." Millie dabbed

her eyes. She liked Lady Dimples. "It means so much to be included into this family. I can't wait to get to know all of you better."

"You don't have long to wait." Patty put an arm around her. "Mom Blythe always plans a girls' bonding time right before the wedding. Kate, Tara and I were wondering what tomorrow's extravaganza will be."

"Tomorrow?" The word squeezed around Millie's heart like a tourniquet. That was her wedding day. "Please tell me we're not doing anything dangerous like jumping out of planes or anything."

"Who knows? There's never a dull moment with Gabby Blythe." Purple Patty nudged her. "Don't worry. We all lived through ours. It'll be fine."

Gabby came up behind Millie and hugged her. "I have Carol wheeling your mother around to take pictures. Look how well she's getting along. Isn't it great?"

Millie nodded. "Not a major outburst all day long. You must be a magician. I love you, Mom Blythe."

"I love you too." Gabby motioned for Carol and Penny to join them. "I have a treat for all you ladies. It's a bachelorette party to welcome my newest daughter to our family."

"Here it comes." Patty squeezed Millie's cold hand. "I just know this is going to be so much fun."

Gabby's eyes widened as she placed her palms on Millie's shoulders. "Since the wedding is tomorrow evening, I thought we girls should be pampered a bit. We'll spend the entire day at the Crowning Oasis Spa getting ready for the ceremony."

"C'mon, guys." Bearded Bart stood and pushed his chair under the table. "This is where Momma and the girls start with their beauty parlor chitchat. Let's go make our own plans for our little bro's bachelor send off."

Metal chairs scraped the floor as the other three

Blythe brothers jumped to their feet and followed their leader.

With a wide grin, Millie watched thick-necked Nick and Spence with a space hoist Lou onto their shoulders and carry him out of the fellowship hall.

Gabby shook her head. "Those boys of mine still act like a bunch of rowdy lumberjacks." She turned to Carol. "We'd love to have your mother join us at Crowning Oasis as well."

"I'm sure my mom would like that, and I appreciate you asking, but going to the spa and a wedding in one day might be too much to handle. She has to save her strength, but I'll tell Mom you thought of her."

Penny snapped one more picture and lowered the cell phone to her lap. "Spa? You mean one of those community bath houses?"

Giggles erupted around the table.

"But, they offer so many other wonderful services, Penny." Gabby cocked her head. "What's the matter? Don't you want to go with us?"

"Oh, I know all about those services, thank you very much." Penny's eyes narrowed. "Lena Mayes, from one of my book clubs, had their colonic irrigation, and it gave her nightmares for months. Do you think I want my colon Roto-Rootered again?" She gave a dramatic shiver, making her wheelchair squeak. "Of course I don't."

Millie tried to swallow her annoyance with her mother and threw Carol a questioning look. Her cousin responded with wide eyes and a tight-lipped smile.

"Roto-Rootered?" Gabby's laugh flooded the room. "Penny Drake, you are such a kidder. How do you come up with these things?"

Confusion surfaced on Penny's face before a spark of awareness flickered. She gave a slight tug on her turban and straightened her shoulders. "Lena also said they do things with hot wax that no woman over sixty should ever have to experience. Or endure."

Lively giggles followed. Penny glanced from one laughing lady to the next. Her mouth crinkled into a half-smile, then turned into a victorious grin.

Millie was . . . thunderstruck. Yes, that was the word. Thunderstruck. She tightly clenched Carol's hand. "Can you believe my mother is adding life to the party instead of snuffing it out?"

Carol whispered back. "I know. Who would have guessed?" She covered her mouth with her hand and snickered. "This proves miracles still happen."

She searched the room to catch her dad's reaction to this phenomenon. He stood slack-jawed beside an equally shocked Frank.

"Thank you for a wonderful rehearsal dinner, Mom Blythe." Millie gave Gabby a hug. "I love calling you that."

"It was my pleasure. Now, go home and rest up for tomorrow. I'll see you at the spa in the morning."

Lou leaned down and kissed the top of his mom's silver head. "I'm a lucky man, I have two women to love." He pulled Millie close. "Ready to go, Sweet Cheeks?"

She wrapped her arms around his waist. "Sure thing. Let's go."

They went to the van. He opened the door for her. "Do you realize this is the last time we'll be alone together before we're married?"

When Millie climbed in, her purse bumped a stack of mail onto the floor. She picked it up and her eyes darted to the feminine handwriting on the envelope sticking out from under her seat. A colorful foreign stamp decorated its top corner.

Lou scooted behind the steering wheel as she placed the mail on the dash.

"Would you look at that?" He tapped on the gas gauge. "We're driving on fumes. Glad I saw it before we ran out."

Millie's eyes homed in on the 5x7envelope with the Caribbean Breeze logo. It was marked: Do Not Bend. Could it be photos from someone on the cruise? Her curiosity burned and a lump rose her throat. The night seemed to grow darker around her, and a shiver surged down her spine. She fidgeted until they pulled into nearby station.

While Lou busied himself with the gas pump, Millie succumbed to the overwhelming temptation. She only wanted to see who it was from. She slowly pulled the colorful print out. Lou was standing behind Gemma. Young, beautiful Gemma. Turning the picture over, she read the words:

This was the day we walked on the shore of Dickenson Bay and you held me close.

I miss your arms around me, my sweet Lou. Give me a call when you're free.

Love always, Gemma

Millie frowned at the closing. Disbelief grew and her mouth went dry. She mentally kicked herself for invading his privacy. Her posture was as stiff as a flagpole as she stared out the windshield.

Trashing it would make it much easier to forget, but one thing Gabby had taught her was to meet problems head-on. Most situations weren't as bad as they seemed. She leaned on the armrest, held her forehead, and squeezed her eyes. Please, Lord, let that be the case. I love this man and can't imagine being without him.

The van door slammed shut, but her back remained rigid. How should she approach this? Last time they cancelled their engagement when the cruise director came for a visit and things got heated. Her stomach rolled. The night before their wedding was the worst possible time for this to happen.

"We're ready to go." He turned on the ignition. "Are you feeling okay?"

She studied his face for a reaction. "Lou, we need to talk."

"Did I do something wrong, again?"

"We need to go somewhere private." She fixed her gaze on the dashboard. "How about the park?"

"Sounds serious." He put the van in gear and headed for the local park. Car lights threw dim shadows into the van as he pulled to a stop and turned to face her. "Now, what's going on?"

"You haven't told me much about your cruise."

He shut off the ignition and cleared his throat. "What's on your mind?"

"Lou, I'm sorry, but I saw your picture of Gemma." She held up the envelope.

"Oh. That picture." He licked his lips. "It was her job to make the passengers feel welcome."

"Did she make everyone feel welcome or just you?" She waved the picture. "Let me put it another way. On a scale of one to ten, how welcome did you feel?"

He leaned his head back, closed his eyes, and took a deep breath. "I was feeling bad about leaving you the way I did. I stayed onboard, wrote you postcard after postcard, and tried to call. It was hard for me to sing in front of that many people and pretend I was happy. The guys couldn't cheer me up, so Gemma came to my rescue. She insisted I go with her to visit her friend in Oranjestad. She helped me pick out that locket for you."

Millie put her hand on the heart-shaped necklace. She would not be wearing it tomorrow.

"It was a while before I figured out why I liked her so much. She reminded me of you."

"A young, beautiful blonde child reminded you of me?"

"Gemma's not a child. She's twenty-seven."

A note of frustration crept into her voice. "And she reminded you of me because...?"

"You may not be blonde, but you're still young and beautiful to me. Gemma is a sweet, caring, and sensitive lady. She's easy to be with, like you."

"That all sounds good, but you're holding her in this picture. And she wrote about you holding her tight on the beach. Why would she send this when she knows we're engaged?"

"You might want to look at the postmark on the envelope. It was sent a week after I got home and must've slid under the seat." He hesitated. "Millie, I had to make a decision before getting off the ship." He took the picture from her, tore it up, and kissed her lips. I chose you, for the rest of my life. Forgive me?"

His pleading eyes quieted her uneasiness and a satisfying wave of comfort washed over her. Gemma wasn't the threat she had imagined. "Yes, I'm sorry for snooping through your mail and doubting again. The question is, do you forgive me?"

Lou leaned over the van's console and gently cradled her face. "Of course I do."

I love you, and only you." Her face heated as they pressed their lips together.

CHAPTER TWENTY-SEVEN

Spa day - morning of wedding

MILLIE PUSHED HER MOTHER'S WHEELCHAIR ASIDE and knocked on the dressing room door at Crowning Oasis Spa. "Don't worry, Mother. I gave them your wig when we first arrived. They promised to have it styled the way you want it."

The silence that followed indicated the woman wasn't buying it.

"Come on, Mother, you look nice in your silky turban. Nobody will say anything about your hair loss." She looked heavenward and took a deep breath. "Let's go and please keep a good attitude. The hostess and the others are waiting on us."

"It isn't my turban or my painted eyebrows that bother me. This place is overrated, Millicent." The voice from inside the dressing room whined. "I'm going home."

"I'm sorry, but no one is going to get dressed to take you home. So, tell me what's wrong?" Millie clenched her teeth. The day had barely started and the first meltdown loomed on the horizon.

"Look at this enormous robe on me. It's dangerous." Her mother opened the slatted door and tugged at the turban on her head. The sleeves of her terrycloth robe draped over the handles of the walker, and the hem nearly touched her slippers. "I'm afraid I'll fall getting into my wheelchair, and the extra fabric will get hung up in the wheels."

"You only have to wear it until they find a smaller one. Let me roll up your sleeves. Maybe if we tie the belt and blouse the top a little?" Millie held her breath and motioned for Gabby to join them. If her mother was hassled too much, she'd blow a fuse.

"What's the holdup?" Gabby gently nudged Millie aside and poked her head into Penny's compartment. "Is there a problem in here?"

"This is ridiculous." Penny stared in the mirror and gathered the heavy material of her oversized robe. She whimpered. "I'm afraid I'll fall and break a hip or something."

Gabby looked directly into Penny's eyes and lowered her voice. "The hostess promised to bring a smaller one as soon as possible." She looked at her watch. "I've ordered the deluxe package for all of us, and it began twenty minutes ago. You have a choice of joining us or hiding in here until your robe comes."

Penny's stenciled eyebrows rose above her red-framed glasses. Millie gave her a hand, and within a few seconds, Penny managed to settle into the wheelchair. Carol and the Blythe ladies had congregated outside the dressing room.

"Why did I have to get a double X?" Penny shrugged and readjusted the robe. "This thing probably came from Acme Tent and Awning."

Giggles erupted from Millie's future sisters-in-law. Patty Blythe snorted and jabbed Carol's rib. "Isn't she a scream? This is going to be a wild day."

Penny's lips quivered into a smile. She gave the sash on her robe an extra tug and then rolled her chair into the middle of the crowd.

Kit, the skeletal spa hostess, smiled. "I'm sorry, Mrs. Drake. Double X was the only size left. The Three Sheets in the Wind laundry truck hasn't arrived with the fresh ones, yet. It should be here soon. Would you all follow me, please?"

Her blue Crowning Oasis shirt with a palm tree logo perfectly matched the blue and green stripes of her tall Mohawk haircut. The odd hairdo fluttered with each step as she led them into the opulent salon area. "It looks like the mani-pedi team is running a little behind. Why don't you enjoy the fruit and juice bar in our lounge while you wait?" She pointed to the double floor-to-ceiling windows. "There's a beautiful view of Bravura Lake."

The seven-woman entourage paraded through the spa's fragrant ambiance to the lounge. Their matching scuffs lightly flapped in sync on the tile floor until they paused to admire a fountain featuring Michelangelo's statue of David in the center of the salon.

"Don't look, Millicent Marie!" Penny jerked her daughter away from the sculpture. "You're not married, yet."

Millie shook her head and grinned. "Oh, Mother, please. I've seen worse on the covers of your romance novels."

The room grew quiet. Penny's mouth snapped shut, and her cheeks turned flamingo-pink as she fiddled with the pocket of her gargantuan robe.

"You know I love you." Millie kissed her mother's forehead. "Let's have a little fun together before I get married."

Gabby winked at Penny and reached for her hand. "C'mon, girls. Let's kick back some juice before Kit comes for us."

Carol grabbed Millie's arm as the others shuffled to the juice bar. "Well, that had to be embarrassing. I'm proud of you for standing up for yourself."

"I'm learning." She grinned. "It felt good."

"It was an awkward situation but you were able to

laugh along with everyone. The peck on her forehead rendered her speechless. Good job." Carol gave her a thumbs-up.

"Gabby's helping me cope by using humor and reaching out to Mother. She says Mother's rudeness doesn't reflect on me, and I don't have to be her victim anymore." Millie smiled. "She also pointed out my great support system, especially you, Dad, and Lou."

"Good for you." Carol turned her head. "I see Gabby's waving at us."

As they approached the group, Tara called from the enormous window. "Look at this amazing view of the lake. It's a perfect backdrop for pictures."

Gabby rounded up the ladies and situated them by height. "I want the bride in front between her mother and me. The rest of you huddle around us." She raised her cell phone. "Squeeze in a little closer, Patty. All together now, say . . . honeymoon!"

"Honeymoon!"

The other guests in the lounge turned their heads to gawk at the group. One woman yelled a hearty congratulation.

Tara pointed to the other window. "Let's get pictures of Millie and her mom over there so we can use the scenery as a backdrop."

Penny clutched Millie's hand. "Millicent, I want you to stand in front of me and hide this ugly robe and wheelchair."

"I will, Mother. Just relax and smile." She rolled the chair to the window and waited for Tara's directions.

"That's good. Okay, get ready, on the count of three . . . one, two, three!"

Right on cue, the other ladies raised their cell phones and clicked in rapid succession.

Patty giggled. "Look, girls. I caught the statue's

reflection in the window. Sorry Millie, you can't see it until your reception. Mother's orders."

"I have David in mine too." Kate gave her phone to Millie. "Don't worry, Penny. Your headgear makes it discreet."

Kit appeared in the doorway holding a robe. "I'm sorry you had to wait so long, ladies. The team is ready for you now." She handed the robe to Penny. "Mrs. Drake, this is smaller than the one you're wearing. I'm sorry for the inconvenience. Let me show you to the powder room around the corner, and I'll help you change."

"We'll wait here for you, Penny." Gabby motioned for the others to have a seat. "This won't take long."

When Penny returned in a smaller robe, they followed Kit into a bright room with eight pedicure chairs, four on each side, facing each other. Each chair had a small tub connected to the foot of it.

Kit placed her hand on the shoulder of an attractive blonde who came to greet them. "This is Becca, our head nail tech. Her team will be pampering you today. I'll be back when your nails are done."

Relief washed over Millie as she studied Becca. Same pastel shirt as Kit, but that's where the similarities ended. Her pageboy haircut gave her a down-to-earth aura, and she appeared better fed than her emaciated colleague.

The nail tech smiled. "'Bye, Kit." She turned to the group. "First, we'll have each of you choose your nail color."

Gabby stepped next to Millie. "You're the bride, sweetheart, why don't you choose the color so we can all have matching fingers and toes."

Millie perused the gamut of polychromatic options and selected a delicate pink, sure to match her attendants' dresses.

"Great." Becca's eyes glimmered. "Frosted Pink-alicious is one of our most popular shades with brides. You may all have a seat and remove your slippers. Put your feet into the tubs of bubbling, scented water, and relax. The team will be with you soon." She moved Penny's wheelchair to the end of the row. "You can stay in your chair, Mrs. Drake. We'll bring a special soaking tub for you."

Millie settled into her seat, removed the white slippers, and dunked her feet into the water. She waved for Carol to sit in the chair next to her.

When Gabby seated herself on end chair next to Penny, Millie breathed a sigh of relief. It was reassuring to know someone was looking after Mother. Millie loved Gabby even more.

"Before you sit down, bring me one of those magazines beside you, Carol."

She reached to the narrow counter beside her and held up an issue of Better Homes and Gardens. "How about this one, Aunt Penny?"

"I suppose that will have to do."

Carol raised her feet from the sweet-smelling water and took three dripping steps to her aunt's chair.

"You're getting water all over the floor." Irritation crossed Penny's face.

"Don't worry, honey." Becca came running to Carol's rescue. "We always have plenty of extra towels."

Penny turned to Gabby. "My stars! Did you see the awful toenails on my niece? They're the most hideous things." She raised her weak voice. "Don't you ever trim them?"

Carol blinked and padded back to her chair.

"That wasn't very nice, Mother."

Leaning closer to Penny, Gabby's stern voice broke the silence. "Penelope Drake. Stop it. That was rude. We want to keep this day pleasant and civil for all of us, but especially for Millie."

Tension crackled like a downed power line. Tara and Kate shrunk in their seats and looked at each other, eyes bulging.

Embarrassment colored Penny's face as she opened her mouth and quickly shut it.

Getting along with the testy woman was like dealing with a temperamental child, and Millie was a happy witness to her mother's verbal spanking.

"I guess my nails are pretty long." Carol shrugged. "I haven't had a chance to work on them since Frank hid the hedge trimmers."

Patty quickly stuck her feet into her tub of water. "Don't look at mine, ladies. My talonesque claws look like I could swoop over Bravura Lake and snag a trout."

An unprotected giggle escaped Millie's throat at the image of Patty snatching a fish from the lake. Bless Carol and Patty for diverting attention away from Mother's rude remark.

Seven nail techs walked into the room and took their seats at the foot of each chair. Their blue spa shirts were color coordinated with their sterile masks, which hung below their chins.

The tech with a red ponytail smiled at Millie. "Hello, Miss Drake. My name is Erin, and I'll be doing your nails today. Are there any areas of concern, like ingrown toenails, athlete's foot, corns, or calluses?"

"Not that I'm aware of."

"That's what I like to hear." Erin flipped the switch on the massage chair and pulled her mask over her nose and mouth. Her red ponytail bobbed as she diligently trimmed and filed Millie's nails.

"This massage chair feels great." Millie wiggled into a better position as Erin scrubbed her heels with a pumice stone.

An hour later, blue and green-haired Kit, the anorexic hostess, came into the room. "I hope you ladies enjoyed your mani-pedis." She tilted her head and glanced around the room. "It's time for lunch, so let me show you to the food court."

They followed her into a rounded glass elevator flanked on both sides by curved marble stairs. Kit's boney index finger hit the second-floor button while the ladies watched the amazing view of sailboats gliding across Bravura Lake. The elevator stopped and doors opened.

Kit checked her watch. "You have about a half hour to eat before our lead cosmetologist and coiffeuse, Ilah Kapree, escorts you back to the salon for your facials."

They ate their lunch of garden salad, fruit cups, and green tea smoothies. Gabby and Penny were deep in conversation as they sat together at a nearby table. Penny pushed her cup of untouched fruit away, sipped at her smoothie, and brought the napkin to her lips.

At the end of their meal, Gabby stood. "Do this for your daughter, Penny. You won't be sorry." She gathered their disposable tableware and threw it in the trash.

Millie was shocked her mother didn't come back with a biting remark.

They all managed to freshen up in the posh powder room before Ilah came to take them to the salon.

"Congratulations to the bride." The dark-haired beauty looked like a youthful Sophia Loren when she smiled at Millie. "I'm sure she's eager to get on with her big day, so if you'll follow me, we can get started on the next phase of your spa experience."

While the others passed, Carol stepped aside to wait for Millie. "How are you holding up, Mills?"

"I'm fine, all things considered." Her hand went to Carol's arm. "Have you noticed Mother's been quiet since lunch?"

"I wonder what Gabby was talking about when she left the table?" Carol repeated Gabby's words. "Do this for your daughter. Sounds ominous."

Before Millie could answer, they rounded the corner to the salon.

Kit gestured to the row of cream-colored padded chairs. "Please have a seat, ladies. My cosmetology team is ready to apply your mint julep masque, and you'll be given twenty minutes to relax in your massage chair." She sent a concerned look to Penny. "I'll send someone to help you into a seat."

After the women tilted back in their chairs, the spa team smoothed cool, wet masques on their faces. It reminded Millie of gooey wallpaper paste. Cucumber slices covered their eyes following the masques.

Millie squirmed in her chair to get comfortable. The thought of her mother's silence resurfaced. Was she storing up her frustrations to explode later? *Dear Heavenly Father, please use this time to breakdown the wall around Mother's heart. Only You can make a lasting difference in her life. Give me peace of mind as we prepare for my wedding, and let our marriage stay rooted in Your love. I pray in the name of Your Son, Jesus Christ, amen.*

A timer rang, and the staff removed the cucumber slices before the mint-julepped faces were unmasqued.

Penny grabbed a mirror from the counter and turned her head from side to side, batting her eyes. "Gabby! Look at this. My crow's feet have been minimized to crow's toes. Check it out."

"Where's my hand mirror?" Gabby found it and squinted at her reflection. "Wonder if this mint julep comes in industrial strength? I'd be happy to buy a couple of gallons."

Giggles turned into guffaws peppered with snorts.

"Maybe this place isn't overrated after all." Penny's eye

fluttering continued. "I can't wait to get my hair back on and go home before the magic fades. Stuart won't be able to keep his hands off me."

"Mother, please!" Millie's hands covered her ears. "Let's not go there."

Gabby's infectious laugh rippled through the room. "Shame on you, Penny. Have you forgotten she's not married, yet?"

Millie held her breath. How would her mother take the good-natured ribbing?

"Touché." Continuing to look at her reflection from side to side, Penny winked and placed a hand over her mouth to stifle a rare giggle.

A lump lodged in Millie's throat. Despite the disease, her mother's face seemed ten years younger when she relaxed and smiled.

Ilah returned and put her arm on the back of Millie's chair. "This sounds like a happy group. How would you like your hair done for the wedding? Will you have a traditional veil, a hat, or anything on your head?"

"I'll have a small veil pinned to the back of my head, so I'd like to have the sides pulled back from my face. That won't be too youthful, will it?"

"Not at all. You'll be a gorgeous bride. Your dark eyes are beautiful."

"Thanks so much."

Before the coiffeuse could reply, Penny piped in. "I hope my wig has retained its poofy hairstyle."

Ilah smiled. "I think we'll be able to please you both."

Within two hours, the women had their makeup completed, and all but Penny had their hair done. They gathered around as the stylist carefully positioned Penny's poofy wig on her head. Millie kept a close eye on her mother's face. What were the chances that her mother would be satisfied with the outcome?

A fog rose around Penny with one final blast of hairspray. As the haze lifted, she looked in the mirror, and her stern expression collapsed and softened.

The hairdresser stood back and smiled. "What do you think, Mrs. Drake?"

Everyone applauded and Gabby scurried to Penny's side. "You look positively stunning, my friend!"

Tears formed in Penny's eyes as she smiled at her beautician. "It's perfect, and so is my makeup." She turned to Millie. "Look, they gave me eyelashes. I've never felt so gorgeous."

"You really are, Mother. Let's take a selfie together."

Everyone pulled out their cells to capture the happy moment.

A glance at the wall clock and Millie panicked. "We'd better hustle. The wedding is in three hours."

The ladies quickly headed to their dressing rooms.

Patty hooked Gabby's arm. "Best bachelorette party ever, Mom Blythe."

CHAPTER TWENTY-EIGHT

MILLIE QUICKLY SLIPPED INTO HER WEDDING shoes, gathered her post-wedding outfit, and put it into her rolling suitcase. Her breath caught at the sheer magnitude at how her life was changing.

Dear Diary,

Can you believe this is my last journal entry as a single woman? I'm so excited my hands are shaking. In a couple of hours, Lou will be waiting at the altar to become my darling husband. It must be official because Mother just gave me the wedding night talk.

Who could've guessed that I, Millicent Marie Drake, would become a part of a devoted, caring family? God is using the Blythes to change all the negative pieces of my former life into joy, love, and acceptance. The happiness it brings me is incredible.

Mother loved to quote the old adage, if something is too good to be true, then it probably is. But Mother didn't have a personal relationship with the Lord. I've found that makes all the difference. Today, I noticed more than ever the quality of her life is slipping away.

Dear Lord, I'm trusting the Holy Spirit to help my mother give her heart completely to You before it's too late.

Please bless Gabby and the family I'm

about to join. Help me to be a blessing to them too.

Millie got out of Carol's car when they arrived at Apache Pointe Community Church. She took a deep breath of the fresh April air. The fragrance was like the promise of spring.

The choir room at the church was large enough to make the perfect dressing room for Millie and her four bridal attendants.

Standing in front of the full-length mirror, Millie admired Aunt Sylvia's pearl necklace against her chiffon lace wedding dress. She added the matching earrings. Here she was, on the most important day of her life, the day she'd been longing for since she was a little girl in pigtails. God had given her the desires of her heart.

"You're so beautiful in your gown, Mills. Let's put your veil on." Carol secured the length of tulle, grinned, and lowered her voice to a whisper. "I'm glad you didn't get that medieval style your mom suggested."

"I know. The dunce cap with a dangling veil was a little over the top." Millie grabbed her cousin's arm. "Although, Lou's reaction was priceless when Mother informed him about the tunic and tights he'd have to wear."

"That would've been a sight." Carol laughed. "How did you dodge that bullet?"

"Mother was happy once I threw her a bone and let her choose the color scheme. I can deal with pink one more time."

The photographer strolled through the feminine maize. He snapped candid shots along with the usual posed photos. The bride's attendants lined up and shifted positions from one side to the other until he was finally pleased.

"Let's get a shot of the lovely bride with the bridesmaids and the mothers in a group hug." He lowered his camera. "Where's the mother-of-the-bride?"

Gabby pointed across the room. "She was getting tired, so I pushed her chair next to the window."

There was a shuffle as everyone turned to where Gabby pointed. Penny hugged her purse as she sat hunched over in her wheelchair. The folds of her former double chin sagged and nearly touched her chest as she snored softly. The bright pink feathers of her lopsided hat fluttered with each breath.

The photographer chuckled and quickly snapped the camera. "You'll want to remember this."

Tara's dimples pierced her cheeks as she went to Penny's side. "Aww, the spa wore her out this morning. She's sound asleep."

Penny's head popped up. "No, I'm not. I was only resting my eyes."

The photographer lowered his camera and a perplexed grin settled across his features. "First, if you ladies are ready, let's have you gather around the wheelchair for that group hug. Then we need to take photos of you lining up for the processional."

Gabby leaned in to straighten the feathers and veil on Penny distinctive hat. "Okay, we're ready. Everyone, pose for the camera."

Once the man lowered his camera, Penny clapped her hands. "This is it, girls, get your bouquets. We're going to take our positions quietly at the sanctuary door. Pinch your cheeks, suck in your stomachs, and smile." She pursed her thin lips. "I'll be watching."

Millie turned to Carol and lowered her voice. "Here we go, again. Somebody needs to get a tranquilizer gun and put her out of our misery."

"Everything's going to be fine, Mills." Carol patted her shoulder as the entourage rushed from the room. "Remember, Lou's waiting for you at the altar."

Millie dabbed her eyes feeling incredibly anxious and wildly happy all at once. She nodded. "And I'm so ready to get married."

When they caught up with the bridesmaids in the hall, Millie heard three members of Lou's group, The Warble-Heirs, crooning, *I Can't Help Falling in Love with You.* The ceremony had begun.

"Just think," Carol whispered. "In a few minutes, you're going to be an old married lady, like me."

Millie's legs wouldn't stop trembling. In the vestibule, a familiar voice was growling last minute orders. Millie was sure she was going to be sick right in front of everyone.

"We can't have this, Stuart. Tuck in your shirt. I expect you to smile and be pleasant. Bend down here and let me fix your lopsided boutonniere." Penny peered over her red-rimmed glasses. "Did Carol make these chintzy things? Who am I kidding? Of course she did. I suppose all the men have the same problem with their lapel flower."

Gabby put her hand on the back of Penny's wheelchair. "Don't stress over something insignificant."

"Insignificant?" Penny threw her hands up. "Our photographs are going to be hideous."

"Forget about the pictures, Penny." Gabby's silvery white hair bobbed as she shook her head. "It's time to take our places up front." She hooked arms with her son, Bart's, and took her mother-of-the-groom walk down the aisle.

With her no-nonsense attitude intact, Penny adjusted her pink, feathered hat, and straightened her shoulders against the back of the wheelchair. Nick slowly wheeled her to the second pew from the front.

Once the mothers were in place, Pastor Frank nodded to Bart and Nick as they found their positions next to Lou and Spence.

It was time for the trio of bridesmaids. Kate, Patty, and Tara, dressed in pink strapless gowns, lined up on the other side of the altar.

With a final squeeze to Millie's shaky hand, Carol walked down the aisle under Frank's steady gaze.

The organ music changed to announce the bride.

The congregation stood as Millie and her dad stepped into the sanctuary and slowly made their way to the front. The photographer's camera flashed with every other step they took. Low chuckles followed Millie all the way to the altar.

The wedding march abruptly stopped on an off-note, and a loud moan erupted from the front pew, bride's side.

Millie clenched her teeth. She'd know that moan anywhere. Mother had to jump at every opportunity to direct attention to herself. Well played, Mother.

Bearded Bart, Spence with a space, and thick-necked Nick doubled over in laughter as they took pictures with their cell phones.

"Remove that beast!" Penny beat on the arm of her wheelchair. "Get him out, Stuart, get him out!"

At least Mother didn't call him a Neanderthal. Millie caught a glimpse of her groom's pale face. Lou nervously licked his lips, and his bulging eyes gravitated to the floor. Was he getting cold feet? Would he leave her at the altar?

The photographer snapped more pictures.

Trying to maintain a semblance of calm amid confusion, Millie gulped and stared at him. Her groom was kissing the air. Not wanting to disappoint him, she blew a kiss back.

Lou approached his bride, put one hand on her elbow, and turned her toward the basset hound behind her.

"Farfel heard there was going to be cake."

Millie's face warmed as she laughed into her hands. "Glad you could make it, Farfel."

"I think the excitement has calmed down." Frank took a deep breath. "Who gives this woman to be married to this man?"

Farfel gave his consent with a resounding. "Bow-Bow-Bow!"

Stuart cleared his throat. "Her mother and I do too." He lifted Millie's veil, kissed her cheek, and shook Lou's hand.

A few chuckles sounded as the bride, groom, and best dog stepped closer to Pastor Frank.

With a nod, the pastor continued. "We are gathered here today in the sight of God and the presence of loved ones, to celebrate and give recognition to the beauty of love. We shall witness the vows uniting Millicent Marie Drake and Louis Elliot Blythe in holy matrimony. Millie and Lou, please join hands."

Millie handed her oversized bouquet of pink roses and baby's breath to Carol. At the moment of handoff, her mother's award-winning sobs ricocheted off the sanctuary walls.

Despite the sound effects from the front pew, the remainder of the ceremony passed without incident. Finally, Frank's voice rang out. "Lou, you may kiss your bride."

After lifting her veil, Lou's arm went around Millie's waist. He whispered so only she could hear. "I love you, Mrs. Blythe." His lips covered hers.

CHAPTER TWENTY-NINE

In the vestibule, the Drakes and Blythes formed a receiving line to greet their guests. Millie put her arm through Lou's. "I can't believe we're actually married."

He pushed a lock of hair from her eyes and his finger trailed down the side of her face. "I've never seen you look so beautiful."

Friends and family members slowly filed by offering their congratulations and best wishes. Millie noticed her mother sitting in her wheelchair, pouting. As usual, something didn't meet the approval of the Grand ol' Duchess.

When the last guest headed for the fellowship hall, her mother's face twisted into a tight-lipped scowl as she veered her chair closer to Millie. "Let your mother fix the back of your dress, Millicent." She issued the order, motioning for her to turn. "It bagged all through the ceremony and nearly drove me crazy. That's what you get for letting Carol talk you into buying a cheap frock from Benny's Bargain Basement."

"It was Benny's Bridal Boutique." Millie was determined not to let her mother's oppressive attitude ruin the joy of her wedding day.

In an instant, Gabby came from behind them, and there was no missing the determination in her voice. "Everyone has commented on how beautiful your gown is, Millie. You couldn't have chosen a more perfect dress." She kissed her cheek. "Where's my son?"

"Right behind you, Momma." Lou squeezed the older

woman's shoulder against his chest.

"Why don't you and Millie join the others?" Gabby pointed down the hallway. "You have a cake to cut and the photographer wants to take more pictures. I'll see to Penny's needs."

Millie kissed her new husband's jaw, raised the hem of her dress above her shoes, and led him into the fellowship hall where Lou's group was singing a medley of love songs in the background.

As he hummed the tune in her ear, she closed her eyes and leaned back against him. She thought of how her life had changed so quickly.

It was here, just over a year ago, Lou got brave enough to kiss her cheek for the first time. Not long after, Mother had brainwashed her into thinking another man was her destiny. Since then Millie discovered dreams change, and the paths her mother picked for her weren't the ones God had in mind.

When the group finished their set, the lead singer, Lonnie Chandler, faced the crowd. "Ladies and gentlemen, please give a warm welcome to Mr. and Mrs. Lou Blythe."

With hands clasped tightly together, the bride and groom bowed to the applauding well-wishers.

Lou took the mic from his friend. "Thank you for joining us today. Everyone here has a special place in our hearts." He kissed Millie's forehead. "My wife—" He grinned. "I like the sound of that. My wife and I have a flight to catch, so we won't be able to celebrate with you very long. Please take time to enjoy the food and each other's company. Again, thank you and God bless."

Recorded background music played softly as they went to the serving table. The cake was adorned with lattice hearts and, as Lou quipped, enough pink frosting roses to enter the Rose Bowl Parade. Cameras clicked as the couple inserted the knife into the cake and gave each other the first bite.

At their feet sat a salivating hound, begging for his share of wedding cake. Lou shoveled a generous slice to a paper plate, and set in on the floor next to Farfel.

Lou's arm went around Millie. He lowered his voice. "I'm going to ask Dooley to take the dog home right away. After all, he's the one who brought Farfel to church in the first place." He grinned. "That rascal owes me."

A few minutes after Lou returned, Millie caught Uncle Max motioning to her. She nodded, grabbed her groom's hand, and headed in that direction.

"This was a lovely wedding, Millie." Max stood and kissed her cheek. "I'm sorry, but it's time to get my sweetheart home."

Millie crouched beside her aunt at the table. "Thanks for coming, Aunt Syl. I'm glad you were both able to join us. It means a lot for you to be here. Be sure to take some cake home with you."

The older woman patted her hand.

"You're a great match." Max pumped Lou's hand. "I'm confident the two of you will have a wonderful life together."

Lou put his arm around Millie's shoulders. "Thanks, sir."

"You're family, so you can call me Uncle Max."

The newlyweds escorted Max and Sylvia to their car in the church's covered drive close to the east exit.

"So p-proud of you, dear." Sylvia's eyes shone with love. "We p-pray for you."

"You're very special to me, Aunt Syl. Thank you for loaning me your pearls." She leaned over and kissed the wrinkled cheek, then waved good-bye.

"Maybe we should get back to our guests, honey." Lou held the church door open for Millie.

Gabby's heels clicked on the tile floor as she came

their way. "Go on to the reception, Son. I want to borrow your bride for a few minutes."

"What's up, Mom? Anything I can do?"

"Not right now. Millie and I need to speak to her mother. We'll join you soon."

When he left, she ushered Millie into a nearby classroom where her mother awaited. She closed the door. "Penny, your remarks to Millie were selfish and cruel. You've put on the appearance of attitude adjustments lately, but maybe you've done it for the wrong reasons."

"Wrong reasons? What are you talking about?"

"There needs to be a heart change and not only a surface change. God promises to take away our stony heart and give us a new spirit." Gabby put her arm on Penny's shoulder. "You know I love you, but I have to ask, are you a Christian?"

"I'll have you know I have been a member of this church for over forty years." Penny crossed her arms. "How dare you ask me such a question?"

"But have you ever asked Jesus into your heart?"

"Stuart said he wouldn't marry me unless I was a Christian."

"Did you ask God to forgive your sins?"

Penny's eyes narrowed and her mouth twitched as if a retort was imminent. She leaned back into her wheelchair.

Prayers filled Millie's mind while waiting for her mother's response, which thankfully never came.

Gabby sat in the next chair and cleared her throat. "We've all done things in our past we're not proud of." Her voice was soft and sincere.

"What have I done that's so bad?"

"Mother, your past has made you angry and judgmental." Millie couldn't believe the boldness she displayed. "You say wicked things that hurt and demean people."

"I was taught to speak my mind. My father abused me until I left home, and I'm not about to let anyone else do the same."

Gabby rested her elbows on the table and looked directly at Penny. "But you're behaving the same way as your father." Her tone was mellow, but the rebuke was obvious.

Penny's face whitened and jaw dropped. "What?"

"Taking out your anger on others before they hurt you is what your father did."

"I've never hit anyone in my life." Penny's voice choked. Her back was stiff as she crossed her arms.

Gabby's eyes closed. "Maybe not, but you of all people should know, hateful words cut into hearts and stay there. For every negative thing you say, it takes six positive comments to mend that one hurt."

"Have I honestly hurt you that way, Millicent Marie?" Penny threw a questioning stare at her daughter.

Millie tried to swallow the growing lump in her throat. She hesitated, unsure of how to answer. A brutal burn ignited in her stomach. It was time to stop hiding and face her mother with the truth. Finally, she nodded.

"Both of you have been internalizing the pain of abuse for years." Gabby sent them a look of compassion. "It's time to release all of the pent-up hurt, anger, and frustration into God's capable hands."

Silence engulfed the room. Her mother's face took on a faraway look as if she was seeing ghosts of a long-ago past. Repentant tears flooded her eyes and a remorseful sob left her throat giving the appearance of an abandoned child.

"I didn't realize I had become as mean as my father. Can you ever forgive me?" With a resigned look, Penny placed her hand in Millie's and gave it a surprisingly strong squeeze.

"You know I do, Mother." Millie kissed her wet cheek. "I love you."

"Gabby's been helping me try to control my tongue lately, but things happen and angry words come flying out." Tears formed as she covered her face. "It's no use. I don't know how to change."

"We can't master some things on our own." Gabby's gentle spirit offered hope. "We need Divine Intervention. If we ask Jesus to forgive us, He does, and then He gives us power to fight negative thoughts and actions."

"I need His help." Penny bowed her head.

This was something Millie hadn't expected on her wedding day. Her heart raced as she witnessed her mother humbled before the Lord.

"Let's pray." Gabby took Penny's hand. "Repeat after me. Dear Heavenly Father, I'm a sinner in need of Your forgiveness."

Penny broke down as she echoed the words.

"I believe You died for my sins and rose from the dead . . ." Gabby waited for Penny's response before continuing. ". . . I accept You as my Lord and Savior . . . and trust You to guide my life . . . Please help me to do Your will . . . In Your name, amen."

Tears flowed as the three women embraced.

The pain in Penny's eyes changed to hope. Her face glowed as she lifted her chin and allowed new confidence and joy to shine through. "I feel so free. I never knew it could be like this." She clapped her hands and laughed.

"I'm so happy, Mother, and very proud of you." Millie leaned over and gave her a tight hug and another kiss. "This is the best wedding gift I could've hoped for."

"Praise the Lord." Gabby wiped the tears and shared a quick smile. "And now, my beautiful daughter-in-law, you need to get back to your husband and guests."

Millie looked at her watch. "Oh, my! Lou and I have to

leave for the airport in a few minutes. I need to say goodbye to everyone." She leaned over and hugged her mother. "My wedding and your salvation. This has been an unforgettable day." She grabbed the doorknob. "'Bye, Mother. 'Bye, Mom Blythe."

As she scurried from the room, Lou approached and took her arm. "Do you know what time it is? I was coming to get you."

"I have a good reason for deserting you." She grinned as they made a mad dash to the reception hall. "Believe it or not, Mother just gave her heart to the Lord."

"What? Really?"

"It's true." Millie vigorously nodded. "I witnessed it all."

"That's amazing. What a great wedding gift." Lou planted a kiss on her cheek. "It's time to leave if we want to make our flight."

"We really need to say a quick thank you to everyone before we go."

They joined their friends and relatives and gave thanks, hugs, and kisses to everyone within reach.

Lou took the mic, tapped it, and pulled Millie to his side. "My beautiful bride and I have a flight to catch. We tried to greet everyone, but if we didn't get to you, thanks for coming to share our special day."

Her dad led them to the church door and the others followed.

Millie dabbed her eyes and tightly hugged him. "Go talk to Mother. Don't worry, it's wonderful. Thank you for the nice wedding and reception. You've been a great father and spiritual leader in our home. Where would I be if you hadn't allowed God to use you?"

Stuart dug out his hanky and wiped his eyes. "You'll always be my special Princess." He embraced her again.

"Thank you for everything, sir." Lou shook Stuart's hand. "You're in our prayers."

"Quick!" Spence yelled. "Grab your bubbles and line up outside before they get away!"

Millie and Lou managed to sneak a kiss while the others stampeded to either side of the carport. She smiled when Gabby wheeled her mother to the front of the line.

The car pulled up, decorated with balloons and Just Married written on the back window. Pastor Frank honked and rolled down his window. "Jump in. Carol and I are taking you to the airport in style."

Following them was a jeep, driven by bearded Bart with Andy riding shotgun. Spence with a space and thick-necked Nick hollered from the backseat.

Millie proudly glanced at her new husband sitting beside her. "Isn't it great to be chauffeured?" When his gaze met hers, she realized her need to escape to fantasyland was over.

His face held a sheepish grin. "Do you like your new name?"

"Mrs. Lou Blythe. Mrs. Millie Blythe. Mrs. Millicent Marie Blythe. I love it."

His eyes glowed with an intense love that sent her heart racing. "That's nice, but what about Mrs. Sweet Cheeks Blythe?"

CHAPTER THIRTY

Late-May

MILLIE STOOD WITH HANDS ON HER hips, surveying her mother's beloved pink and white dream kitchen. It seemed strange to create a full meal without the Grand ol' Duchess watching over her shoulder. Millie grinned. What would Mother do if she knew Farfel was in her pristine kitchen?

The basset hound sat behind her on a large throw rug, tongue hanging out, and a hungry look in his eyes. She was learning to read his distinctive personality.

She looked at the wall clock. Dad and Lou would be here in four hours. Where did Mother keep her slow cooker? Fortunately, the second cabinet on the left yielded the small appliance, among the rest of her electrical cookware.

Once she had supper started, Millie, followed by Farfel, climbed the stairs to her old bedroom to begin the wearisome process of sorting through her belongings and packing keepsakes to take back to her new home. Of course starting a throw away pile was inevitable. The dog did his best to sniff or sneeze on each item.

She pulled a box from the back of her closet and unfolded the flaps. One could only imagine what horrors lurked inside the tightly packed carton. On the very top was her dark green gym suit from her freshman year of high school.

She held it up. The atrocity had an elastic waist and

leg bands, causing the rear end of the athletic wear to balloon out. The whole gym class looked like a flock of Daisy Ducks. It was first into the trash heap. Her old 1980s retainer was a quick second. She shuddered. What an unglamorous decade. For everybody in general, but for her in particular.

Millie tossed Victoria, her old fake diary, into the trash. It had served its purpose. She remembered her real diary hiding inside her hollow closet door. She scooted her desk chair around the sleeping dog and to the closet to retrieve the book.

She sat at her desk, picked up her pen, and opened the journal to a fresh page.

> Dear Diary,
>
> I haven't had time to write since my wedding day. So much has happened in our family since March. It seems more like two years have passed instead of only two months.
>
> There are a couple of beautiful reasons why I'll never forget that first Saturday in April. First, I married the love of my life and became Mrs. Louis Elliot Blythe . . . Mrs. Millicent Marie Blythe . . . Mrs. Sweet Cheeks Blythe.
>
> Lou is the sweetest, most attentive, and selfless husband in the world. He loads the dishwasher and even puts the seat down. His momma raised him well. He didn't complain once when we decided to postpone our honeymoon cruise due to Mother's failing health and funeral. Instead, we spent a long weekend in Tucson.
>
> We'll be going on the cruise in eight weeks, for my birthday. Last year, that day ended with Lou walking out and the start of a miserable

time. This year we're married and my birthday will be remembered as the beginning of our honeymoon and happy memories. What a difference a year makes.

The most important thing that happened on our wedding day is Mother asked the Lord to forgive her for hurting so many people because of her anger. Not only that, but she became a completely new person in Christ. A warm, loving heart replaced her cold, negative demeanor and we were there to witness this miracle. I've marked 2 Corinthians 5:17 in my Bible. "Therefore if any man be in Christ, he is a new creature: old things are passed away; behold, all things are become new."

Gabby gave Mother and Dad a beautiful wedding vow renewal and reception. It was Mother's last request. Dad was happy to go through with the ceremony. He said she had become a brand new bride. Gabby caught the bouquet.

The Lord blessed me with six wonderful weeks of caring for Mother before she died. We cleared a lifetime of cobwebs and skeletons and forgave pain and disappointments. The first forty-three years of my life, she never once said she loved me, but the last forty-three days of her life, she told me over and over. Her tears of repentance that fell on my shoulders were honest and sincere.

I've never seen such a remarkable change in one person. God truly worked a miracle in her life.

After three additional hours of sorting and tossing,

Millie caught a whiff of their pot roast supper. Her dad and Lou would be here soon. She stood and glanced at Farfel, who was sleeping on his own pile of discarded treasures.

The dog ignored her as she scooted boxes into the hallway. The guys could take them to the trash while she set the table and heated the dinner rolls.

"Come on, Farf. Let's get supper ready before Grandpa and Daddy come home."

The dog gave a squeaky yawn and stretched his lazy bones. He wagged his tail and trotted down the steps after her. The sound of keys in the front door drew a deep, protective bark from Farfel.

The door opened. "There's Grandpa's Farfie. What a good boy." Stuart scratched the hound's long ears and then kissed his daughter. "Hi, Princess. Something smells good, and I'm starving. If I don't eat soon, I could get dangerous."

"Supper will be ready as soon as Lou gets here."

"I saw his van right behind me on the way home." He pulled a dog toy from his pocket and tossed it to Farfel.

"Better go wash up, then." Millie gave him a hug. Her dad's eyes were tired and drawn. His gait seemed slower than before. Mother's death took more out of him than Millie had realized. He needed time to rest, gather strength, and be around his loved ones.

The dog came running and stopped at the storm door. He shivered with excitement as Lou approached.

"Wait a minute, Farfel. Mommy first." Lou reached over the baying hound and kissed Millie. "How was your day, sweetie?"

"Very busy. I managed to pack a lot of things in my room." She kissed his cheek. "I do have a few boxes for my strong men to take out to the trash."

Lou finished loving on the dog, stood, and flexed his muscles. "I can take care of it. Shouldn't take long, right?"

"I'll take the lighter stuff." Stuart patted his son-in-law's shoulder. "I'm older than you."

After the meal ended, the men talked about the possibility of getting season tickets for the Phoenix Suns.

Millie gathered the dinner plates from the table and loaded the dishwasher. She washed her hands and filled the coffee pot with water, then carefully measured the Italian-roast grounds into the filter.

She gazed out the kitchen window waiting for the coffee to brew. Nothing in her life had stayed the same. She and Lou were married and living in a home of their own. Mother finally made peace with God and her family before she died. Millie was thrilled to have good memories of her, something that never seemed a possibility. Despite the many hardships her family had faced the previous year, it was amazing how the Lord had blessed them.

Tears of gratitude filled her eyes as she placed the coffee pot, mugs, and a plate of Grizzly Bars on a tray and took them to the table.

"Yum. Thanks, honey. These bear things are my favorite." Lou blew her a kiss and then looked at Stuart. "The last time we talked you mentioned helping out at the reservation. Is that still in the works?"

She poured the coffee, sat with them at the table, and waited for her dad's reply.

"Yeah, it's on the back burner. I need to get with Ethan and Rikki's administrator, but it'll probably be sometime in early October before I can do anything." Stuart sipped his coffee and reached for a Grizzly Bar. "That being said, I need to talk to you both about the flower shop. For the last year or so, Max and I have been mulling over the idea of selling Floral Scent-sations and retiring."

Millie's mouth dropped. "I can't imagine you and Uncle Max not being at the flower shop, Dad. I've helped you there since I was six-years-old."

"You and Carol were the best little helpers we ever had. Let me explain. Max doesn't want everyone to know, but since he and Sylvia had their accident, he hasn't totally regained his strength. Heavy workdays take a toll on him now, and he wants to spend more time with Sylvia because of her failing health. When your mother got sick, I understood where he was coming from."

"Besides working on the reservation, what else would you do to keep yourself busy?"

"Don't get upset, but I'd like to sell this place. With the exception of my memories of you growing up, there's nothing to keep me here." Stuart wiped his hands on a napkin. "We bought it because your mother had her heart set on it. At this point, I'd like to have a smaller place. I don't need much, just a few rooms on one floor. A ruffle-free bachelor pad."

Alarm squeezed the air from Millie's lungs, and her mind reeled from a lack of oxygen. She wouldn't allow another change to overwhelm her.

"But what if you find someone later on?" In the back of her mind, she was thinking of Gabby Blythe as a distinct possibility.

"Why would I want to bring anyone into this pink monstrosity? It would be a constant reminder. Anyway, I need to move on." He chuckled. "And in case you're wondering, I have no intention of getting remarried any time soon."

Millie covered his hand with hers. "If you ever change your mind, please take your time to weigh the pros and cons. They say you shouldn't make any major decisions during the first year after a spouse passes. I don't want you to jump in with both feet and then realize you're not happy."

Stuart placed his coffee cup back on the table. "Good point, Princess. I might want to see if the shop's new owner would let me work part-time later on. But for now, letting go of those responsibilities is what we need."

"We'll help you pray about finding the right direction." Lou clapped his hand on Stuart's shoulder. "We're here for you no matter what the decision, Dad." He polished off another Grizzly Bar and wiped his mouth.

Stuart washed down his fourth cookie with one last gulp of coffee, then pushed his empty cup to the side. He leaned back in his chair, stretched his legs out, and crossed one ankle over the other. "Thanks, I knew I could count on both of you."

Millie's room looked abandoned. She picked up the box of keepsakes, turned the light out, and stared into the darkness.

"Thank you, Lord." As she voiced the short prayer, her lack of confidence began to dissipate, replaced by a warm blend of assurance and strength. Certainly not through her own power or abilities, but in Christ, the One who carried her to this time in her life.

She closed the door on the first forty-three years of her life and turned into Lou's outstretched arms.

Now—A Sneak Peek at Book Three

The Call of Indian Summer

Chapter One

August 15th had finally arrived, and the wedding reception at Powder Ridge Community Church was winding down. Sue North scooted her chair away from the table to get a better view of her only daughter throwing the bridal bouquet. The precious minutes left with Rikki ticked by unbelievably fast. She pushed the thought away as the bevy of beautiful single ladies clustered in front of the bride, their arms waving frantically to catch the posies of hope.

Alberta Gilbert, Powder Ridge, Vermont's least-likely-to-get-married, pushed up the sleeves on her polka-dot dress, licked her lips, and stood ready to block anyone in her way. The mere presence of the beefy high school gym teacher had a way of intimidating her former students. Coach Gilbert took the stance and clapped her hands over her head. "Pass it over here, North."

With a chuckle, Sue aimed her cell phone, ready to catch the play-by-play action on video. She heard Rikki call over her shoulder. "It's Mason, now, Coach. Get ready. Three . . . two . . . one!"

The bundle of blossoms flew across the room, ricocheted off someone's fingers and landed in Sue's lap. Alberta lunged for them, knocking Sue into a blue sequined heap on the floor.

"Sorry, North. Now shake it off." The coach lifted the

now-frazzled bouquet over her head, did a victory dance in a shower of petals, and then disappeared into the crowd.

Masculine hands gently helped Sue to her feet and guided her to another chair. "Are you okay, Suzie-Q?" His comforting voice sounded familiar.

Sue blinked several times and peered into the man's eyes. "Stuart. Thank you." She patted his hand and smiled. "I'll be fine once the bells stop ringing."

Rikki and her new husband, Ethan, came to the table. She knelt and tucked a stray blonde curl behind her mother's ear. "You must have taken quite a hit from the coach. My back was turned so I didn't see it happen."

"Neither did I." Sue shook her head. "I was focused on filming you. The last thing I remember was the bouquet landing on my knees."

"I'm sure Coach Gilbert didn't mean any harm." Ethan gave her a kiss on the forehead. "She's one determined woman on a mission to land Mr. Dinkus at Dinky Donuts. She's probably there by now."

Ethan stepped aside making room for several friends and neighbors to gather around the table. They offered well wishes to the newlyweds as well as shared their concern for Sue.

After assuring everyone that nothing was hurt except her pride, Sue quietly excused herself and hurried to the powder room. She stood in front of the full-length mirror and checked for damage. No blown out seams . . . check. Zipper intact . . . check. One earring . . . MIA.

Carol Mason-Bailey rushed in. "Sooze! Glad you're okay. I couldn't get to you any sooner." She gave her a hug and held out an earring. "I think this is yours. Uncle Stu found it on the floor."

"Thanks. I'm glad he was here to help me to my feet. I've never been so embarrassed." She took the jewelry from

Carol, wiped the post, and fastened it to her waiting lobe. "I couldn't believe Stuart made the long trip from Arizona for the wedding."

"Dad felt he should stay with Mom, so Uncle Stu decided to come in his place. He needed a break from the detailed paperwork and loose ends after Aunt Penny's death. Poor man's been overwhelmed." Her eyes softened. "Both of us remember the legal hoops you have to jump through when a spouse dies."

Sue added a touch of lipstick and looked at Carol's reflection in the mirror. "I'm glad he was able to come. It's good to see him again."

"What a day! I'm whipped." She put a hand on Sue's shoulder. "Everyone's been sharing memories of Bob and how much he meant to them. Of course, they all wanted to meet my new husband." She shook her head. "Bless his heart. Frank's a good sport."

"You're the one who's a good sport. He only has one afternoon to be sized up, but you're under the microscope 24/7 at his church." Sue took one last glance in the mirror. "Are you ready to hit the reception scene again?"

Carol consulted her watch. "Absolutely. I don't know about you, girlfriend, but it's hard to wrap my mind around the fact our babies are married. In a couple of hours they'll be on their way to sunny Cape Cod for their honeymoon."

"And to think it all began in college. God's timing is perfect. If my schooling hadn't been delayed for a couple of years, we'd never have been roommates." Sue nudged her, thankful for the longevity of their bond. "We've spent twenty-three years watching their relationship grow into true love."

"Ethan and Rikki are meant for each other. I'm proud of them for trusting in God's promises and following His will for their lives by working with the orphans at the reservation."

"I agree. That gives me peace in letting them go." Sue released a deep breath as they hooked arms, left the bathroom, and walked across the reception hall.

"They'll love working at the Mustang Ranch." Carol gave her a little squeeze. "Those kids need a lot of TLC."

The two friends headed for the table where Frank and Stuart were laughing and drinking coffee.

Sue sat and scooted her chair close. "With the wedding over, I'm staring at an empty nest, and it has me thinking of my future."

"That's where our faith comes in."

"You're right, and the Lord's stretching me." Sue pushed the wayward lock of hair behind her ear and pointed. "The kids have changed their clothes and are motioning for us."

Frank jumped to his feet, took Carol's hands, and pulled her up. "Come on. If we want to see them off, we'd better make a mad dash."

"Let me be a gentleman, Suzie-Q." Stuart held the back of the seat as she stood.

She grabbed Stuart's hand, and together, they took long strides to catch up to the others.

The women's heels clicked on the polished tile as the quartet headed for the door. Once outside, everyone blew a flurry of bubbles as the newlyweds passed.

Following hugs and kisses, Sue blinked back tears of mixed emotions. Life was about to change once again. Rikki and her childhood sweetheart were married. Their eyes held the absolute purity of the love they shared, but it went beyond that. They were following the Lord's direction.

Sue wiped her damp cheeks while she and Carol waved their final goodbyes.

After the decorated car drove off, Frank hugged his

wife. "Most of the guests are leaving. If you ladies don't mind, Stu and I thought we'd stretch our legs for a while. Call my cell when you're ready to go."

Sue tossed her house keys to Frank. "You guys can go on to the house. Carol and I will take my car." Arm-in-arm, she and Carol returned to the table.

"Moving to Arizona really worked out for you, didn't it, Carol?"

"Sure did. Aunt Penny caused quite a few doubts, but Frank and I persevered." A good-humored grin appeared on Carol's face. "Now that you're an empty nester, why don't you think about moving out west?"

"I've been giving it a lot of serious thought lately. Vermont has always been my home, but with Rikki moving to the reservation, what's keeping me here?"

"Are you staying because of your bakery? You've only had the Pie Hole a couple of years."

"My main concern is Crystal Peak Resort is expanding. Again." Sue shrugged, trying to hide any evidence of the mounting stress. "They prefer working with one company, and my bakery isn't equipped to handle that much productivity. I don't want to get in over my head at this stage of my life, but without the resort's business, I'll go under."

"Why didn't you tell me earlier?"

"Sorry about that, but you've had quite a few things going on in your life too." The corners of Sue's mouth turned up in a smile. "However, the people at church surrounded me in prayer, and the Lord heard them. Last month the Lovin' Oven Bakery Company contacted me. They want to buy the Pie Hole facility."

A brief look of surprise crossed Carol's face. "Really? That's wonderful." She grabbed Sue's wrist. "Lovin' Oven is a huge outfit."

"Listen to this, the price they quoted was double

market value. Can you believe it? All I have to do is sign on the dotted line and it's a done deal."

Carol squealed and clapped her hands. "How can you pass that up?"

"Who says I did?" She put her finger to her lips when the last two guests stopped at their table.

Elsie rubbed Sue's back. "What a beautiful wedding. Rikki was the prettiest bride I've ever seen. Herb and I wish them well." Her silent husband nodded in agreement and shook their hands.

When they left, Sue lowered her voice. "I haven't told anyone else yet, but Lovin' Oven also put an offer on the house along with the furniture. The company says it's the most impressive home they've seen in the Powder Ridge resort area. They're buying it for the local head honcho."

"What an opportunity. You won't have to go through a realtor."

"Their offer was very generous." She tilted her head. "Actually, they asked me to take an administrative job, but I'm a baker, Carol, not executive material. Business stuff wears me down."

"Can't blame you there. You just hit the half-century mark in June." She giggled. "Why take on extra stress in your golden years?"

"Golden years?" Sue's mouth split into a grin as she crossed her arms. "Why did you have to bring that up? Remember you're only three years behind me."

"Excuse me, three and a half years."

"All right, then. Three and a half years." Sue nibbled on her lower lip. "I can't wait to get out of that humongous house and leave all the bad memories of Grady behind. It'll be nice to have a place small enough to take care of myself." Her mind wandered to a warm cottage with a picket fence, flowers, and a cobblestone walkway.

"We have condos in Apache Pointe with all the

amenities you could ask for. I've heard the price is a little salty, but worth every penny. You're the widow of Powder Ridge's answer to Perry Mason, so that shouldn't be a problem."

"It's not the cozy cottage I pictured, but I promise to give it more thought." Sue pulled a lock of hair back. "Grady did a lot of terrible things during our marriage, but at least, he was a good provider. Rikki and I each inherited more than enough money to live on if we use it wisely."

"Sounds like the puzzle pieces are falling into place." She cocked her head and gave a teasing grin. "So, was that a 'yes' for moving to be with your daughter, best friend, and future grandbabies?"

"Grandbabies? Talk about the ultimate trump card."

Carol giggled. "This is a decision you have to make on your own." She hesitated. "But come on, Sooze, Millie and I could use a third musketeer."

As she and Carol laughed together, the caterers swiped the azure coverings from the round tables. "Speaking of your cousin, how are she and Stuart doing since Penny died?"

"Millie loves being married. Lou's unconditional love is what she's needed all along." Carol fiddled with the button on her navy jacket. "You're not going to believe this, but Uncle Stu and Dad are thinking about retirement."

"Really? Now, that surprises me. They're both so full of energy it's hard to think of them being ready to retire."

"Dad's sixty-five and Uncle Stu is sixty-four, so they're old enough to consider it."

Sue shook her head. "Still hard to think of them slowing down. The last time I talked to Stuart, he was interested in Native American Missions. Has he looked into it?"

"He's been working a little on the Maverick Ranch whenever possible." Carol wiggled her shoes on and stood.

"I'd like for him to find new friends, but he doesn't see the need. He's fallen in love with all those kids, and they pretty fond of him too. When Rikki was there last summer, she called him Poppy, and most of them have picked up on it."

"How sweet." A warm sense of nostalgia engulfed Sue. "She used to call my dad Poppy. I bet Stuart eats it up."

"He does and always has gum in his pockets for the kids. It costs them one hug. You should see it, Sooze. They swarm around him like hummingbirds to nectar."

"You and I know how important it is to find a niche in your life after losing a spouse. I'm glad Stuart found his." She gathered their plates and cups from the table then glanced around the room. "Looks like the caterers are ready to clean up. I guess we'd better go."

Sue pulled her car into the drive-thru, rolled down her window, and ordered a large Coke. The tantalizing smell of onion rings made her mouth water. She reached for the ringing cell phone in her purse. "Hi, Carol. I haven't heard your cheery voice in two weeks. You called at a great time. I'm about to go crazy sitting in a long line at Jumpin' Jack's."

"Let me guess. The onion rings, right? Glad I can save your sanity. How are things going with the negotiations for selling Grady's law partnership?"

The yellow van behind Sue honked, and she inched her car forward. "Jillian Ingram is helping me, and things are going great. I honestly feel more comfortable with a lady lawyer. She takes a lot of gratuitous cases, so that tells me she's not in it for the money."

"It's good that you finally have someone you can trust. Fortunately, not all lawyers are like shady Grady."

"It's difficult to keep that in mind when it's all you know." Sue tapped her fingernails on the steering wheel while the smell of deep-fried onions penetrated her nasal passages. "Jillian said the Lovin' Oven contracts went through. I have six weeks to vacate my home." She paused as her stomach growled. "The only thing left is to have Grady's law firm onioned . . . I mean, audited."

"Girl, get yourself something to eat."

Sue nodded as if Carol could see her. "I have more news. As of October first, Apache Pointe, Arizona will be my new home."

Carol screeched. "Do you mean it?"

"I do. Hang on a minute, the drive-thru line moved, and I'm next." Sue pulled next to the window, handed money to the cashier, then reached for the drink. "You know, Carol, the farther away I can get from Powder Ridge the better."

"That makes me so happy. My best friend will be living close by just like the good ol' days."

"In a month my world will be a lot different. I look forward to the change."

"Who knows? There might be a wonderful, compassionate hunk to escort you through your twilight years."

"Okay, knock it off. I'm going to hang up now. Talk to you later." Sue chuckled and turned onto the main drag and took a sip of Coke. Where would the changes in this new life lead? Her thirty-year marriage to Grady left many harsh regrets. Having a romantic relationship with any man, hunk or otherwise, made her stomach cringe.

She vowed never to go down that rocky road again.

Author Note

Dear Reader,

Our Heavenly Father's love is readily available for everyone. How fortunate we are that no person or sin is outside the reach of His forgiveness. God gives us the ability and desire to back away from sin by talking to Him. Our best shield is His grace. This amazing gift offers a new nature and outlook on life. The inward makeover results in obvious outward changes.

In *The Promise of Spring*, Millie Drake witnessed this remarkable change in her mother as explained in 2 Corinthians 5:17. "Therefore if any man be in Christ, he is a new creature: old things are passed away; behold, all things are become new." What a great hope this is to anyone who thinks they're beyond redemption!

In Millie's story, our goal was to illustrate life for someone raised under a parent's oppressive thumb. Verbal and emotional abuse is often incapacitating, leaving one without a sense of purpose. As a result, the victim often acquires many coping strategies to escape its tortures. Millie's diversion of choice was her daydreams.

Our stories have a sweet romantic element, but the storylines are more about the ups and downs life throws at us. Real life events are difficult and even painful, yet God offers the assurance that He is with us and will always make a way.

The two of us know these peaks and valleys first hand. While going through final edits for our first book, one of Linda's daughters was fighting breast cancer. The Lord saw the family through the horrible months of chemo, radiation, and multiple surgeries. (We're happy to report she's now cancer-free.)

At the completion of *Come Next Winter* and the beginning of *The Promise of Spring*, Deb's husband, Ray, wasn't feeling well. He went in for tests and the doctors found stage four pancreatic cancer. Sadly, he lost his battle on Christmas Day 2016. It's been an emotional roller coaster for Deb as she adapts to her new life.

However, it's in those times when we feel abandoned or burdened with heavy problems, we need to be reminded again to trust and ask the Lord to lift us up and bear our load. He's waiting for us with outstretched arms.

We hope you enjoyed your second visit to Apache Pointe, Arizona. Please stop by next time to catch up with old friends and make new ones in *The Call of Indian Summer*, book three in the Seasons of Change series.

Our readers are welcome to contact us on Facebook at www.facebook.com/groups/Thebooknookoflindaanddeb

Linda Hanna and Debbie Dulworth

Discussion Questions

1. Penny's domineering personality affected Millie's life. Knowing she didn't have the finances to move out, how did Millie cope with her mother's abuse? Why did she resign herself to a life of pleasing her mother even though it made her miserable? Why didn't Stuart take control of his marriage?

2. Did Lou do the right thing by silently walking out the door on Millie's birthday rather than getting involved? Would it have helped if Lou had stayed to face Penny? What else could he have done to better defend Millie?

3. In the beginning of this novel, Millie's self-esteem had grown because of the love she and Lou shared. However, on her birthday, her confidence took a hit. How did this sense of unworthiness affect her ability to make decisions? What role did her lack of confidence play and how did it affect the outcome of the story?

4. Even though Lou's parents were affirming, he had a shy and introverted disposition. How was his backward personality different from Millie's?

5. How could Lou have tried harder to contact Millie? Why didn't he?

6. Describe Millie and Kent's relationship. How does he view his relationships with women? Could Millie ever fit into his sophisticated world? Would she ever want to?

7. Which hurt Millie the most? Was it Lou walking out and

not contacting her or the fact her mother paid Kent to date her?

8. Kent took Millie to a racy movie, which made her uncomfortable. Have you ever been in her situation? What did you do? If she didn't like any of the dates with Kent, why did she continue to go out with him?

9. Penny manipulated everyone around her. She thought her opinions were more important. Have you ever acted in a way that wasn't in your own best interest? What do you think motivated you? What lessons did you learn from that experience?

10. Gabby helped Penny work through her abusive past. Penny was able to tell Millie she loved her and to ask for forgiveness. Do you think Millie had doubts about her mother's sincerity? Have you ever given someone a second chance? Have *you* ever needed a second chance?

11. Millie found peace for her bruised heart when she surrendered her life to God. Have you trusted Him with control of everything in your life?

12. Who in this story deceived themselves the most? What truth did they have to tell themselves in order to change their path?

CPSIA information can be obtained
at www.ICGtesting.com
Printed in the USA
LVOW03s1448201117
557025LV00012B/1172/P

9 781943 959358